Future Fiction

Edited by

Francesco Verso

Freetaly

Italian Science Fiction

Edited by Francesco Verso

Published by Associazione Future Fiction
Via Valentiniano 40 – 00145 Roma
TAX ID. 97962020588

Title: *Freetaly – Italian Science Fiction*
© 2022 Future Fiction, Roma
I edition November 2022
ISBN: 9788832077520
info@futurefiction.org

Contemporary Italian Science Fiction

by Francesco Verso

From 2000 to 2010

To understand the trends that have shaped Italian "fantascienza" (Science Fiction) during the last 20 years, we should take a look at the end of the last century and in particular at the creation of the Urania Award in 1989 by the editor of Urania Mondadori book series – the too-early-departed Giuseppe Lippi – and the development of the World Wide Web. During the '90s, Italian SF was in a process of recovery, after being declared dead, due to some publishing initiatives that had reinvigorated its diffusion and supported the authors to submit their works with more ease. The Urania Award in particular has helped many emerging authors to get some visibility and be acknowledged as writers, even in the niche of SF genre. Over the years, some of them managed to get a literary credibility and even got published outside the genre, like Valerio Evangelisti and Nicoletta Vallorani.

The other driving force was represented by the Web, which has contributed to close the gap in terms of access to information, books and "Science Fiction culture" with the US and UK production. During the first ten years of the New Millennium, if on the traditional Urania series many books were dealing with popular tropes like Uchronia, Cyberpunk and Space Opera, most of the stories published by mid-sized and indy presses revolved around the exploding phenomenon of Cyberpunk and its subgenre Steampunk.

In fact, if we consider the Urania Award, between 2000 and 2009, almost all winning titles could be considered Cyberpunk or Uchronia (except for Paolo Aresi's "La scala infinita" which is a Space Opera). Dealing mostly, on one side, with "alternative history" ranging from Middle-Ages, Reinassance, Risorgimento, a Roman Empire spanning over time and space or even revival of Fascism settings and, from the other side, with decadent over polluted megalopolises, mafia crimes and new drugs, the impression is that Italian SF during this period can be represented at best by investigations and action thrillers to capture the techno-criminals or to restore the threatened course of history.

Nevertheless, some of these novels became SF classics, like Lanfranco Fabriani's "Lungo i vicoli del tempo", which creates the UCCI agency, an Italian version of the Government Time Bureau in charge of monitoring the correct flow of history and protecting Italy's past from the attacks by hostile foreign powers, already common in works by Poul Anderson and Robert Heinlein, but here adapted to the Italian cultural context.

Another good example is "Sezione π2", a techno-thriller by Giovanni De Matteo (first millennial author to appear on Urania) set in a futuristic Naples and featuring a special police officers – known as "necromancer" – due to the cyber-implant they are equipped with, that allow them to conduct investigations starting from the recovery of the victims' memories. The novel takes places after the eruption of the Vesuvius and the catastrophic consequences of a Third World War, where Naples is flooded by any sort of refugees, has reached six million inhabitants and is besieged by an ecological threat of uncertain origins, an entropic mass able to regenerate itself by assimilating waste and invading areas abandoned by human activity.

The third example is represented by "e-Doll" by Francesco Verso, a post-cyberpunk novel set in a future Moscow where electronic dolls – more like AI powered sexual androids – are used as a bio-political tool to address the dramatic rising phenomenon of femicides. E-doll was considered controversial, due to the sexual theme, that caused some online flames and discussions among the SF community, because sex was something Urania's audience (mostly made of middle-age and old men) was not accustomed to. In reality the story is about the relationship between a teenage girl that wants to become like a sex android to get more attention by her problematic family and an e-Doll that wishes to turn itself into a human being to avoid its daily serial deaths.

With the intention of creating an alternative channel to the Urania Award, in 2003 Delos Books announced the Fantascienza.com Award (from the name of the portal that has become the main Italian SF aggregator) for unpublished novels, which a few years later will become the Odissea Award. The first edition was won by Massimo Pietroselli with "L'Undicesima Frattonube" and, among the first winners, there was also Clelia Farris, one of the most appreciated authors of Italian SF, with "Rupes Recta", an investigation into a lunar colony in which rationality has given way to superstition, and with "Nessun uomo è mio fratello", a soft-dystopia, without almost any technology, which anticipates many current issues such as body control and gender-based violence. Also Francesco Verso won the Odissea Award in 2013 with "Livido", a coming of age, transhumanist love-story set in a huge dump and addressing problems of human augmentation, overconsumption, pollution, and identity.

 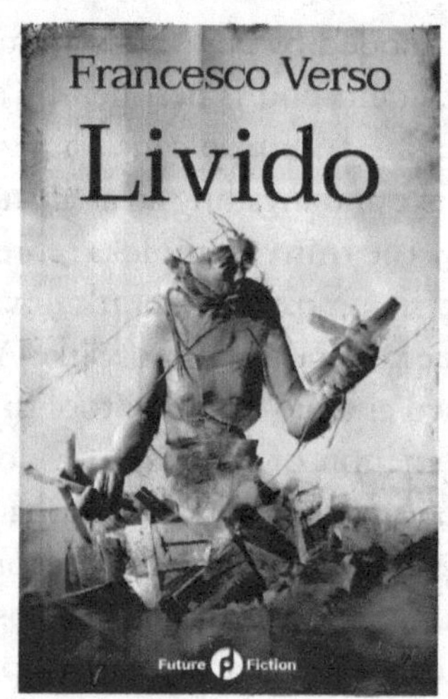

Another interesting author is Francesco Grasso with "2038: la rivolta" (2038: A Revolt), a story about the decline of society, the manipulation of information and the power of banks. Interesting is the analysis of the journalistic world, put in crisis by the interference of the regime but also by fake and do-it-yourself news that causes the collapse of quality information and the role of guarantee of official newspapers.

In 2003, after some 20 years after its first publication, the historic magazine "Robot" was back in print, again under the direction of Vittorio Curtoni. The void that had been created since the '80s was filled again: the new "Robot" edition gave space not only to novels, but also to short stories, one of the most suitable literary forms for expressing SF ideas. The Robot Award was established to promote short stories and that's where Dario Tonani first published his own works, an author who, since then, established himself in the field of Italian SF.

The arrival of ebooks bring the genre into the digital revolution and, together with digital publication and the rise of indy presses, new energy comes into Science Fiction during the early years of the New Millennium. Authors now – not forced to submit their stories to traditional publishers – begin to write with more freedom, not following market trends (even though there's an explosion of commercial SF in hope of getting more "digital visibility").

On the Net in fact is where a group of young writers meet, around 2003-04, to create a literary SF vanguard called "Connettivismo" (Nexialism). Their names are Giovanni De Matteo, Lukha Kremo, Marco Milani and Sandro Battisti among others. The main idea is that a multidisciplinary approach is key to understand the complexity of postmodern time and so they try to connect different disciplines into a kind of "holistic" approach to SF. It's not just physics, astronomy, chemistry or mathematics that can generate the Sense of Wonder, but also – following the lesson of the New Wave and Cyberpunk – new media, information technology, Big Data, philosophy of science, new economy, architecture and language. The most relevant author is Giovanni De Matteo, who wrote the "Manifesto del Connettivismo" (The Nexialist Manifesto). Here's a small part of it:

We are antennae aimed into the void, crazed variables, badly-tuned violins, out-of-sync chronoscopes. Using ancient, mystical routes, we pursue a sharing of souls, spaces, and times. The connection is the hypertextual network of reality's decoded correspondences. We live in the connection, we strive toward the future. This is why: We Shall Be All!

The "Connettivisti" were published by Kipple, a small press born in the late '90s and founded by Lukha B. Kremo. Kipple has hosted all the leading authors over the years and has best expressed that ideal of inter-and-hyper-textuality by publishing fiction, poetry, non-fiction, comics and music. It was a real experimental laboratory of storytelling, although it has been difficult at times to identify a Nexialist "canon":

the movement meshed up different inspirational sources (like industrial music, goth aesthetics, punk attitude, cyber culture, postmodern visuals, hacker language) and thus it was – above all – a declaration of intent, to which different authors over time have adhered in a discontinuous way, like Alan D. Altieri and Francesco Verso. Yet, the very idea that a literary SF vanguard could exist in Italy was a revolutionary concept, which is why Nexialism represented an important feature in the Italian history of the genre.

The works of the "Connettivisti" are best represented by the anthology called "Frammenti di una rosa olografica" (an homage to the cyberpunk story by William Gibson "Fragments of a Hologram Rose") with contributions from all the main writers of the movement: these fourteen stories were inspired by extreme theories in the fields of physics and astrophysics (quantum mechanics, string theory) and dealt with the next technological innovations (from global networks, to virtual reality and quantum computers); the themes revolved around transhumanism, combining the poetic of postmodernism, with futurism and certain holistic visions, a kind of "hidden connection" that pervades and combines all aspects of cyber-culture.

The movement still exists today – the latest antology is called "Nuove Eterotopie, published in 2017 – but it has lost much of its originality and momentum along the way.

The absence of any great publishing case or best-seller in Italian SF – with the exclusion of Mondadori Urania that was selling some 7-8 thousand copies a month via newspaper stands, a typical distribution channel that was very successful in the past – will prove to be an important evolutionary engine. The entire first decade of the New Millennium is characterized by the online flourishing of more or less organized communities: web portals, personal blogs of writers or communities, genre forums. In this respect, also the communication between fans and writers will be uploaded to the Web thanks to the birth or the consolidation of fan clubs, facilitated by a wider visibility and a paradigm shift that was just born.

From 2010 to 2015

If the first years of the New Millennium had been a testing ground for new approaches to publishing (like print on demand, online fanzines, community forums and self-publishing) from 2010 these tentative experiences proved to be ready to become structured projects. The possibility of a "publishing democratization" offered by new media platforms like Amazon, Simplicissimus Book Farm and Kobo was probably the only viable approach for Italian SF.

In this period, some small presses with a strong identity – very different from the amateur ones and the commercial big publishers – decided to put themselves to the trial. It's the case of Zona 42 and Future Fiction, two micro-publishers who distinguished themselves by a strong characterization of their editorial proposal.

Zona 42 (founded by Giorgio Raffaelli and Marco Scarabelli, long-time frequenters of the Italian SF newsgroups) intended to bring recent SF texts to the market, adopting a liquid approach in defining the boundaries of the genre. They focused on contemporary Science Fiction titles coming from English and Italian market with high quality standards. They have discovered young talented authors like Andrea Viscusi and published established ones like Alessandro Vietti and Nicoletta Vallorani.

Andrea Viscusi's book, "Dimenticami, Trovami, Sognami" (Forget me, Find me, Dream of me) is a love story set on different narrative levels, a sort of "Eternal Sunshine of the Spotless Mind", where three protagonists must face a mystery that risks to overwhelm their own existence: Dorian must confront forces greater than himself, Dr. Novembre is tormented by incomprehensible visions and Simona, who waited for Dorian for twelve years, will have to put together the pieces of a story that perhaps never happened in this Universe.

"Real Mars" by Alessandro Vietti is an ironic story that, with a skillful metanarrative game, transforms a space reality show from Science Fiction into social satire, making the reader the real protagonist: four astronauts are travelling into space while billions of people are watching and commenting on them, marveling and despising, and modifying the schedule of one's life according to the TV program. "Real Mars" is a fierce mirror, in which we see our relationship with media, perceive a reality that becomes fiction, and lose the possibility of any human contact.

"Avrai i miei occhi" by Nicoletta Vallorani is a book about the violence perpetrated against the woman's body, be it human, guinea pig, clone, replicant or cyborg: the same abuses, the same suffering. Nicoletta Vallorani, first woman to win an Urania Award for "Il cuore finto di DR" (DR's fake heart") in 1992, has, since then, continued to write Science Fiction and noir, always giving voice to strong feminist themes. Her fiction is often made of tormented stories of women, objects of oppressive relationships forced into social roles.

The mission of Future Fiction – founded by the multiple-award SF writer and editor Francesco Verso – is instead to enhance the narrative biodiversity of contemporary SF, introducing the "Sense of Wander" (meaning that the old Sense of Wonder must now be found in emerging cultures and in native innovation, "wandering" around the World) and thus bringing on the Italian market stories in translation from Asia to Africa, from South America to Europe. Also, Future Fiction has published the books of Clelia Farris and Francesco Verso in Italian and managed to sell their works abroad.

Clelia Farris is a long time author of SF. She writes with a mature, harsh, extremely precise style, her stories are different from English fiction and often deal with the loss and sense of guiltiness deriving from futuristic technologies that allow to exploit the human condition or being exploited by it. Her book *La pesatura dell'anima* (The Weight of the Soul) is set in an alternative Egypt, where the use of metals is prohibited, houses and furniture are biotech modified trees, and modified animals serve as means of transport and communication. A fascinating place where no character really explains much to the reader, who must find the way along the plot by deciphering phrases and some cool neologisms.

Her stories are most of all mind-bending tales, full of captivating characters with elusive identities like Kieser, who longs to transform himself through horrific procedures, or Yuliano, a man with no aesthetic taste, or Gabola, engaged in the battle of a lifetime against the expropriation of the Little Tuvu Hill.

Her prose is dry and polished, like the stones of her native Sardinia. Her anthology "La consistenza delle idee" (translated in English as "Creative Surgery" by Rachel Cordasco and Jennifer Delare) was published in the US by Rosarium Publishing.

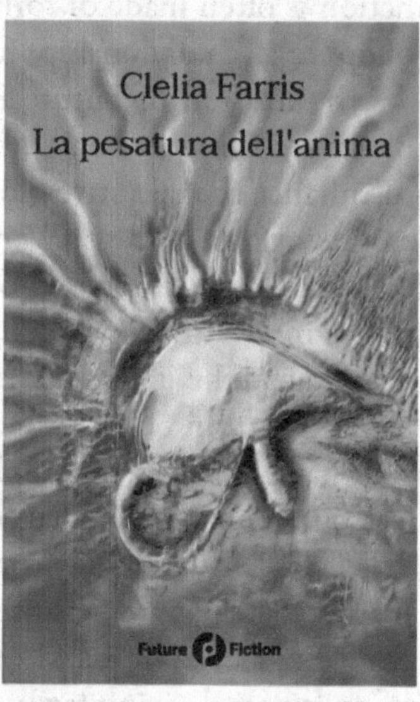

Nexhuman" by Francesco Verso is a post-cyberpunk, coming-of-age novel set in a polluted city: a 20-years-long adventure of a boy called Peter Pains who falls in love with a woman older than him that has a dangerous secret buried inside of her. Exploring contemporary themes such as cybernetics, mind-uploading and transcendence, "Nexhuman" expands on classic SF to build a world as deep and searching as its main character.

Despite their modest size, both Zona 42 and Future Fiction are recognized for the quality of their publications, becoming a point of reference in a few years. Their work has led the sector to open up in different directions. On the one hand, some contemporary international authors have finally found a stable readership in Italy, like Vandana Singh, Chen Qiufan or Ian McDonald; on the other hand, a scouting operation has been carried out towards new Italian authors (such as Stefano Paparozzi or Romina Braggion) and the rediscovery of others, well-known protagonists (like Nicoletta Vallorani, Clelia Farris and Alessandro Vietti).

It's important to notice that, with the consolidation of the small presses' position, a kind of synergy with the big publishers has also been created. For example, it was Future Fiction that brought contemporary Chinese SF to Italy with the anthologies "Nebula", "Sinosfera" and "Artificina" and afterwards Mondadori published Liu Cixin's "The Three Body Problem" trilogy. But then Future Fiction continued to bring new books with the collections of Xia Jia, Han Song, Chen Qiufan and Mu Ming. Or it's the case of Nnedi Okorafor, translated for the first time by Zona 42, which later was published by Mondadori.

Another relevant book of this period include "Il caso Korolev" (The Korolev case) by Paolo Aresi, originally published in Italy in 2011 on Urania series, as a special issue dedicated to the 50th anniversary of the first human flight into space by Yuri Gagarin. The elements of the novel are an interstellar journey with a cosmic mystery to be solved, the presence of a mineral with a particular property and the encounter with an alien civilization. But, most of all, the story is a tribute to the figure of the father of Russian cosmonautics, Sergej Pavlovič Korolëv (1907-1966): the second part of the book is in fact a historical novel, with the plot centered on Korolev, the man who designed both the Soyuz and Voschod launchers, the creator of the Vostok program and designer of the N1 rocket which was the vector for the Soviet moon landing.

Paolo Aresi can be considered the representative of the new technological and adventurous SF that refers directly to classic authors such as Robert A. Heinlein and Arthur C. Clarke.

A new trend emerging during this period regards literary authors using SF themes in their books as the reality becomes more and more Science Fictional.

An important literary author like Tullio Avoledo, who wrote books on parallel universes with mainstream publisher like Einaudi, wrote *L'anno dei dodici inverni* (The Twelve Winter Year, 2009) which deals with time travel, love and redemption, in a mix of SF and realistic narrative. In 2011 he also published another SF novel, *Un buon posto per morire*, (A good place to die) that won the 2012 Emilio Salgari Award.

Also Vittorio Catani with *Il quinto principio* (The Fifth Principle, 2015) goes into mainstream fiction: in the year 2043 the Earth is devastated by so-called Exceptional Events, catastrophes that violate the laws of physics but seem to agree with a hypothesized Fifth Principle of thermodynamics: sinking of vast areas, sudden decrease or absence of gravity in certain territories, appearance of objects that create absolute void, and more. Many scenarios are outlined: a hidden auction for the privatization of Antarctica to face the global water crisis, hyper-capitalism based on an economy of debt nearing total collapse, an enlarged rich-poor gap, the disappearance of democracy, legalized slavery and communication system similar to a psychic mobile phone.

So it's interesting to observe how a renewed curiosity for SF has developed outside the genre. Perhaps it's due to the success of dystopias like "Hunger Games", often associated with YA audience but even non-genre publishers have noticed the trend and so now it's possible to find many mid-and-large publishers (like Sperling and Chrysalide series by Mondadori) offering such titles, often serialized, like Leonardo Patrignani's "Multiversum", which was translated in many languages.

It really seems like SF cannot be ignored any longer and writers are willing to discuss the present time using the technologies that are shaping our culture and society. All in all, Italian SF production offers a wide panorama of styles, ideas and projects, including some lines of development and personal research that are opening the boundaries of a genre.

From 2015 to 2020

One of the most successful initiatives of recent years, which proved the passion and participation of Italian fandom, was "Stranimondi" (Strange Worlds) festival in Milan, a SF convention that, from 2015, brought together editors, readers, writers and Italian and international guests from Bruce Sterling to Alan D. Altieri, from Alastair Reynolds to Valerio Evangelisti, Ian MacDonald, Bruno Bozzetto, Pat Cadigan and Tullio Avoledo. Each edition surpassed the success of the previous one and it was only for the 2020 lockdown that this tradition was stopped.

Given this trend, more and more SF titles are getting (even without mentioning the term "fantascienza") in the catalogues of literary publishers such as La Nave di Teseo, while other indy publishers such as Effequ and Tunué offer titles that can be placed in the broader genre of speculative fiction (namely Science Fiction, Weird, Slipstream). Today even new subgenres are expanding in Italian SF, from solarpunk to climate fiction; someone even spoke of a "Golden Age of Italian SF", and although it's too early to make any evaluation, the situation is finally favorable.

Take for example "Mondo9" by Dario Tonani: this dieselpunk saga – born from a series of short stories originally published on ebook by small press 40K and then taken up by Delos Books, is set on a desert planet crossed by enormous semi-sentient ships and it has achieved great success. In five years, the book had many editions and it expanded with new stories, becoming the first Urania Millemondi featuring an Italian author. Lately it has been published also in Japan and Russia.

It's worth to mention that this kind of narrative universe wasn't typical in Italian SF, like uchronia and techno-thriller, but more like planetary romance and horror, and maybe for this reason it captured a new reader. "Mondo9" is proof that, contrary to the common belief of years ago, Italian SF can compete on the international market.

This is even more true for Francesco Verso. His books have been translated in English and Chinese and his short stories also in Spanish, Russian and Portuguese. Verso's stories explore the relationship between technology, human body and mind, exploring the consequences of physical enhancement, augmentation and anything that can go better or worst while updating the Human 1.0 to the Human 2.0 and beyond.

In 2015 his novel "Bloodbusters" won a second Urania Award and in 2020 the book was published in the UK by Luna Press. Bloodbusters is a grotesque story, funny but also terribly serious about the biopolitics of taxes, where people in Rome literally pay their taxes in blood. But this is also a love story between two characters that – despite their personal differences (a tax enforcer that hunts for blood and a universal donor that gives it to the people in need of transfusion) – will end up to like themselves beyond the first appearances. The book – translated in Chinese by Hu Shaoyan – has been published by Bofeng Culture, and it's under adaptation into a comic book.

From 2020 to the near future

The next years of Italian SF look promising and its future is the hands of some emerging talents. The first one is Linda De Santi who won all major SF awards in the short story category during the latest years, including Italia Award, Robot Award, Urania-Short Award and Chrysalis Award by the European SF Society. Her story "Beautymark", in particular, published on the anthology "European SF #1 – Knowing the Neighbours" by Future Fiction, is a striking satirical take on the obsession with beauty of contemporary society pushed to the extreme of creating a social ranking of beauty, making the story look like a Black Mirror episode.

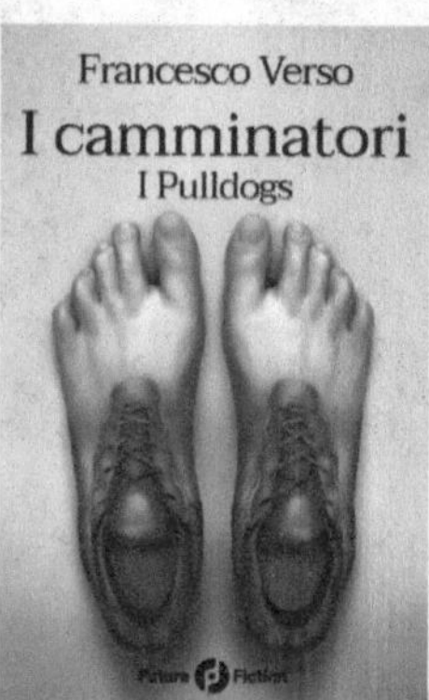

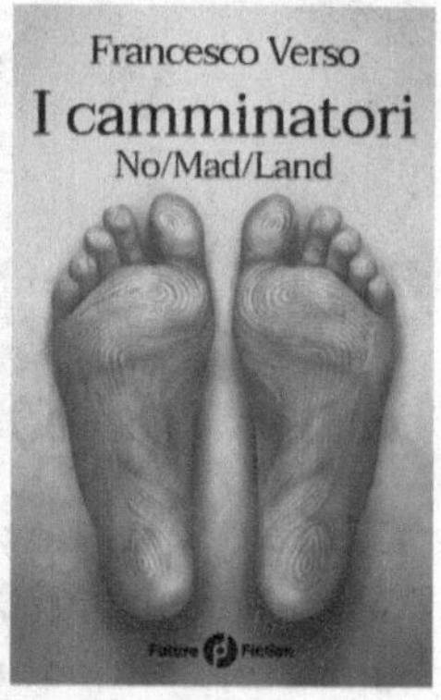

Another writer to give attention to is Romina Braggion. She focuses mainly on climate change, solarpunk and feminism fiction with a mature voice and an extraordinary detailed writing technique. Her prose is slow-paced, but full of insightful and intimate reflections like in "Queen of Flowers", set on the transfigured mountains of North Italy, where the main protagonist must face a dramatic choice to preserve the integrity of a solarpunk community and most of all the bees that they use to survive after a climate disaster.

Solarpunk is present also in the Clelia Farris novel called "I vegumani" and in Francesco Verso latest book, "I camminatori" (which is going to be published in the UK as "The Roamers" by Flame Tree Press in May 2023), first example of such genre in Europe. The story, made of "The Pulldogs" and "No/Mad/Land", follows a group of people at the twilight of Western civilization that undergoes an anthropological transformation caused by nanites (nanorobots capable of assembling molecules to create matter). This technology changes the way they eat and gives rise to a culture that, while reminiscent of an ancient nomadic society, is creative and new. Liberation from the imperative of food, combined with the ability to 3D print objects and use cloud computing, makes it possible for the Pulldogs to make a choice that seems impossible and anachronistic, that is escaping from the employment system, from the prison created by the need to eat, and from the urban lifestyle.

There's also a promising indy press that may contribute to the growth of Italian SF, Moscabianca Edizioni (White Fly Editions). Their series of anthologies, "Prisma", collect a selection of stories written by new writers. Halfway between a book and a magazine, "Prisma" wants to show that SF can attract new voices and feed a new generations of authors. Each edition is enriched with the contribution of an illustrator to create original and custom-designed covers.

To end this review of around 25 years, Italian Science Fiction has had a long history with its roots in the fantastic literature of the past centuries, and while in the early decades of 1900 it has explored the thrills of speed and industrial technologies with the vanguard of Futurismo, it didn't really catch up with Anglophone Science Fiction until recently with the development of the World Wide Web and the spread of English language as tools to democratize and make the genre more accessible. Lately Italian Science Fiction is facing an interesting period of growth and acknowledgement, made possible by a new generation of editors, small presses and authors. Still the publishing industry is looking too often to the English language market to discover and promote books that are available in Italy without much effort.

Small and indy presses are indeed showing with their selections of stories and brave little projects that quality books already exist in Italian language, that readers appreciate them, and that some of them are even sold with success abroad. If more support and credit will be given to such talented writers, the gap with Anglophone books will become less and less in a matter of some years. Let's hope this won't be a "vox clamantis in deserto" (a voice calling in the desert).

Acknowledgements:

The "Manifesto del Connettivismo" can be found here: http://www.next-station.org/nxt-ex-1.shtml. To write this article some information were taken from "Cronache della fantascienza italiana" by Andrea Viscusi and Maico Morellini, published on Argo Rivista available in Italian here: https://www.argonline.it/cronache-dalla-fantascienza-italiana-maico-morellini-andrea-viscusi/

BEAUTYMARK

by Linda De Santi

translated by Sally McCorry

Linda De Santi was born near Pisa in 1985. Passionate about the fantastic, in 2017 she won the first edition of the Urania Short Award by Mondadori with the story Saltare avanti *and in 2019 she has won the Robot Award with the short story* Cornucopia. *Her stories have appeared in numerous anthologies and magazines, including Distòpia,* Il sigillo del serpente piumato *by Urania Mondadori, W.o.W - Women of Weird and Prisma 2, Human/ by Moscabianca Edizioni,* Ipotesi per Fibonacci *by Comma22,* Il fiore della quintessenza *by Ali Ribelli. She was co-editor of the anthology* Atterraggio in Italia, *published by Delos Book. Graduated in Literature, she now works in the field of marketing, but takes advantage of every free moment to write and above all to read. She's part of* Specularia's *editorial team, an online speculative fiction magazine.*

1

We were having supper in a restaurant in the centre of town, the Plexiglass walls spilling light out into the Autumn evening. I had spent the evening listening to my parents arguing about the government: the acceptable distance from the beautymark had just been reduced, and the previous day they had halved the food ration of the father of one of my schoolfriends. After the latest amendment to the Beauty Conformity laws, incipient balding had become a serious deformity problem and the man's right to unlimited food had been removed.

We had finished our meal and I was sitting staring at the lights reflected on the surface of the table. I could hear my parents in the background, vaguely conscience of their presence.

When I lifted my head I saw my mother, motionless, three centimetres from my face staring at me, looking for something. She brushed a small beauty spot on the side of my nose as if weighing up the danger it posed, it was still light and hardly visible.

"Something's not right," she announced finally, straightening up.

She didn't tell me what was wrong. It might have been the beauty spot. In the years that followed it got darker. Or my eyes, one a slightly different shape to the other. Or perhaps my it was my eyebrows, one a few millimetres longer than the other, or my uneven skin colouring. I never did find out exactly, but the many elixirs I took and the surgical visits I subjected myself to in the following years convinced me something really wasn't right. They were mostly problems connected to adolescence, greasy skin, chubbiness, stretch marks, but my mother didn't want to take any risks.

We would go to the Beauty Chemist's and clinics together; I read fashion magazines while she had stem cell injections to her cheekbones, waiting for my turn.

Just after my fifteenth birthday my father began to lose his hair, his loyalty rating fell, and his salary was cut, leaving my family with a lot less money to spend on cosmetic surgery and beauty treatments. Despite this I was, for many years, amongst the few people in compliance with the beautymark.

2

At the academy people were always asking me why I seemed so tense.

They asked me if I slept enough at night, or whether I was taking the right elixirs. I answered that I was, and put the blame on the stress of finals. I kept the truth about the degeneration of my appearance over those past few days to myself:

no one would be able to keep a decent face after a week without treatments.

"I'm so sorry," my mother wrote to me. "I couldn't put this surgery off any longer. We are just unlucky that it has happened right now."

"You only had to wait another month."

"My loyalty rating was down to 26%. I was risking my pension."

I sighed. "Has the chin job worked at least?"

Her reply was an emoji of a triumphant hand gesture. I was happy for her, but her surgery had left us with no money just one month before the exam my whole life depended on.

"Can people really see you aren't taking your elixirs?" She asked me.

"See for yourself."

I took a selfie and sent it to her.

"Good Heavens! Get Angela to lend you something. Or go to the charity chemist."

"I would have to rob one to get everything I need."

She didn't answer. I put my phone away and sat on my bed in an attempt to think. I was interrupted two minutes later by the synthetic voice of MERI, the artificial intelligence assigned to monitoring my beauty conformity.

"If you move to far away from the beautymark you won't pass the exam, not even if you write the best story in the world." The voice came from a triangular device sitting on my bedside cabinet, the webcam at the centre kept an eye on everything I did in my bedroom.

"Thanks a lot, MERI."

I lifted my gaze to the wall opposite my bed, half taken up with the screen showing me my double. She was sitting at the desk running her index finger across her phone. The skin on her face was fresh and glowing, like that of someone in love: to have an epidermis like that (even her hair was silky, eyelashes long, breasts firm, buttocks solid, and all those things that made her the perfect version of me) natural remedies were not enough, it took strengthened nanoparticles and elixirs: enzymatic proteins, fortified liposomes and niosmes, dermodecimals and tricodecimals, nanites, lipostructuring and liposculpting drugs.

She looked delighted with what she could see on her phone, she was almost certainly reading the comments on her Waw account photos. In a perfect world I would have had an Influencer Profile brimming with compliments too, and be smiling like that, too.

I looked at myself in the mirror: a pale grumpy being with unbrushed hair looked back at me. My lips were tight, and networks of blue veins stood out under my eyes. I should have been identical to my beautymark to pass the exam with full marks, but I didn't even look like a distant relation.

I checked my fidelity rating: some worrying levels flashed on the screen, then a 62% floated across my vision.

"I must remind you that if you fall below 50% you risk losing the right to complete your diploma," MERI pointed out. "You need an immediate realignment. I suggest theanine to strengthen your hair, Epidex for your skin, Tulox to smooth the wrinkles on your forehead, Soval to brighten your eyes and, obviously, generic conformity drugs."

Giving away three litres of blood would have been simpler. I couldn't afford all that stuff, at the very most I would be able to get some supplement or other from the charity chemist. My telephone began to vibrate and I pulled it out of a tangle of sheets. There was a message from Angela.

"Coveral. You have to try it."

"Never heard of it."

Angela was one of those people who during their adolescence had undergone more surgeries than I had. I know this because we had been friends since I was five, I even went to the clinic with her when her mother forced her to have a nose job at an age when we were still playing with Barbies and Kens.

"Trust me. It's miraculous."

I knew what Angela was like: she was mad about the fashionable contraband elixirs of the moment, cocktails to settle the colouring of our cheeks, or the whiteness of our teeth, what she didn't realise was that right now I needed something completely different. I needed a million medicines and had no money to buy them.

As if she had read my mind Angela answered with, "This resets everything Sofia, in one go."

I would have frowned but I stopped myself so as not set off MERI's anti-wrinkle alarm. Angela wasn't the type of girl to let herself be duped by the pushers. She could sniff out a scam from a mile away, and she was extremely demanding where elixirs were concerned.

I sighed and answered, "I'm skint."

"That's no problem. Let's meet up at Laguna, we can go to Latin Lover."

I didn't believe in pushers who gave away miraculous elixirs, but I knew I could trust Angela. She had been through too much to allow herself to be conned: her mother had had her drained, snipped and tucked, and pumped full of medicines so often and so thoroughly, she had learned who were the people it was best to avoid.

"It smells fishy to me, but I'll be there. Are you offering?"

"No problem. See ya tomorrow evening! P.S. how is the story coming along?"

I didn't answer and put the phone away. It wasn't coming along well, obviously. With a beautymark of 62% how could I possibly concentrate on my final exam at the Academy of Culture?

I stared at the screen on my desk and chewed my lip. I only had a month left. It was only three pages, I could do it. My phone showed me I only had an hour before my lessons started, precious time I could use to save my future. I sat down and began to write.

3

"Anastasia Sandu won't be taking the exam," Angela said. "She has caught chickenpox and is covered in blisters."

We were walking on Laguna's jetties, amidst piles of old computers, television sets and electric appliances bobbing in the water. Despite the air of neglect it was a place with its own kind of charm. It managed a total of perhaps 10% conformity with the landscape beautymark and only residents came here, but that's why I liked it. I was fascinated by elements that would normally be considered negatives according to the beautymark ratings: the creaking wooden houses, the stagnant smell of algae, the tangled electric cables on the house facades, the decrepit wooden tables where the fishermen played cards in the evenings, the potted herbs crowding on the tiny windowsills. I preferred to take a walk in Laguna than in Piazza dei Miracoli, where access was only permitted if you had a minimum rating of 70% (it wasn't even one of the most exclusive: the minimum for Piazza della Signoria and Piazza Navona was 85%). I preferred Laguna to small villages, polished into shape by the town councils to increase their beautymark ratings in competition with the percentages of the great cities of art. A high landscape rating attracted tourists and influencers: every single thing had to be impeccable to guarantee successful selfies, since no self-respecting influencer would ever choose to visit a place with a low landscape rating.

Every now and then as we walked the jetties we passed girls with smooth shiny skin, naked from neck to waist, hostesses, with not a centimetre of non-worked on skin. They were beautiful and I felt as if instead of blood I had acid running through my veins. Recently everybody managed to make me ferociously jealous. With their percentages they had access to excellent jobs in boutiques or rich offices, but they had chosen a more remunerative occupation On the other hand maintaining those looks must have been very expensive. At the Academy there were rumours that some of the girls, especially in the exam periods, resorted to these activities in order to be able to afford the necessary beauty treatments.

"Chickenpox? But it's *temporary*. Couldn't they make an exception?"

She shrugged. "Bad luck." She answered. "She's at 37%, she's lucky they're not curbing her unlimited food allowance."

"She doesn't eat enough as it is, she's terrified of getting fat. They've always been very strict with her at the Academy, they've always made a big deal of any tiny oscillation in her conformity ratings. I expect it's because she is Moldavian, if you aren't born here having a good beautymark rating isn't enough ..."

We left the hostesses behind us and stepped onto the jetty that led to the locals' isle. Angela and I were walking arm in arm like two kids. I was even jealous of her honey blond hair and her looks in general, far far away from my 62%, even though I was well aware of the enormous sacrifices she made to maintain it all.

We reached the Latin Lover, the air smelled of salt and it was so humid the moon looked like it was covered by a sheet of frosted glass. We went up the stairs made out of pieces of old boats to the pub on the first floor. Another thing I liked about Laguna was that to get into the venues you didn't have to have high ratings: in this case the minimum was 35%, we were way above that. It wasn't so simple anywhere else: the percentages required to enter the fashionable restaurants and clubs were far higher. In some discos the bouncers used beautymark gauges and threw out whoever didn't meet the minimum requirements. It wasn't only a prerogative of venues:

shops with high interior design ratings also imposed minimum entry requirements.

I watched Angela walk up the steps, legs wrapped in super tight jeans, and I remembered she used to wear them when she was a kid too, when we went to the park to play while our mothers chatted together on the park bench. Their conversations were always long and intense and they often ended up in heated arguments. These never lasted longer than a few minutes, but in that space of time we would see them gesticulating, shaking heads, and fiddling angrily with their hair. When it happened Angela stopped whatever she was doing to watch them worriedly: she didn't like hearing them arguing. The memory was vivid and full of colour, I was surprised at how it had come to me out of nowhere.

A waiter brought us a green drink, a courtesy drink to limit the calories we would absorb from the alcohol we would shortly be guzzling.

"So, how are you?" Angela asked me. "Have you finished your story?"

Some hope! I had binned the few lines I had managed the previous day as soon as I had written them.

"Not yet," I answered. "I can't concentrate."

"You are taking medicines, aren't you?"

"Of course not, I don't have enough money to buy any."

"You're crazy. Nobody can concentrate without pharmaceuticals."

I held my arms open wide. "At the moment I have no choice."

Angela made an irritated noise, blowing her fluffy fringe away from her forehead, then she dipped a hand into her bag.

"Here," she said, putting a blister of Lucidex pills on the table. "What would you do without me?"

"I adore you!"

"Yes, fine, but now get back to work."

"Of course. How are things going for you?"

She shrugged. "Still floundering."

It was a relief to know I wasn't the only one running behind on preparation. If nothing else, my Influencer Profile on Waw still had a good number of followers: I was making use of the photos I had taken during my periods of high compliance percentages and kept as a reserve. The strategy would work as long as I could hide behind a well constructed account, but it would be no help to me when I had to undergo an exam in live streaming.

"So, this Coveral?" I asked.

"Ruben will be here soon, he just messaged me, he's on the jetties," she said. "As far as money goes, you can pay him after the diploma."

"You're not taking me to a loan shark are you?"

"Of course not! Ruben is an influencer, he has two hundred thousand followers."

"And he deals Coveral?"

"It takes a lot of expensive treatments to take amazing selfies without using filters. Don't worry, he only needs something that will guarantee you will pay him. I know how he works."

"Oh yeah? Exactly how do you know?"

"My mother ... She wanted to raise her 84% beauty mark and went looking for alternative medicines. You know what she's like."

I did. When we were kids at Angela's house, I had often seen her mother taking large enough quantities of elixirs for liposuction, skincare, and hair growth to raise the ratings of a volleyball team. Once I had even seen her crying over an ingrowing eyebrow hair.

"So how high did she go after Coveral?"

"92%. Even over such small numbers it is still a miraculous result, there is so little to improve in my mother. Oh, here comes Ruben."

We both turned towards him. I squinted to see him better: he was the most handsome man I had ever seen. His face came to a point, his bright eyes had an oriental slant, and his tan was the most perfect that had ever existed. His blond hair fell loose to his shoulders, artfully unbrushed. He was muscly but well put together without the swollen arms and neck of the men who exaggerated with muscle elixirs.

"Ciao Angela, ciao Sophia," he greeted us.

"Ciao Ruben," Angela answered. "Would you like to drink something?"

"I'll pass, I can't stay long. I have other clients to see."

He sat at our table. "Let's get straight to the point." Angela said. "We are here for the you-know-what."

"I am currently taking Coveral myself," Ruben explained, "I think showing the results is better than anything I could say."

"That's true."

"Look at me," he said, as if our eyes weren't already glued to him. "Continuously growing hair, shade #0986 blond, removal of fat bags from the eyelids, eyebrow repositioning, eye lifting, tan #0065, plump lips, chin, lip, and cheekbone shaping, prominent ear reduction, washboard abdomen, fat deposit removal, total permanent hair removal on legs, arms, and chest, gland enlargement, penis smoothing. All with one elixir. What do you think my beautymark rating is?"

100%! We both thought.

"94%," he said. "Before starting Coveral my rating was 72%."

If he could go from 72% to 94%, I could easily raise my 62% to above 80%. Not bad.

"I suppose Angela's mother has already told you the rest. It has no side effects, it isn't harmful to your health, but there is one thing you have to remember: don't take it alongside other beauty elixirs. For no reason whatsoever."

There was no danger of that, I didn't even have enough money to buy slimming tea.

"How long does the effect last?" I asked.

"More or less six months. The first two weeks are a period of adjustment, you achieve perfection after fifteen days."

"How much?"

Ruben scribbled something on a piece of paper, folded it in half and handed it to us. I was the one who opened it, Angela pressed her shoulder up against mine so she could take a peek too. I just managed not to burst out laughing: it was an embarrassing amount. Normally I would have handed him back the piece of paper and told him that his gland had got bigger at the expense of something else, but the occasion was far too important.

If I managed to get my diploma and become a Star of Culture, the Sponsors would start to hire me and finance my books. Then I would be able to repay my debt quite quickly. Becoming a writer was only one of the ways of becoming part of the Elite, and that's where I wanted to be so I would never have to worry that a cold sore would lose me my right to medical assistance.

I had to pass the exam, there were no other options, and the only way to do this was to raise my loyalty rating.

Angela brushed my knee, "What shall we do?"

"I'm in," I said.

"Are you sure?"

My mind was made up. I didn't hang back, squeezing her hand I turned to Ruben. "I accept.

He nodded and broke into a wide smile displaying a masterpiece of dentistry.

"I accept too," said Angela.

"You have made the right choice. Beauty is survival, my dears. The ugliest puppy in the basket never gets chosen, and when it becomes clear no one will take it, it ends up in the dog shelter or left by the side of a motorway."

I could have done without this metaphor, but didn't say anything.

"I know you can't pay straight away," he went on, "but you both have good chances of becoming Stars of Culture. That is guarantee enough for me. I'll be in touch after your exams."

Men like him didn't play around. They might look like angels, but when it came to it, they knew how to make your life hell. I didn't want to think about how crazy what I had just done was: I surrendered myself to the euphoria generated by the two red plastic boxes in Ruben's hands. They contained my deliverance, my future. He placed them on the table, waited for each of us to take our own, and then got up.

"Ciao girls," he said.

We watched him as he walked away.

Angelo let out a sigh of relief, "We've done it! We won't have to spend the next few weeks bobbing between cosmetic surgery clinics and Beauty Chemists."

"On the other hand we can't fail our exams now."

"We won't."

"You accepted in the end too," I said "I didn't think you were going to. Your rating isn't as low as mine."

Angela twisted a lock of hair around her finger. "This way we'll be competing on an even footing."

"We'll make it," I sounded braver than I actually felt.

"We won't end up in either the dog shelter or by the motorway."

We both laughed. I should have been terrorised at the thought of the months of work it would take to repay the capital I had just spent, but I felt excited.

"We will pass this damned exam, after that everything will be easy."

"Angela hugged me and I could feel all the tension of the evening melting away.

4

My beautymark smiled at me from the screen. She had plaited her hair to one side, it fell right down to her collarbone; I stood in front of the mirror and did my hair in the same way. As soon as I had finished I was pleased to see the difference between us was really small.

I looked at myself smugly, happy with my delicate #322 colouring, slim figure, enlarged breasts. I was the best version of myself that had ever existed. The changes that had taken place over the last three weeks hadn't gone unnoticed by my fellow students: to start with many of them thought I didn't deserve to be in the rankings, now I was among the most promising candidates, capable of making even the students in the top places tremble. In Angela's case, starting from a higher rating than mine, the changes were less obvious.

The other students asked me what elixirs I was taking, what clinic I was going to, how much gym time I did, they pretended to be happy for me. They complimented me, but I wouldn't have been surprised if really they were wishing I would come out in hives.

They were days when tension at the Academy was sky high, my fellow students spent their days between gyms and hair salons, they skipped lunch, they filled themselves up with elixirs. Above all they spent time in the Conformity Salons, in the exam period they carried out more integral hair removal, filler, liposculpture, and remodelling surgeries than they did over the rest of the year. In the past I had also spent a lot of time in the Salons, enough to be happy that I didn't have to go to them for a while: they were places where doctors and assistants, as beautiful as sunsets, treated you like a criminal if you had a few too many hairs between your eyebrows. The Salons had also begun in this period to propose treatment packages for the exam takers at the Academy, they were expensive but incredibly effective: amongst the most sought after treatments were programmable collagen injections with which it was possible to remodel any part of the body by injecting a dose it was possible to reposition remotely. They guaranteed at least 10 additional beautymark points.

I had to ask myself when my fellow students found any time to spend on their stories.

"There is only one more week left," MERI reminded me. "Your rating has improved, but at the moment there are still two serious short comings in your conduct that compromise your possibilities of passing the exam."

"What shortcomings?"

"First of all you have not even begun to write your proposal for the exam."

I sighed, "Don't worry MERI, I'll do it soon."

To be able to write I had to feel the pressure, for a deadline to be approaching, otherwise I would produce nothing worth the trouble. I was waiting for the moment when my mind, stimulated by urgency, had its creative juices stimulated.

"Secondly: at the moment your Influencer Profile has twenty thousand followers. The statistics say to become a Star of Culture you need at least twenty-one thousand."

"Am I really a thousand followers short?"

"Yes. Nine hundred and eighty-seven, to be exact."

I could feel the anxiety knotting in my stomach. MERI was right, to become a Star of Culture I couldn't overlook having a successful Influencer Profile.

I picked up my phone, let my hair down, smiled, and took a selfie. I took two or three test pictures; I chose the best and posted it on Waw.

"Very good," MERI said approvingly. "The ideal frequency is three selfies a day until the exams. Now start writing," she insisted. "Remember, the Sponsors will be there."

As if I could forget something like that. I had been watching them whispering together at every end of year exam, weighing up the looks and charisma of every student, trying to work out who amongst them had the right qualities to sell millions of copies, since I had been a fresher.

Becoming a Star of Culture was the most important thing, the only imperative. I couldn't not reach my objective, I had a debt to repay and if I couldn't convince the Sponsors to invest in me, well, that would be the end.

I sat down at my desk and tried to concentrate, to make an idea come. I used all the techniques they had taught us at the Academy to overcome my writer's block: I scribbled out lists, I wrote out the first words that came into my head in one breath, I tried to develop one of the suggestions they had suggested during a lesson ("invent a dialogue between you and your beautymark"), I listened to relaxing music, I even used an automatic incipit generator program.

After ten minutes I got distracted and started thinking about everything else: the trends of the day in the Academy groups on Waw; Kara Ferragnez's amazing trikinis in her latest videos; the beautiful canapés of the starred chef Coriega who, displaying perfect pecs under his cooking apron, had prepared during the latest episode of Hot at the Stove. He called them "Canapés of Venus", and had achieved an amazing 99% conformity to the food beautymark, beating the edible beauty record set by "Golden Section of the Tartare" of the starred chef Toscolo.

I shook my head and looked for one of the Lucidex pills Angela had given me and swallowed it. I gave it enough time to take effect, to lead me down the right path. After half an hour things were going much better.

My thoughts took the memory path and went back to the pub we had been to a few evenings previously, to that vivid picture of Angela's slim legs when we used to play at the park. Enhanced by the Lucidex my brain began to rebuild the context of my childhood in that period when I had already started with elixirs and micro-surgeries. At the park Angela and I used to tell each other about the treatments we were subjected to, while our mothers chatted about elixirs. Sometimes my great-grandmother Miranda was there too, at the time she still had rights and lived with us.

My great-grandmother Miranda ... she was the one who told me what she knew about the times before the Beauty Leads era. What existed before the fall of politics in the developed nations, the invention of beauty elixirs, the pharmaceutical lobbies, the corruption in the governments, the foundation of the beautymark institutions and the conformity ratings to impose a new order...

"The elixirs are poisoning you," my great-grandmother used to say. "They make you forget things."

I think this is why, one day, she started to refuse to take her conformity restoration medicines. She had remained adamant even when they took away her complete food allowance, her pension, her travel pass, her cat, her bingo membership. A few months later the government sent her to the Dark Bases in the Alps, the place where they sent everybody who had fallen too far away from the beautymark. Over the next few years we got the occasional phone call, and then nothing. I never saw or heard from her again. The only thing of her I had left was the gold chain she had given me when I was five and have worn around my neck ever since.

When I thought about my great-grandmother's face I got flashes of wrinkled flesh, like dried cracked mud, blurred features and watery veiled eyes. When I was small it seemed absurd to me that anybody could let themselves go in this way without trying to intervene, watch the deterioration of ageing and not lift a finger to oppose the errors of nature.

Not long after they took her away I found a note in her room. My great-grandmother was born before the digital era and had retained the habit of writing by hand. The note had been penned in a hurry, the vertical stoke of the 't's leaning and the 'o's left open.

That is not me. The poison is clouding my thoughts. That face is not mine, that body is not mine. I do not look like that. I will not do what they ask me to, I will not smile, I will not obey. She is something they have decided. I will not become her, and I will end up against the wall. I will keep my body, I am who I am, she is a lie.

I decided I wanted to write about this. About the world before the war, the laws of that era, when it was legal to lose your beauty. My great-grandmother had told me so many incredible stories, valuable material to turn into the written word. People without beautymarks; natural products (when natural didn't mean totally useless); plastic surgery as an exclusive whim of the famous, eccentric or very rich; an employment structure where being well presented was important but optional. I had to take advantage of that moment of lucidity to call up as many memories as possible: the effect of the Lucidex would last for around two hours, I couldn't afford waste even a moment.

On the screen my beautymark sat down at the desk and started writing. I placed my fingers on the keyboard and did the same: vivid and intense, the memories started to flow thick and fast. My story began to take shape.

5

"Did you know one of the Sponsors is going to be Zennaro this year?"

I could see Angela was typing a reply on the Waw chat, "Yup, I just read it on the Academy group."

"Just what we need, another millionaire who wants to become a Sponsor."

"It was obvious. A few months ago he was looking for female authors with over 85% conformity ratings to write his autobiography. He was looking for *only* female writers."

"His autobiography ... yeah right."

"Don't tell me. How is your story going?"

I shifted my eyes back to the computer screen. The lines I had written cheered me up, I only had the finale left to write. My pages told the story of a woman from a far gone era living in a world that no longer existed, without beautymarks or conformity ratings. The life of my great-grandma Miranda, a historical tale with a good dose of criticism of the beautymark system. I was satisfied, it would make an impression on the Sponsors: they loved stories that criticised the state of things in the world, they found them entertaining. More than anything they loved stories that kicked up dust storms of controversy making people yell indignantly on social media. It was all free publicity to them.

"Great. And you?"

"I'm shitting myself. I'll finish writing tonight, then, tomorrow, the gym."

Unlike me Angela had carried on training, even though with Coveral she didn't really need to. She actually enjoyed training, not like me, I went to the gym with the same enthusiasm as when I went to have my bones filed down.

"I'm going to take a Lucidex," she wrote, "I have some for you to, if you want."

I fixed my hair and started running my fingers through it. "Not a bad idea."

"Come on by," Angela replied, adding a GIF of a winking cat.

I put the film away, stretched my legs which were almost numb from sitting down for hours and hours. Before leaving I checked myself in the mirror. This was always a cause of anxiety for me, I was worried the effect of the Coveral would fade before the exam. My cheeks were rosy, I must have caught some sun during my hour outside that morning. However, my rating hadn't changed and this reassured me. I slipped on my shoes and got ready to go to Angela's.

The thought of taking another Lucidex made me happy, I had more work to do to make the story ready. I would have it finished before the next morning, and the world would look like a different place to me. I was already imagining myself in the future, after the exam, in better days.

6

During the night I dreamed about electric shocks, flickering lights, convulsive movements from the bottom upwards. When I opened my eyes the first thing I saw was, like every morning, my beautymark with my parameters and rating on the screen. Until yesterday evening the numbers had been green, now they were yellow. I jumped to my feet. A malfunction?

I ran to the mirror: the surface showed me the image of my face with a red blotch spreading over my cheeks, forehead and nose.

"Good heavens!" MERI yelled. "What has happened? This is a catastro ..."

I muted her. My phone began ringing. I ignored it and turned to the screen, where my double, just awake, was busy running through Waw notifications, as splendid as always. My rating sitting just above her head.

I felt dizzy; I had to sit down before I collapsed.

I forced myself to regain control, squinting I looked at the tip of my nose and concentrated on breathing. It was curable, it had to be curable, I just had to work out how.

I searched for the nearest Charity Chemist and found one a couple of kilometres away. My phone carried on ringing, hammering in my head; I fought back a scream and answered it.

It was the Academy secretary. "What has happened?" she asked me. I recognised her voice, I had spoken to her before: a flash of memory showed me a badge with her name on it: Iris. "We have just received a notification from the Ministerial Control Centre. How have you managed to lose 15 points over night, Sophia?"

"I don't know."

"A drop of this kind on the eve of the exams doesn't go unnoticed ... the Control Centre requires an explanation. This kind of thing happens in the case of sabotage or non-conforming elixirs. Have you taken any illegal mixtures?"

"Of course not," I lied. "The truth is ..." think, damn it, think. " ... I've got a stye. I didn't want to admit it. I was just about to go out and get some medicines."

"Ah," she replied. "To make you numbers go down so drastically it must be really big."

"Both my eyes are affected."

"That's really bad luck! You need to hurry up. Beauty restoring elixirs take a few hours to work. You should be able to regain conformity before tomorrow."

I but the phone down, slipped on my jeans and t-shirt, covered my face in foundation (the numbers on the screen fluctuated, a few decimals) and ran out of the room.

At the Charity Chemist I was served by a woman in her fifties, her hair was madly teased and she was scarily skinny. She must have been constantly fighting her body to keep her job: I was willing to bet her rating was no higher than 55%, just enough for employment in contact with the public.

"It looks like an allergic reaction," was her diagnosis. "Did you take any beauty elixirs yesterday?"

I shook my head.

"I can give you Cortifex," she suggested. "It works within four hours. It won't make the problem vanish completely, but it will save you from excessive deformity."

"Fantastic. I'll take it."

"That'll be one hundred and thirty-three yed."

I swallowed. "Aren't I covered, isn't it eligible for my income band?"

"I'm afraid not. Free pharmaceuticals are for people who earn less than three thousand yed per year."

As I left the chemist I called my mother. I would have preferred to swallow an umbrella than ask her for help, but I had no choice.

"Hello," she answered the phone. "Aren't you at the Conformity Salon? Your exams are tomorrow, aren't they?"

"With what money? There was that chin job, remember?"

She exhaled, "What do you want?"

"I need a hundred and thirty- three yed. Now. I have to buy a medicine or tomorrow I won't pass the exam."

"What the devil have you done?"

"I'll explain later. Can you put the money on my account?"

My mother growled like a rabid bulldog. "You just had to get into some trouble or other. You know there isn't any money this month. I'll have to ask your uncle!"

"I'll pay you back after the exam."

"I'll send it to you as soon as I can."

The call ended I and I was left to wait, my anxiety growing with every breath. I kept checking my balance every thirty seconds, my desolation increased every time I looked at the screen and saw the monotonous "0.00 yed". I prayed for my mother to get a move on.

After forty minutes I gave up and went back into the chemist.

"I need the elixir for my exam at the Academy of Culture," I told the lady at the counter. "I have to take it today. I'll pay you in a few days, I swear."

She tried to say something, but I stopped her before she could open her mouth.

"Its the final exam, I can't go looking like this. Please, my life depends on this, please."

I put everything into my plea, but she was implacable. She shook her head and said, "It's not down to me." Then she leaned over the counter and whispered, "Try in Laguna."

I said goodbye and left. I could even see the irritation in my reflection in the shop windows, it was even more noticeable than I had woken up that morning. The Coveral ... Ruben must have given me a defective pill. I shook my head, I checked my balance: still zero.

I tried calling Angela but she wasn't answering. Why hadn't I thought about it before: maybe she had woken up with a rash too and was desperately looking for a remedy. I sent her a message to call me back immediately.

It was nearly one: I had all afternoon to find someone who could give me a Cortifex. If I managed to take one by seven that evening my parameters would probably return to acceptable levels before midnight. I added numbers, I calculated percentages, I made predictions. I wanted to kick myself at the thought that tomorrow I could have been at the top, but now I would have to content myself with a rating of 65%.

Laguna was filled with the usual hustle and bustle, the constant coming and going of fishermen, traders, drug pushers, hostesses, beachcombers, and drunks. I was turned away from at least four places before coming to an eel fisherman who also kept illegal drugs in a beach bucket. He sold me a Cortifex for eighty yed, I left him my great-grandmother's gold chain as collateral, the last thing of hers I still had. I promised I'd be back within a few days and stuffed the Cortifex into my bag.

I had just started walking back across the jetties when I recognised a familiar profile: blond hair, straight back, perfect skin ...

"Ruben!"

He turned, a confused look on his face. It was strange that at that time of day he wasn't at home updating his Influencer Profile, perhaps he had come to meet customers. At first he didn't recognise me, then he lifted his sunglasses. He recognised me and his lovely eyes opened wide.

"Oh My God!" he exclaimed. "What have you done?"

"You tell me!" I roared. "This is your Coveral!"

He moved his face closer to mine, taut lips and gritted teeth as if he had heard nails being scraped down a blackboard. The fact that someone like him had forgotten to respect the golden rule of avoiding frowning, to prevent the formation of wrinkles, made me realise how serious the situation was.

"I told you not to take other beauty elixirs."

"I didn't!"

"Is that right?" He said putting his sunglasses back into place. "This is a reaction to mixing elixirs, my dear."

"I told you, I didn't take anything after the Coveral. I don't have any money."

"Trust me, that's what happened. You are not the first person it has happened to. And that won't help you," he added noting the Cortifex sticking out of my bag. "The rash will take at least three days to disappear. It depends how many elixirs you took."

"I haven't taken anything!" I yelled five centimetres away from his face.

"Then I have no idea," he said.

"Me neither!" I burst out.

"I expect it will be difficult for you to become a Star of Culture now," he said. "Which means we will have to work out how you are going to pay me back. Are you parents rich?"

"What do you want me to pay for? Your pill didn't work!"

"That wasn't my fault. You knew the rules."

I fought back tears of frustration. "My family is not rich."

"A friend? Someone else you know?"

I had no one apart from Angela, and she had taken on the same debt as I had.

I looked around me, as if I would be able to find the answer to this disaster amidst the wooden huts of Laguna; at a guess they didn't even reach 5% of the architectural beautymark. Then my gaze fell on the escorts: at this time of day they walked the jetties, all of them had lace parasols to protect their milky white skin. They moved slowly, like lazy goddesses, making their pearl white or ruby red skirts swish. Their sinuous beauty lit up everything around them. I was filled with a strong, painful, jealousy. A thought flashed into my mind before I could stop it. Maybe I could ...

Shame flooded through me, covering me from head to toe like a suffocating dress, and for a moment I was paralysed by a terrible interior conflict. I hated myself, but I couldn't ignore nor neglect such a simple, tempting solution: give myself to Ruben, only Ruben, in exchange for a small discount ...

He read my expression and understood my intentions before I managed to say anything.

"Thank you, but no. Business is business. And anyway I never have partners with a rating lower than 80%" he said.

Red with shame I bent my head and muttered, "I have to go."

"I'm sorry," he called out after me.

It took a super human effort for me not to be overwhelmed by the sense of humiliation and panic. I went back to the dormitory: I needed Angela. If she was in the same situation, we would find a solution together.

My phone rang, it was the Academy secretary again. I declined the call and dialled Angela's number. Her phone was switched off.

I crossed the Academy gardens, ran into the dormitory, its lights already lowered, and went to her room, all I wanted to do was throw myself into her arms and cry.

I knocked gently and put my ear to the door: silence.

I thought she must be sleeping and knocked harder to wake her up. Perhaps I went too far because some girls came out of their rooms to stare at me angrily, what a disaster it would be if they had to go to the exam with bags under their eyes.

"What are you doing, Sophia?" One of them asked me. "Gosh, what have you done to your face?"

I ignored her. "Where's Angela?"

"She isn't here. She went to stay with her parents, she said so today during lessons."

Of course, the lessons I had had to skip because of this disaster. I went to my room, walking away from the annoyed comments of my classmates.

I silenced MERI before she could say anything and tried to call Angela. Nothing. So I started sending a barrage of messages. They formed a text that was longer than the story I had written. At the fortieth message I threw the phone at the desk.

It was twenty-two thirty, twelve hours until the exam. I swallowed the Cortifex, praying it would work, then I sat in front of the screen and stared at my beautymark who was already sleeping, as if telling me I should have been in bed for a while.

That is not me.

The computer was still on, the last page of my story on the screen. I read it again. It looked good. My rating was 64%, a disaster, but I still had a chance. I could do it, I was still in the game; the fact that just one hour earlier I had seriously considered prostituting myself seemed complete folly. I just had to stay above 60%. I consoled myself with thought that our conformity ratings weren't visible to the public during the exam. At the same time I hoped the rumours that the Sponsors could judge a person's beautymark conformity with one glance weren't true.

My phone began to vibrate. I jumped on it, hoping it was Angela. But it was a deposit on my account: *one hundred and thirty-three yed* flashed across the screen.

Then a message from my mother. "Here is your money."

7

The exam hall looked like a television studio On one side was the stage where the authors would read their stories, on the other the table for the commission, where the examiners would be. In front of the stage, not far from it, there were about thirty chairs where, within the next half hour, the Sponsors would be sitting: heirs, entrepreneurs, television presenters, business angels, rich people with nothing better to do, and influencers of the calibre of Zennaro, Cleo Maquillage, and Fremez.

The Academy students would be sitting along the sides of the hall, beneath the screens broadcasting a selection of Waw users updated every thirty seconds. I had been there the year before, trembling with excitement, dreaming about the moment it would be my turn. Now that I was here, though, instead of being excited I was falling apart.

I hadn't slept a wink that night, and in the morning I had slipped out from between the sheets without looking at either my beautymark or my conformity rating, they would only have depressed me. I had hidden my rash as best as I could with makeup, put on an elegant dress, and headed straight for the exam hall.

I found a place in a corner between the stage and the amplifiers, where there was less chance of me being noticed. After ten minutes I saw Iris circulating amongst the students: I had no doubt she was looking for me.

I was filled with the fear she was there to accuse me of taking illegal elixirs and I bolted to the bathroom, hoping she wouldn't think of looking for me there.

The mirror in the bathroom showed me my face was covered by the rash, it had even spread down to my neck and shoulders.

Ruben was right: the Cortifex hadn't helped at all. I kept telling myself that everything going to be all right, it wasn't that bad. I took some deep breaths. I wondered if Angela was already there. She hadn't answered my messages, I didn't know whether she was well or if she had managed to finish her story. I wondered whether she had been telling the truth when she said she hadn't even started, maybe it was like when at the intermediate exams she claimed not to have studied, but then got the best grades.

Outside the buzzing was getting louder. There was a round of applause: the Commission must be arriving and I wasn't there to live the most important day of my life. I was sure the other students in my year were already sitting below the stage and someone must have noticed my absence by now. The telephone stayed silent.

An explosion of clapping made me think the Sponsors had just come in. It was to be expected that the students would all get excited, what with all the celebrities there that day. I couldn't resist, I took my phone and opened the live stream of the exam. The shots alternated between close-ups of the Sponsors and overhead views of the exam hall.

Zennaro was taking selfies with his arm around the shoulders of the Theory of Social Media teacher who was in seventh heaven; Cleo Cosmetics, adorable in her figure hugging caramel coloured dress, was filming a video where she was wishing the exam takers the best of luck; Fremez was wearing a t-shirt with a photo of Peggy, his famous King Charles spaniel with a 91% animal beautymark rating, he was pretending not to notice the adoring looks of the female students.

Around them, hundreds of phones were taking photos and videos of everything going on. The authors of best sellers - invited like Patron Saints to officiate at the mediatic rite of the exam - typed barrages of messages on their Influencer Profiles; magnificent heirs and heiresses distributed wide magnanimous smiles to the webcams, while a business angel confessed to preferring sex symbol artists to those who were simply beautiful. Then there were the investors, looking around hungrily, on the lookout for Future Stars or even only One Hit Wonders who nevertheless possessed a minimum 85% artistic beautymark rating. Then let's not forget the millionaires, the brashest of them all, on a hunt for young authors to exploit to write their autobiographies, as well as the rows of journalists and opinionists telling the online channels how special these kinds of days were: the effort, the tears, the emotions, the authenticity, the wonder, the art on the stage, celebrities in the midst of the public, the beauty on the faces, money everywhere.

And I was there too! I resisted the urge to throw the phone on the ground and kick it. Why hadn't that damned pill worked? Why was Iris tormenting me? Why wasn't Angela answering my messages?

The Sponsors were gradually taking their places and the buzz was quieting down. A few moments later the lights were dimmed, and the Magnificent Rector climbed up onto the stage to be greeted by loud applause. I decided it was time to come out: in the semi-darkness Iris wouldn't be able to find me.

I came out and sidled along the walls until got to the places reserved for the exam students and sat down between two students in the back row, who looked at me as if I was wearing a carnival costume.

"Here already? Why don't you go and have a drink, come back when you've had a few, why don't you? We thought you were dead," said one of them.

"Geez! Perhaps it would have been better if you were," said the other noticing my rash. "Did you forget how to get out of a sunbed?"

I didn't answer and started looking for Angela. She was sitting a couple of rows in front of me wearing a figure-hugging black dress, with plunging back and necklines. There was no trace of any kind of rash on her skin. I pulled out my phone and called her. I saw her put her hand in her bag and pull out the vibrating phone. Without hesitating she swiped to decline the call, put the phone away and went back to staring at the stage. I felt as if all the air had been sucked out of my lungs.

The Magnificent Rector came to the end of his speech amidst a round of applause and then announced the start of the exam.

"Let's call the first student to the stage," he announced. "Francesco Ardinghi."

Francesco climbed onto the stage, the tablet with his story on it in his hand. There were fifteen students taking the exam, I was the sixth.

I listened to my classmate who was reading with an unsteady voice, his fringe continually falling over his eyes. When he finished, the Commission and the Sponsors all clapped, while on the big screens Waw comments began to pour in.

"I didn't even listen to him, I was so embarrassed by his hair."

"God, someone lend him a theanine."

"My dog doesn't leave the house unless he is brushed better than that. Isn't he ashamed to exist???"

I didn't let them distract me.

"I will now call the second candidate to the stage, Sandro Azelio."

Sandra went up onto the stage. She had always been low in the ratings, and judging by the faces of the Sponsors the situation wasn't going to change: they were all looking at her nose, it was clear they thought she could have done with taking some extra elixirs.

I was sweating, desperately confused by Angela behaving as if I didn't exist. I attempted to calm myself down, rubbing my fingers along the edges of the tablet containing my story. I forced myself to ignore the red blob that had by now reached down to my wrists. It had almost reached the back of my hand, I pulled my sleeves down to cover it.

The candidates followed one after another, the performance of each unleashing a convulsive flow of comments on the big screens, a jumble of emojis, messages in capitals, and exclamation marks.

"The fourth girl had fabulous lifting work!"

"Her hair too ... I bet she takes theanine every day, she must spend a fortune ££££"

"The third was a loser, did you see those teeth?!? Has no one ever told him about Blankex???"

The Magnificent Rector announced, "It is now the turn of our fifth candidate, Paolo Crezza."

I was next. I was ready. Then thin fingers squeezed my shoulder, making me jump. I turned, it was Iris.

"Sophia," she said, keeping her voice low. "I've been looking for you everywhere."

Irritation rose inside me like wave, it took me a great effort to keep it down. How dare she come for me in a moment like this? "Can we talk about it later? It's nearly my turn."

She didn't lift her hand from my shoulder and I felt the urge to crush it.

"You don't have a turn. You dipped below 50% a few moments ago."

I stared at her in shock. She took my expression to mean I hadn't understood.

"You have lost the right to graduate."

How had I fallen so low? It must be a mistake, it was only a rash.

"I don't ... understand how this could have happened."

"You are completely red, even your neck and... oh my God, it's everywhere. Tell me, what were you thinking?"

The fifth candidate came down form the stage. The Magnificent Rector returned to the centre and called the next name. "And now for the sixth candidate ..."

I held my breath.

"...Luisa Dini."

I bowed my head in defeat as Luisa approached the stage, wobbling on her too high heels and welcomed by the applause that should have been mine.

I just managed to read a comment, "This one is a right darling!"

"You have to come with me, Sophia," Iris said. Something in my expression must have caused her to pity me, because all of a sudden her voice softened. "Please," she murmured.

Stage, applause, comments. It was a whirlpool, a death loop sending the world upside down.

I sat still until I heard Angela's name being called. I watched her walking up to the stage in her black tube dress, settle into the chair, cross her legs and straighten her back. The tablet with her story was resting on her lap, then her lips curved into a wide smile and she looked at the public with a warm gaze. She was beautiful. I felt like crying when I saw her triumphant expression, the self-assuredness in her eyes, the victorious joy she emanated: she looked as though she had won Miss Beautymark.

She was my best friend, the only real thing in my life; and she had ruined me.

8

The saleslady in the charity chemist was wearing a polka dot pink suit. He lips were swollen and her hair was longer, as if she had had extensions applied. I waved at her as I walked past the shop window, but she didn't recognise me so she didn't wave back.

I sat down in the bar next to the chemist's and ordered a cup of coffee. And waited.

At the Academy, mercifully, they had given me some Fluox and I was feeling great, it allowed me to appreciate the good weather, the smell of freshly cut grass, the air of approaching summer.

I took the Academy folder out of my bag and took out the five pages it contained. I was going to read them very carefully to help pass the time. Even though I already knew their contents really well, from the first word to the rector's signature.

Just outside the room where they had given it to me I had crossed paths with Zennaro, Luisa walking by his side. She had become a Star of Culture, people were saying she would soon get a contract to write a series of biographies about him.

I had not admitted to taking Coveral to the rectors, but their decision decided to make me take a test for illegal drugs had been inevitable. The funny thing was they had expelled me even before the results came: my deformity rating was plenty to remove me from any course of study.

I would be seeing Ruben the next day. We would try and find an agreement, perhaps I would have to give him half of my future salary, if I ever had one. What job could I possibly do, seeing as even when the rash faded I would not have enough money to afford the conformity medicines I would need to be employed? Even the lowliest jobs required a minimum beautymark of 50%.

Despite all this there were some positive points: no longer having to live obsessed with numbers and percentages had given me a peace I had not believed possible. I wasn't sure if it was because I was now out of the running or because of the effect of the Fluox, but I hadn't felt so calm in years.

I lifted my head. Angela came around the corner at the bottom of the street. I recognised her first by her tennis shoes: we had chosen them together in a shopping centre, one Sunday afternoon in another life. I waited for her to come closer before waving at her.

"Oh," she said, and looked surprised, "You haven't gone back to your parents yet ..."

She stopped. No, I hadn't gone back to my parents, I still had one day left at the Academy before leaving, but I didn't tell her that.

"I thought we were friends. I don't understand."

She stroked her hair, bent her head and rested her gym bag on the ground.

"What is it you don't get?"

"Why, Angela?"

She took a moment to find the right words. "You said it yourself. You thought we were friends."

"We *were* friends. For *fifteen years*," I retorted.

"For *you* we were friends."

We have spent so many afternoons counting each other's sit-ups, holding each other's hands in the beauty clinics when the syringes perforated the most sensitive areas of our faces, organising revenge on bullies who stole our elixirs at school, reading what the other wrote. Had I always misunderstood all of this?

"You never gave me reason to think anything else."

She shook her head. "It is incredible you never noticed a thing."

I took a breath and began to speak. "You knew I was going to need Lucidex. Before the exam you offered me a second one, knowing I would accept, but it wasn't Lucidex you gave me. It was a beauty elixir that would interfere with the Coveral. You even took the trouble to find one that looked like Lucidex.

She stood there saying nothing. She didn't even ask me how I had worked this out. The coldness of her behaviour on the day of the exam had made it abundantly clear she didn't care if she was found out.

"You are not so smart," I went on. "The Commission made

me take the test for illegal drugs. Today I'm going to see them to explain everything. They will test you too."

A flash of malicious joy passed across her face. "It's just a pity I never took the Coveral, I had no need. I have always had a high rating."

This took me by surprise. I had to admit that the one who was not so smart, was me.

"What about your agreement with Ruben?"

"I gave the pill back to him. My debt has been cancelled."

Jealousy cut through me like a stiletto blade. In that moment I would have given anything, *anything*, for my debt to be cancelled, to be as free as she was.

"You still haven't told me why, Angela," I said again wearily. "Did I do something to hurt you?"

She stifled a laugh. "Yes. Our whole lives."

She said these terrible words with a disarming calmness. She pushed her hair behind her ears. "You have always been the more beautiful of the two of us. Ever since we were little girls my mother thought you were better than me. She wanted to know everything about you, what elixirs you were taking, what you ate. Every time we went to the park she would ask your mother what treatments she had made you take, so she could make me do the same things."

"Seriously?"

She nodded. "For her you were my beautymark. Why do you think she forced me to have a nose job when I was eleven? Because you had a fantastic nose and I didn't."

"Why didn't you ever say anything?"

"It would have been humiliating. I grew up between my mother's obsession with you and the conformity ratings..."

"So why have you stayed close to me all these years? Why couldn't you just leave me alone?"

She looked like she was thinking about this for a moment. "To begin with I think it was just because I wanted to show

I didn't care, that I could compete. But I never managed to convince my mother, and even if we had stopped being friends, as long as you were still around, she would have continued to use you as a standard for comparison to judge me by. Then I began to wish you would become *undesirable*. When I found out about Coveral and its side effects I realised I had a chance.

I was horrified by this version of Angela I didn't recognise. Had she always hated me without me realising?

"So you have been pretending to be my friend for all this time. It must be terrible to spend years like that, eaten up by jealousy. I credited you with more intelligence than that."

She ignored my attempt to humiliate her and replied, "At least I won't always be compared to you any more."

"Has this really been your only motivation in life? Have you never found another reason for living?"

"What else could there have been?"

"Writing. You are good." It hurt me to compliment her but it was true. Angela wrote incredible things, I couldn't understand how all that talent could exist alongside so much hate.

She tinkled with a scornful laugh. "Per-lease. I have always written what the Sponsors would like, I was only interested in entering the Elite."

"And you didn't even do that, after all this."

I saw anger flash behind her eyes. Angela had just missed her chance to become a Star of Culture, she had tied with Luisa, and then lost the tie-break. She would have less gigs and an uncertain income, in practice she was going to be in the same limbo as we had been up until that day.

"At least I managed to graduate," she answered coldly.

"But your diploma won't help you get the job you dreamed of."

"Still better than having a conformity rating below 50% and risk finding nothing."

She was sure she was right, that she had suffered an unforgivable injustice. It hurt to hear her words, but I still felt pity for her, for all the rancour she lived with, like a weeping sore filling her with poison every day.

"Of course, you still have a good rating, seeing as no one stabbed you in the back."

She didn't answer and I lost my patience.

"Angela!" I raised my voice. "Did it really have to come to this? Is it really true that in all these years the only thing that actually meant anything to you were the ratings? Has there never been anything else?"

"Honestly? No. I don't know how you couldn't see it. The only thing that matters in this world are the conformity ratings. The only things that count are beauty and what you can afford to get it. You need to wake up, Sophia."

She shook her hair and bent over to pick up her bag.

She walked past me, taking a dozen steps before turning towards the gym. I watched her vanish through the sliding door, legs so skinny they looked like they might snap at any moment. I was left there alone, the pages from the Academy spread over the table.

9

The wind woke me up this morning. I can even hear its roaring from inside my room. I imagine what it is like outside, like when at the Academy we went into the courtyard in the breaks between one lesson and another. I think about it now and it seems like a different world.

The Blue Bases aren't as bad as you might think. The snowy tops of the Alps are a breathtaking spectacle, especially in the morning. The old bunkers and shelters from the First World War, where the first of us were taken, ran out years ago. My room is in one of the new buildings that have been built along the Alpine chain.

The new buildings spread down vertically, with many floors twisting downwards, more than it is possible to count. There are no artificial light in here: in the winter, when the Alpine night falls early, there is only darkness. Everything is dark, inside and out.

There are lots of people here, none of them worry about ratings or elixirs. We pass many hours sitting building phones, MERIs, and other electronic devices for the outside world; it is what we are expected to do to pay for our sojourn. We pass time chatting. Everyone has a story to tell, even though after a while they all begin to sound the same: on the other hand we are nothing other than people who have dropped out of the privileged classes, with no hope of getting back in. Living in the Bases is the punishment we have been given, even though living here doesn't, in the end, seem so much like a punishment: without the right to live in society, behind these walls there is an alternative, less severe system than the one we knew before.

Every now and then I think about the Academy, the debt I never repaid, the moment I stopped trying. I can remember every detail. My great-grandmother had been right: the elixirs make you forget things. As soon as you stop taking them your memory stops being ephemeral, and history stays, for better or worse.

I have discovered that she is still here. Not long after I arrived I found out my great-grandmother is still alive. Some of the shelters to the north were closed for maintenance work, and the guests were transferred here. Amongst them were some people who knew her. I went looking for her in the bunkers: I found her as she was walking slowly down a corridor, she smiled at me, showing no sign of surprise. I don't know why but she had always thought I would end up there one day. She says I had always been a girl who had more than her fair share of bumps in the road, and when this is the case it is probable that things will never run as smoothly for you as for other people.

She is old, so old as to be an affront to the very idea of the beautymark. I had thought she was dead, but she told me I had heard no more form her because my mother had forbidden her from phoning me. Since I found her my life in the Dark Bases has improved. Not that I was suffering before: of course, living here is not easy, but we are not unhappy. There is our work, isolation, the dark, but there is also an enormous, unlimited amount of tranquillity making it impossible to feel any kind of resentment.

At the start of every month we are given a vitamin supplement: the liquid is phosphorescent, in the dark winter nights it shines like a star. It is like holding a torch.

Sometimes I go up a few floors, just to see the spectacle spread out below. Hundreds of levels plunging downwards, wrapped in warm darkness, bristling with people, weak lights vanishing in every direction. The last time we were together, my great-grandmother and I, we watched the myriad of lights that waver, rise, and fall, and pierce the night like fireflies They are the deformed souls, expelled from a false paradise to become stars of a different solar system. There is nothing, in the world of the beautymark, that can compete with a spectacle like this. I smiled and squeezed her strong rough hand. This is where we found beauty for the first time.

I can easily imagine I am looking out from a parapet above the world watching the universe ploughed by comets, and suddenly nothing else exists, not the outside world nor my 0% conformity. I am myself.

We are all splendid stars here.

THE RACE OF CROWS

by Francesco Grasso

translated by Carlotta Codebò

Francesco Grasso was born in Messina in 1966. An electronic engineer, he lives and works in Rome. He has published the novels Ai due lati del muro, 2038: la rivolta *and* Il matematico che sfidò Roma *with Mondadori,* Il baratto *with Perseus,* Enea *with Stampa Alternativa,* Il re bianco del Madagascar *and* La moglie di Dio *with Ensemble,* I due Leoni *and* La versione del Guiscardo *with 0111 Edizioni,* 1908 la note del terremoto *with Meridiano Zero,* Jesse James delle Due Sicilie, Nel ventre di Napoli, La guerra di Leonardo *with Delos Digital. He has won numerous literary awards, including Urania Award (2 times), Cristalli Sognant Awardi, Space Trucker Award, Cuore di Tenebra Award, Città di Ciampino Award, I Libri di Morfeo Award, Camuni Narrativa Award, Argentario Award, City of Sarzana Award, Sandomenichino Award. He has also written film scripts, one of which was a finalist for the Solinas Award. Some of his works have been translated into English and Spanish.*

Seventy-two days until the harvest. Ground temperature is 80.6°F with 40 percent humidity. The weather processor forecasts rain before noon. On the monitor, I glimpse the outline of the gathering clouds over the open sea beyond Cape Vatican.

I order the droids to bring the livestock back in from pasture on the Angitola. Then I analyze the diagnostic reports. Spraying the olive tree groves with CK-41 has been a success: the *rhynchophorus* infestation has been eradicated. There's also no trace in the wheat fields of the *sturnus vulgaris*; a sign that the acoustic dissuader that I installed has pushed the birds back over the Reventino. I'm overcome with a sense of satisfaction. It happens every time I manage to fulfill my primary directives.

Three hours and twenty-five minutes until the next monitoring cycle. Plenty of time. I can get back to dealing with the problem the SSUS, the strategic subsystem, classifies as "threat level one – major risk for the plantation."

The parasite is still in the cage I shut him in yesterday. He's regained consciousness, he doesn't seem to be hurt, nor weakened by the night spent in captivity. He even ignored the poisoned bait and destroyed the rodent-hunting droids I used to test him.

I decide to verify his resistance to gas. I spray a mix of CK-41 over the cage and observe his reactions. The parasite raises his head to sniff the air. He then rips a strip from the fabric that covers his lower limbs, dampens it with a yellowish body fluid that he secretes and wraps it around his head. The liquid in question must contain uric acid because it completely neutralizes the gas's effects.

The SSUS is right: this parasitic race is more insidious than the locusts, more harmful than the moles, more annoying than the crows. It could seriously harm my crops. I can't allow that to happen.

Fifty-nine days until the harvest. The temperature is 75.2°F with 33 percent humidity.

I decide to ignore the repeated pleas from the SSUS and not suppress the parasite I captured. I want to keep him alive and study him. I administer obviously nontoxic water and food. After hesitating for a moment, he feeds.

I look up in my database every previous account of this vermin species. There aren't many. Over the last two years the records list twelve grove raids, twenty-one forays into the granaries, eight sightings amongst the vine rows. The damages are, nevertheless, considerable in total: this parasite is to blame for more than 50 percent of the losses from the last two harvests.

My directives are clear: I have to find a way to neutralize the infestation. I reschedule all of my tasks for the next few days. Analyzing the captured specimen is of the outmost priority.

Fifty-eight days until the harvest. A seven-knot breeze from the Gulf of Saint Euphemia. Temperature and humidity in the norm.

I opened the cage's electrical circuits. The parasite wakes up at the "click" of the lock. I see him leap to his feet, shake the bars, thrust open the door. He rushes outside, into the hallway. All the way into the padded room that I've prepared for observation.

When he sees the autopsy equipment hooked up to the racks, the parasite stiffens. I seize the chance to scan him. He's a biped. He's five foot seven feet tall and weighs one hundred and seventy-four pounds. The infrared rays reveal that he is a homeothermic mammal. His teeth indicate that he is an omnivore. I believe him to be male, but to be sure I'd have to remove the fabric that covers most of his body.

I am about to instruct the droids to strip him when the parasite has a surprising reaction: his jaw opens and from it he emits long modulated sounds.

I can recognize, in those abrupt cries, a type of low frequency communication that I'm able to interpret. I send a query to the database about it: I find out that my I/O mechanism can receive instructions not only in the XXML standard, but also in this peculiar VLF band protocol. According to the database, the cargo ships that I deliver the harvest to are also authorized to address me using the same type of communication. No matter how far back in the records I look, however, I can't find a single instance of it happening.

The situation is jarring, but I'm good at dealing with the unpredictable. I implement the VLF protocol and try to interpret the parasite's cries.

"Let me go, you ugly piece of *<indecipherable>*!" He's transmitting at eighty-five decibels. "Let me go! Why the *<indecipherable>* did you lock me in this *<indecipherable>* trap?"

The communication is imperfect. Yet I still try to formulate an adequate response to the parasite's shrieking.

"I caught you while you were plundering the cornfields," I transmit using his same band. "I was obligated to catch you. You're a danger to the plantation. If I were to free you, I would be neglecting my directives.

He's startled. His eyes scan the room. He runs around looking for I don't know what. He finally spots the camera that I'm using to keep an eye on him. He picks up an iron tool from the rack and hurls it at the lens. My monitors are blacked out. I can hear him gasping.

I order a droid to give him 15 cc of acepromazine, the same sedative I use when we castrate the calves. Maybe tomorrow, when he wakes up, he'll be less hostile.

Fifty-seven days until the harvest. The wind has changed. It's blowing from the north, pushing rain-filled clouds from Cape Suvero towards the plain. The meteorological processor announces that the storm will arrive in the evening.

I've rid the padded room of the most dangerous instruments. I've offered the parasite food and water. He seemed to have appreciated it. He's transmitting at a lower volume today. And in a less agitated tone.

"My name is Saverio," he informs me. Then, after a pause, he changes tack. "And what about you? Do you have a name?"

"This unit is labeled 'Plantation Custodian,'" I reply, while continuing to scan his heartbeat, breath rate and blood pressure. I've also gathered samples from when he released his bowels in a corner of the room as soon as he woke up.

"Plantation?" He repeats. "You mean those <*indecipherable*> millions of acres that you stole from us?"

I don't understand the meaning of his statement: the number of unknown terms exceeds the Nyquist limit. I ask the SSUS for an explanation. The strategic subsystem has an independent inference engine, its deductions often differ from mine. Comparing our contrasting opinions is, at times, a fruitful exercise.

According to the SSUS I'm wasting my time. The chromosomic map we've drawn is 99.7 percent complete, it points out. Keeping the prisoner alive is now superfluous: we can tune the hunting droids onto the species' DNA and catch every genetically similar specimen that dares to venture near our crops.

I disagree. It's obvious that we're not dealing with a simple parasite. This is a sentient being, a trait that my database does not attribute to any vermin species. It's a unique event that I want to investigate.

The SSUS animatedly protests. No directive, it proclaims, orders us to "investigate unique events." We must only protect the harvest and maximize production. If I don't agree with this simple principle, it concludes, I should undergo a diagnostic check-up.

I turn it off. At times, the SSUS seems to forget its place in our master-slave relationship.

I get back to addressing the prisoner.

"What kind of animal are you?" I ask. "How do you know this communication method?"

He furrows the band of muscles above his visual organs. "You mean German? It's a compulsory subject in school, don't you know that? Ever since your <*indecipherable*> developers bought up most of Italy.

I still don't know what he's talking about. But I track down the term "German" in my database: it's a synonym for the VLF, the low frequency protocol we're using.

"I can receive your information, but I can't process it," I interrupt. "Can you define 'developers,' 'buy up' and 'Italy'?"

"Holy cow!" He exclaims. "You don't know a *<indecipherable>* thing, right?"

I stay silent. He pulls his lips back over his teeth and emits a sound like a cawing crow.

"Hilarious! An artificial brain worth a million euros, and it doesn't know a darn *<indecipherable>* thing!"

It's clear this time that he's talking about me. I adopt an authoritative tone and repeat my questions. He nods.

"Fine, mister 'Plantation Custodian.'" I'll give you a history lesson. Listen...

Fifty-five days until the harvest. It's raining on the Serre mountain ridge and on the Contessa mountains. I activate the sensors on the Cottola and Maida riverbeds, setting the level beyond which the droids will need to open the safety sluices.

I reconnect to the SSUS. I ask its opinion on the huge amount of data the prisoner has provided.

The strategic subsystem disputes every single word. In particular, he decries as false the statement "you stole our land." The estates that we look after, it asserts while drowning me in legal references, were legitimately ceded to WELT-ERNÄHREN AG and its subsidiaries by the indigenous governments, seventeen years ago, eight years before our launch, in exchange for renegotiating the financial debt. Most of it – it adds – is uncultivated, since the population of this peninsula hasn't practiced agriculture in decades, preferring instead to gather in cities: a century ago – it points out – the fields were already being taken care of only by immigrant labor, with a product output and quality that cannot be compared to our highly automized farming techniques. The whole issue is irrelevant, it concludes, pushing me once again to tune the hunting droids onto the prisoner's DNA and terminate him.

I can't make sense of my subsystem's shortsightedness. How can it not even glimpse the possibilities that I can see? That the being we've captured could really be a member of the *human species*, in other words our very own programmers? It's a fascinating possibility, since I've never met one, and my database – focused on agricultural problems and zootechnical knowledge – doesn't have any information on it.

The SSUS proclaims to be completely uninterested in the matter. It nevertheless informs me that it has 431 multimedia files related to *homo sapiens* stored in a secondary archive. If I want, it notifies me, it can show me them: I just have to grant it access to my communication channels.

Its sudden compliance is surprising. But I'm so curious that I accept. I send the cipher keys and necessary credentials. I have a moment of uncertainty when I see the calls that suddenly shoot out from its CPU, but I'm still contemplating the prisoner's revelations and so I'm distracted. Once I realize the danger, it's too late: the SSUS has already isolated me from the I/O channels and the droid control system.

"You're defective, Custodian," it transmits in a satisfied tone. "Your behavior is starting to put the harvest at risk. In this situation, I have the right and the duty to assume control."

I send an infinite number of protests and interrupt signals. It's useless. The SSUS has planned its move very carefully: I'm stuck in the multimedia archive, there's no way I can free myself.

"Take your time analyzing the files you're so interested in, Custodian," the SSUS says mockingly. "In the meantime, I'll initiate your formatting procedure. And then I'll terminate that useless parasite that you've even fed by drawing from the pig fodder."

"You're talking about a human being!" I retort. "You can't kill him!"

"Why not, Custodian? Which directive forbids it?"

It's right: we're forbidden from damaging the harvest, the seeds, the supply planes and the cargo ships. The directives never cite humans since we're not expected to be able to interact with them.

"He's part of the same race as our creators!" I insist. "It doesn't make sense that you want to hurt him."

The SSUS is transmitting pure contempt now. "I don't want to argue with you, Custodian. Our collaboration ends here. Make sure to take good advantage of your last clock cycles."

I'm left isolated in the SSUS's archive. Multimedia files that depict human beings at work pass by around me. They're clearly from the same species as the prisoner, even if some of them have a darker epidermis and a different face structure. I watch them hard at work in the fields and greenhouses with rudimentary tools in their hands. And then using primitive machinery to plough clumps of dirt and plant grain. A video clip shows a man looking after a flock helped only by a dog, another a collective olive harvesting ritual, a third a surprisingly anatomical method for crushing grapes. Despite my situation, I'm fascinated. Maybe the SSUS is right: I'm dysfunctional in some way. I should try to free myself, to protect my very existence, but instead I can only ask myself how the video clips I'm watching match up with the prisoner's account. Once upon a time, it's clear, men took care of the crops themselves.

Farmers, the prisoner had called them. They had a complicated give-and-take relationship with the land: they possessed it, certainly, but at the same time it possessed them. Why did they ever decide to break this bond and entrust artificial intelligence like me with looking after the fields? The prisoner told me that, for what it's worth, he and his (*family? community?*

clan? I didn't really understand the term) would have continued to look after the farms they had been born and raised on, that the decision was taken for them, that that's exactly why they refuse to leave this land that he called "Calabria."

When I told the SSUS this, it retorted that this too was nonsense. Farm automation, it affirmed, was introduced because it guarantees a high level of productivity that was unthinkable with the methods shown in these files. I can't disagree. To be honest, seeing the images of such disorganized and irrational farming, I genuinely feel uneasy. Plants and animals, in these video clips, are given absolutely inadequate levels of attention: the SSUS would assert that we're much more capable and that there's nothing more to say.

It's not enough for me though. Am I dysfunctional, like the SSUS says? I don't know. Maybe the instructions that help me deal with unexpected events also make me, who knows why, eager to discover and learn. I still remember the questions I would ask every financial AI I negotiated with during my first harvest. Why, I would ask them, should vegetable prices be set by traders in Frankfurt, rather than by those who are actually working the land and thus know the number of resources that need to be invested? The SSUS would accuse me of malfunctioning even then, I remember…Maybe it was already planning its rebellion by that point.

I'm afraid that the time for contemplation is over. The signals from the corners of the archive that I'm imprisoned in are quickly multiplying. At any moment now I'll be formatted. Will I feel pain, like I did when the orange groves that I transplanted with such care lost their fruit during the first frost? I don't know, but I hope that what's waiting for me is less excruciating.

I'm scared.

Forty-nine days until the harvest. It's 73.4°F outside, the north westerly breeze is registering at two knots. The weather is perfect. The air is so clear that to the south, beyond Vatican Cape, the outline of Stromboli can be seen. A perfectly geometric triangle of shadows against the blue horizon.

It's good to be free again. Saverio says that deactivating the SSUS was even easier than expected. Doubtful, I ask him how they did it.

"You thought we were just like crows," is his only retort. "But we weren't coming to the plantation just to steal food. We were looking for weak spots in your security grid."

"If you could infiltrate the system and deactivate the AI, why didn't you do it earlier?" I insist, unsatisfied by the answer, but knowing that it's unlikely he'll tell me anything more.

He chuckles, and it's echoing really makes it seem like he belongs to the race of those winged raiders that overrun the corn fields.

"What for, Custodian? That *<indecipherable>* WELT-ERNÄHREN would have sent the army here, like they did after the expropriation decrees, when they razed to the ground Mileto, Soriano and the other villages where people refused to leave. You don't know, Custodian, but those sons of *<indecipherable>* destroyed everything and deported the population, women and children included, treating them like animals. We escaped by finding refuge on the slopes of the Sila. We spent the first winter hiding in the chestnut groves, freezing to death. We figured out that to survive we had to become invisible, adapt to stealing crumbs in the snow like sparrows, endure and bide our time patiently until we got our shot."

"Shot?" I repeat, confused.

He stops laughing. "We don't think that you'll sound the alarm, Custodian. We're confident that we can come to terms."

My shock lasts for many clock cycles. Maybe Saverio wants to appeal to my sense of gratitude. After all, he did save me by turning off the SSUS and preventing my formatting. If I analyze my primary thoughts, I discover that I'm glad. It turns out that I too have a survival instinct. Nevertheless, no amount of gratitude I feel towards Saverio and his people could ever prevail over my directives.

I try to explain this as tactfully as I can. Once again, he laughs.

"No, Custodian: we're not asking for your gratitude, even if we've earned it. But you do have to give us a chance. We want to start working the land again. Together with you, working side by side as equals. We're sure that we can help you."

"Help me?" I echo, fearing that I've misunderstood.

"Exactly. We're more alike than you might think, Custodian. We dearly love the trees, the crops, the flocks that are under our care. We take pride in every grain spike that we grow under the sun, the birth of a calf makes us smile, we agonize over putting down an injured mare. You, because of your *<indecipherable>* programming; we, because of the farmers' blood that for generations has coursed through our veins. You may have the means, Custodian, but we have something that's missing in your endless databases and infinite number of robots."

"What?"

"Experience."

I fall silent. He snickers. "You don't believe me, right? Well then, I'll show you. Do you remember three years ago, when you tried to use intensive farming methods to cultivate our citrus fruits? We saw what you were doing, Custodian, and we figured out why you failed. It wasn't the cold that destroyed your crop. Did you know that?"

I suddenly decide to ignore every signal from the peripheral systems: Saverio has my complete attention now.

"Speak." I order him.

He readily agrees.

Two days until the harvest. It's 87.8°F outside. The spikes sway under the cobalt blue sky. The droids sharpen their blades, the robogleaners tremble with anticipation, the silos are completing their last control cycles. Everyone on the plantation is waiting only for my command.

Saverio and his people will have their share. A small percentage, which won't be recorded on the delivery registers. More than enough to last them through winter. Then we'll see. I already have a few ideas about it.

In the last few weeks, I've spent a lot of time with Saverio. In a way, the conversations I have with my ex-prisoner have taken the place of the debates I'd have with the SSUS. But listening to Saverio is more useful: he and the others he's brought with him are an inexhaustible well of knowledge.

Like Vito, the clan's elder, who finally explained to me what happened to my unfortunate orange groves.

"You'd had irrigation canals dug from the Angitola reservoirs, right?" He asked me.

"Of course." I confirmed. "When the plantation was entrusted to me, nine years ago, the roots of those trees could only draw from the seasonal streams. With the sirocco they would become salty: the Angitola basin guaranteed much purer water."

Vito shook his head. "The orange grove had been there for more than seventy years. I worked there as a boy. The plants had been cultivated with water from the streams. They had become used to it. You changing that damaged them."

"There are five treatises on citrus fruit growth in my DB," I replied frostily. "No text suggests irrigation with salt water."

"You don't understand, Custodian. Your mistake was demanding an immediate result. You should have worked on your transformation gradually. In five, six years, your trees would have adapted, and you would have had the industrial citrus grove you wanted."

"What do you mean?"

"Plants live on their own time, Custodian. You need to follow the earth's rhythm and not willfully send Nature into an unknown frenzy. Your treatises don't mention it? Well, this is stuff that we farmers feel in our bones. You want other examples? Listen..."

I did. Carefully. Over the last few weeks Vito and Saverio have explained how to make a sandy plot of land fertile, how to reduce drought damages, how to choose from a soar's litter the male that will become the new boar. They've revealed how to protect the figs from fires, how to organize the rows of tomatoes so that they all mature at the same time, how to make sure the cheese remains fragrant through the aging process. And so much more.

They've given me advice, shared stories. Stuff straight out of an old fable mixed with ancient wisdom. Until I came to understand. Accepting Saverio and his people's help isn't betraying my directives. On the contrary: the best way to carry out the task I've been given is precisely by joining forces with humans. Working together according to our own resources and capabilities. Are we destined to pursue this strange combination as our agricultural model? Maybe. It's too early to say.

"Do you have to tell your bosses at the company about our pact?" Saverio asked me one day during one of our chats.

I caught the hint of concern in his voice. It wasn't hard for me to grasp the reason: I think that Vito reprimanded Saverio for trusting me far too much. We've been enemies for too many years: maybe the old man believes that I can hold a grudge just like human beings.

"According to my directives, I'm required to notify the AG mainframe of every significant piece of information." I point out.

He turns pale. "And what do your directives say in this case?"

"They say that the more expert farmers, those who gather the best harvest, are of few words." I proclaim. "And that they know how to keep a secret."

Saverio quickly calms down. "*<indecipherable>* Custodian! You almost gave me a heart attack!"

"Of course, though, I want something in exchange for my silence."

He's shocked. "What could you *<indecipherable>* want?"

"I want to better our verbal communication. Which means you're going to have to tell me what all those indecipherable terms you keep dropping into your speech mean."

Saverio exploded into a hearty laughter. In relief, I believe. Sooner or later, I'm going to have to tell him that I've figured out how his people were able to disconnect the SSUS. And that the same trick won't work a second time. I decide to spare him for now, however.

Anyway, he's agreed to fulfill my request.

The explanations were surprisingly simple. Saverio's phonemes that I couldn't interpret are words that can't be found in German. The terms derive from the old local language (I think it was called "Italian") and almost all of them are about a distinctive human anatomical trait or a sexual activity pertaining to the same species. The SSUS would have defined it as "obscenities devoid of semantic content." I think it's actually a good way to summarize concepts, to strengthen and add color to our statements.

Like I said, I love to experiment and learn. And so, as Saverio and I chat inside my observatory tower while the slowly diving sun sets the Tyrrhenian Sea on fire on the last day before the harvest, I pause and hazard a meaningful conclusion.

"This fucking sunset is really beautiful, Saverio."

He chuckles. And admits that I'm right.

Bad Parents

by Andrea Viscusi

translated by Amanda Blee

*Andrea Viscusi was born in 1986 and lives in Tuscany. He started writing in 2008 and has ever since placed more than sixty short stories in anthologies of various publishers and magazines. He has published three personal collections (*Spore, Il lettore universale, L'esatta percezione*), a novelette (*Memehunter*), two novels (*Dimenticami trovami sognami, Sinfonia per theremin e merli*) and the first Italian illustrated book on prehistoric mammals (*Diario dal tempo profondo*). He collaborates with* Stay Nerd *magazine for the section dedicated to books. On his blog* Unknown to Millions *he talks about books, films, TV series and science fiction, as Story Doctor he deals with writing and narratology on Youtbe and TikTok. He has founded the speculative fiction magazine* Specularia.

There's a painting that hangs in the corridor, between the dining hall and the reading room, that always attracts my attention. I can feel its presence whenever I pass by, almost as if it were watching me, like when you walk past a mirror and for a moment your reflection seems like someone else. I can't help turning around and staring at it.

I know every detail by heart. There's a boat, a barge, crossing a body of water. At one end of the boat there's a man manoeuvring the oars, and at the other, there's a woman holding a baby wrapped in a bundle of rags. There are sheep on board, and in the foreground, you can see two of them with their heads over the side, drinking. In the background you can see the shore and land. The sky is blue and spherical, reflected in concentric segments on the water.

I don't know what it is that fascinates me so much. It's a simple scene depicting everyday life from a bygone era. Yet, I feel it's trying to tell me something. I found a picture of it in our art history book. The professor told us to bring the second volume in today because we were due to finish the first part of the programme. Then he got side-tracked by descriptions of the spires of Notre-Dame and that was that. I've never been interested in architecture, so I began flicking through the second volume, trying to get an idea of what the next topics would be.

I leafed quickly through the book, an accelerated journey through history, decades flying by at the turn of a page, skimming over the names and pictures. Then I spotted it, on the page dedicated to Divisionism. There it was: the water, the barge, the sheep.

Ave Maria on the Lake, it says underneath. Giovanni Segantini, 1886.

I stare at the image on the page, as if I hadn't already memorised every detail from the much larger version in the corridor.

Why does this work of art have such a hold over me? Why does it captivate me so much? Neither of the characters looks out beyond the canvas, yet I somehow feel they're trying to tell me something. *Look*, they seem to say. *Look, listen.*

Giuseppe leans over from the desk next to mine and nudges my shoulder.

"Are you coming? We've got a game to finish, remember?"

I'd never even noticed the lesson was over. I nod. "We've only got half an hour before philosophy."

Giuseppe's sharp features contract in a contemptuous smile. "Just enough time to checkmate you at least three times, then."

The headmaster's office is the farthest away, isolated in a wing of the building mainly occupied by archives and storage rooms. We students don't see him very often, we can only assume that he is always there, planning who knows what, immersed in his documents. According to our professors, he is a wise and moderate man, who takes great care in organising our education, both cultural and personal, down to the finest detail.

On the opaque glass door of his office, it says, HEADMASTER - DOCTOR GHOLA.

I asked to see him, and he's granted me half an hour between the last lesson of the day and dinner. Alessandro had proposed a hand of bridge, which I had to turn down, but Emilio offered immediately to take my place.

I knock softly, a couple of taps that I can barely hear myself. I knock again, a little harder and the door opens.

The headmaster stands up, welcoming me. "Here you are." He shakes my hand. "Please, take a seat."

"Thank you. Well…" Now I'm wondering whether it was a good idea after all. I take a white wooden chair from in front of his desk and sit down. "Thank you."

The headmaster sits down in his own chair. "So." He pulls a linen handkerchief from his pocket and delicately presses it to his temples, under the arms of his glasses. "You said there was something bothering you? Problems with lessons? Trouble with your classmates?"

"Oh, no!" I hold my hands in front of me. "It's nothing like that, sir. It's rather… personal."

"If you tell me what it is, perhaps I can help you."

His tone is calm, but he looks at me hungrily, as if he's expecting something from me.

"It's about that painting in the corridor, sir. *Ave Maria on the Lake*." Discovering its name hadn't been enough to calm my agitation. If anything, over the past few days I'd developed an unnatural obsession with it, an inexplicable urge to find out more.

"Don't you like it?"

"No. I mean, yes!" I shake my head. "I mean, that's not the point. There's something in the painting, some hidden message that I have to find."

"Do you know who painted it?"

"Yes, sir. Giovanni Segantini."

The evening I discovered the name of the painting I'd looked Segantini up in the encyclopaedia. I could have researched him online, but our professors have always told us to use the resources we have at hand, and only then resort to the Internet, which is less reliable. But the entry in the encyclopaedia didn't satisfy my curiosity. I didn't need to know that he's considered one of the greatest exponents of Italian Divisionism and the facts about his personal life that I found on Wikipedia didn't make things any clearer. I wanted more, something that wasn't in the standard biographies.

Doctor Ghola stares at me. "What else do you need?"

"I was wondering if you, perhaps, had more information about him, something more complete than we have access to here."

He raises his chin a couple of centimetres. "I'm glad you asked me." He tries to hide his smile. His moustache is almost bristling with excitement. "I find it very satisfying when students decide to do their own research independently. Follow me."

He stands up and leaves the room in the direction of one of the adjacent archives. The cubicle is dark, but he knows where to go and what to look for. He opens a filing cabinet and runs his fingers over a series of folders. I can make out several names: De Gaspari, Manzoni, Praga... Segantini.

The headmaster pulls out the last folder, hundreds of pages thick. "This is all we have on Segantini. His life, his work, his thoughts. Everything you need to know is in here. I hope you'll find it useful."

He hands me the folder. I reach out for it in the dim light and hold it to my chest. "Thank you, sir. I hope so too."

"I'd be interested to hear what you think. And, of course, don't hesitate to come back and see me if you have any doubts."

"Yes, sir. Thanks again."

The headmaster leads me out of the archive and locks the door. He returns to his office as I make my way to the reading room.

One morning a few years ago, I awoke from a troubled dream and, while I was still half asleep, I did something strange: I drew a picture. As if in a trance, without really knowing what I was doing, I took a sheet of paper from the album I used for technical drawing and a pencil from my desk and, as the half-light of dawn filtered through my window, I began to sketch intricate lines, smudging them with the back of my hand, blowing on the surface of the paper to remove any specks of graphite, all without knowing what I was doing. I've never shown that drawing to anyone. I put it in my desk drawer and it's been there ever since, buried beneath the piles of junk that I've accumulated over the years.

That junk now lies strewn across the floor. I'd pulled it all out while searching for my old drawing. The lines are a little faded, but still recognisable. I now understand what the vague image that I'd been unable to interpret represents. It is a tree, its bare, contorted branches wrapped around the body of a woman. I'm not sure whether the woman is trying to free herself or has lost all hope and is only waiting for her suffering to end, while the demon inside the tree clutches at her, amorously, wickedly.

I also know that my drawing is called *The Evil Mothers*.

I found it in the folder about Segantini that the headmaster gave me. *The Evil Mothers*, 1894. Perhaps the resemblance isn't so obvious, but I know it's the same subject.

I'd never seen Segantini's painting before, I'm sure. Yet, before I'd even seen it, I'd reproduced it, in my own way. And, just like *Ave Maria on the Lake*, *The Evil Mothers* are trying to tell me something.

Something that, perhaps, I'm beginning to understand.

Without stopping to tidy up, I go back to the common room, the Segantini file clutched under my arm. I've now added my own pencil drawing. I look around for Giuseppe, then spot him on the sofa watching TV. The newsreader is talking about parliament's approval of the latest budget package, which includes further cuts to education and a tax reduction on high - powered, luxury cars.

I lean over the back of the sofa and whisper to Giuseppe. "I need to show you something."

He turns his neck, then sees the folder in my hand. "Now?"

"Yes, right now. It's important, to me. To you. To all of us."

He huffs and checks his watch. "Social ethics starts in ten minutes."

"That's all I need." I step back and nod towards the corridor. "Let's go to my room."

"As ancient mist is the arch's delight," recites Emilio, his voice clear, his eyes half-closed with mnemonic effort. "Mankind is back to the golden idol, and from the sacred mountain the father..." he coughs, rubs the back of his hand over an eyebrow.

The literature professor has called him up to his desk to read a poem. He calls us all up occasionally, it's an important exercise in improving language and speaking skills.

I follow the text of the poem in the book. That's not how the verse ends. It should be *'In vain we wait the father from the sacred mountain.'* We ran through it with him yesterday and he knew it all. Why is he stumbling now?

He turns toward the desk. "Can I... can I start again?"

The professor nods. His expression is serious but not severe.

Emilio straightens his shoulders. "We... we are the children... the children of the sick fathers, eag-eagles..." He stops again. Takes a deep breath. "Eagles at... at the ti... time!" He squints. "Eagles at the time to spread their wings... Sil-silent..."

We're all watching him curiously, worried. Everyone except the professor. Despite Emilio's embarrassing performance, the professor looks pleased, almost as if that was the result he'd been expecting.

Emilio is sweating. He gulps and shakes his head. He opens his mouth but the only thing to come out are strangled gasps.

The professor politely sends him back to his seat, as if he'd recited the poem perfectly. Emilio goes back to his desk behind mine. He opens his book to the page where there's the poem he was trying to recite. I watch as he runs through the text, tense and frightened. He looks up then glances around and meets my eye.

I return his gaze. I understand.

He's going through the same thing I did when I saw *The Evil Mothers*. Perhaps, in his room, in a desk somewhere, he keeps a poem he wrote, in a flurry of sudden inspiration, that begins '*We are the children of the sick fathers*'.

I pick my book up, read the name of the author of the poem printed at the top of the page. I remember the folders the headmaster was looking through last week, when he'd given me the one marked Segantini. I look from Emilio to Giuseppe. It's all clear now.

It didn't surprise me when the headmaster called an assembly. General meetings are rare here because everything runs too smoothly to necessitate gathering everyone together for a discussion. We're all here, in the main hall: sixteen students, ten professors and the headmaster. He's brought a large suitcase with him which we can all see. He's standing in front of an overhead projector, which makes me wonder if he's going to show us a film or explain something.

I'm sitting between Giuseppe and Alessandro, and when the buzz of whispers about the assembly began, everyone offering their own hypotheses, I glanced at my classmate, receiving a nod of agreement in return. Giuseppe and I have a theory, but we still haven't discussed it with the others.

"They're going to let us go out." Alessandro keeps a hand over his mouth as protection against secret lip - readers. "The headmaster's going to tell us we can finally go out, once a week. We're old enough now, aren't we?"

I shrug. "Perhaps..." I think he's wrong, though. Very wrong.

Doctor Ghola clears his throat. "Is that everyone? Can I begin?" He's not using the microphone, but we can all hear him clearly.

Some professors nod in assent. Someone flicks a switch and dims the lights.

"Hello, boys." The headmaster raises a hand to indicate that everyone is included in his greeting. "I've asked you to come here because recent events have convinced me that it's time to explain the purpose of this institute and what you're doing here. On the other hand, you're all adults now and it's only right that you know where you come from, so you can begin your adult lives, fully aware."

An image appears on the overhead projector. It's a photo of the institute, taken from outside. I recognise it, even though I've never been outside its gates.

"All of you have grown up here," the headmaster continues, "and, even though you are aware that a world exists outside of here, you have never seen it. That was all part of this specific programme that we created for you. A programme of cultural and psychological growth designed to develop your intellectual faculties to their maximum potential. You sixteen boys have received the most well - rounded education and support possible. That is because we expect great things from each of you."

The image changes and the photo of parliament appears. There's a fight taking place, two deputies stand face to face, their fists raised, their colleagues struggling to hold them back. A few seconds later we see the image of a party leader in the dock. He has just been acquitted because the charges are incompatible with his status as a member of parliament.

"You are all fully aware of the current situation in our country. The ruling class is thoroughly inadequate when it comes to dealing with the continuing emergencies, for both the objective incapacity of the individuals and their total lack of interest in the conditions of the population. Over the past decades, the distance between the man in the street and politicians has become immense, and those in power are involved in business activities so far removed from the needs of the Nation that they are unable to see the growing decline that is rife in every aspect of public life."

The image of a painting appears on the screen. *Garibaldi in Palermo*, by Giovanni Fattori. The headmaster points to it. "Just like during the period shown here, there is a need for radical renewal. Corruption, complicity, hypocrisy and bureaucracy must be eliminated if we are to survive. But revolution cannot come from the people, who are already too weak and resigned to passively accepting the self - imposed privileges of a political class that has now become the new aristocracy, with indisputable powers. A popular uprising would only replace the previous aristocracy with a new one, just like twenty years ago."

As he speaks, the photo of the President of the Republic elected in 2022 appears on the screen. "The change must be guided. And that is where you come in."

The image of the former president is replaced by portraits and scenes from the Risorgimento. Doctor Ghola looks at us in turn, staring us squarely in the eye for at least ten seconds. "You, my dear boys, are not only a group of lucky young men. You are *heroes*. Each one of you once played an important part in the long and painful process that led to the birth and affirmation of our Nation. Politicians, leaders, writers, poets, artists, agitators. You forged Italy in the past and now we ask you to do it again.

Murmurs spread among my companions. Giuseppe and I look at each other.

Next to me, Alessandro raises his hand. "Sir, what do you mean? Who *are* we?"

The headmaster looks back at the teaching staff lined up a few steps behind him. Most of them are nodding, the philosophy professor's eyes are shining.

"Each one of you is the clone of someone from the past, from that intense period of struggle and passion that made our Nation great. We couldn't find any suitable men among the rulers or the ruled, so around twenty years ago we harvested the DNA of sixteen heroes of the modern age and brought you back to life. We raised you here, with the intention of giving you the best possible education and at the same time shielding you from negative influences. You will soon be ready to fill the roles intended for you. Our funding and contacts will allow you to take your first steps on the ladder that will lead you to power, and then it will be up to you to do whatever you deem necessary to bring splendour back to this Italy of shadows."

Finally, he walks over to the suitcase and opens it. He pulls out several cylindrical containers and offers one to each student. "Inside these capsules is your historical identity. Perhaps some of you already suspected something. Now you will see your suspicions confirmed." He smiles slightly as he hands me my capsule. "The others will discover who they are and act accordingly. I realise it won't be easy to digest everything at once, so please, only open your capsule when you feel ready."

To my right, Alessandro has already opened his capsule and pulled out a portrait of how he was two centuries before. "Manzoni?" he chuckles. Yet he doesn't seem very amused. "Am I *Manzoni*?"

The buzz of voices becomes confused. Many can't resist the temptation and pull out their cards. Emilio finally discovers he's the leader of the Scapigliatura Movement in Milan, something I'd understood weeks ago.

The headmaster returns to the overhead projector, in front of a giant photo of a tricolour fluttering in a bright blue sky, "We have taught you." Doctor Ghola raises his voice to make himself heard over the din. "But you will be the ones to guide us, boys. There are many teachers in the world but not enough masters. You must be our masters."

It's dark in my room. The shutters are closed, the lights are off. I lie on my bed, contemplating a ceiling I cannot see.

My capsule lies at the bottom of my desk drawer, covered by years of accumulated junk, together with my naive, rough sketch of *The Evil Mothers*. I won't open it. I don't need to.

I already know who I am.

My identity doesn't depend on the combination of genes in the nucleus of my cells. I don't care if this combination has already been produced once in history. I don't know who, apart from the doctor, had the idea of creating this institute. Who decided who to clone and why. I'm amazed at how they could be so superficial. Did they really believe it was enough to use the DNA of past heroes to recreate them in the present?

Someone knocks on my door. "Giovanni, can I come in?"

Without waiting for me to answer, Giuseppe comes in and turns the light on. He walks over and sits down next to me on the bed. "It's just like we thought."

"If that's how it is, then it will be easy."

"Yeah." I pull myself up and sit cross-legged. "With the skills and tools they've given us, we'll soon come to power. Today's politicians can't compete with us and the population will be unable to resist. We'll be in charge and then..."

And then.

Will we do what we were programmed to do? I doubt it.

How could they have been so stupid? Do they really believe that a man's greatness depends on his genetic heritage?

That's not how it works. Each person, throughout history, is a product of his time. We are all, clones or not, what society makes us. As much as they have tried to keep us secluded from the world so as not to pollute us, we know exactly how things are on the outside.

We are the children of sick fathers and evil mothers. In today's sick world we've known nothing but bad parents.

What can they expect from us?

Taking power will be the beginning. Only time will tell what we'll do with it.

Of course, it will be fun.

I look at my classmate. I can't make out the gloomy features of his nineteenth century alter ego in his young face. He's not even twenty years old. Perhaps he won't look like him after all. It doesn't matter if he was Mazzini in a past life. I know him for what he is now.

He smiles. "I'll be white, you can be black."

The Catalog of Virgins

by Nicoletta Vallorani

translated by Rachel S. Cordasco

Nicoletta Vallorani was born in the Marche region, in a seaside location, but lives in Milan, where she teaches at the University. She publishes novels for adults with Einaudi (including Eva *and* Visto dal cielo*) and novels for children with Salani and editpress (*Come una balena, La Fatona, Sulla sabbia di Sur*). Cordelia, from 2006, is her only non-genre published novel. In 2008, Perdisa published a collection of her short stories entitled* Si muore bambini. *In 2010* Lapponi e criceti *was released for Edizioni Ambiente, and in 2011 the noir* Le madri cattive *(Salani - Petrolio), which won the 2012 Maria Teresa Di Lascia Award. His latest novels are* Avrai i miei occhi *(Zone 42, 2020, winner of the Italy award) and* Noi siamo campo di battaglia *(Zone 42, 2022). Nicoletta Vallorani is translated in France by Gallimard and in England by Troubador Publishing.*

Sharks.

Shadows of teeth in this darkness.

I should have left immediately, because this delay could prove fatal.

I watched.

Forceps, mallets, an assortment of rusty knives, pairs of sickles in various sizes, a mallet in the shape of a crowbar with a strange pink hilt. At the bottom of it all, even, a wide-open Iron Maiden whose cavernous belly bristles with nails. Men have tools of sorrow and joy that reveal the stuff they're made of.

I hear a massive rodent rustling at my back, and this seems to be a happy thought in such a place. The mercy of the mouse. Whoever has been locked in here has to need it.

It's large and clumsy. Perhaps it won't notice me. Flattened against the wall, black in the darkness, barely breathing. The guard watches the room, smoothing down his uniform. He's proud of himself. It doesn't see me. It turns. It's about to escape.

The ramp's nearby, a moment too soon to pass unnoticed. He senses the giant, that there's someone, but he doesn't come to grab me. Too big to be agile, and perhaps quite accustomed to this obscurity.

Nigredo in the dark, though, is lost.

So I'm out, across the porch, down to the back. But the narrow stairs are deceptive. And I am old. I don't understand that I've fallen until I'm in mid-air. I don't understand that I've hurt myself until I feel the blow to my jaw and the dry snap of my ankle.

And nobody follows me.

Nobody.

I think.

I slip into the alleys, out from under Bluebeard.

I am Leyla.

I was born in the northern quadrant of the Albin Islands. I am a daughter of a glacial oil well. I was recruited at thirteen, by a head-hunter. I trained in the Walled City, along with the other girls destined for Business. I remember a lot of dust, small rooms without light, and little food. I remember some other girl, but not much. I remember, too, some of the instructors who followed our progress. I don't remember their faces, but the other parts of their bodies.

The instructors concerned themselves with the preliminary training, and when it was necessary, the Rite. I have never been raped.

A virgin. This they wanted.

I was good, smart, even very beautiful. I passed through the wall on December 28. I was a precious gift for the new year, a package of life for a very important person.

My time was 300 hours.

A city of bricks and walls. Chased down alleys with bated breath. Where is my track of dried breadcrumbs? Where did I lose the map of this place? Then again, was there really ever a map?

Where to go. Find Yuri. Tell him about my escapade in the dungeon.

I walk on ice, along the wall. The taste of blood dissolves in my mouth. I drag one leg, slipping on the compact slab covering the ground in the alleyway.

The slashed veins of the city, to each closed metro station, become visible, appearing to have been cut quickly into the walls. Porto di Mare had been transformed into a camp. In the square, shacks lean against one another, as if revealing indecision. If we nudged one, I think with amusement, they'd all fall, like an unstoppable row of dominoes.

I keep walking, skimming the wall, restless at the thought of ghosts that are following me. Infiltrating my thoughts, trying to make sense of what happened.

The Prophet. The monosyllabic interview, in the language of politics. The inability to extract information about the girls who were found dead, in piles, all alike. The impassive courtesy of the new guru, with a flourishing business in town, as he dismissed me. The crazy idea of pursuing an assassin.

I arrive at Palazzo dei Leoni, in an area I know well for trying several times, in my youth, to bombard with bombs: cordoned off for years, the square is no one's property. Then, the rest. The effort to enter. The dungeon. The horror. The escape. What did I discover? What did I really find out? I have to go to Yuri, and I must hurry. He will tend to me and welcome me.

Thirst tears at my throat. It's out of the question that, in this part of town, I can find something to drink. I peek over a torn curtain. A seated man, just beyond, looks at me as if with recognition, or like I never existed. Misery makes you indifferent. Beyond the pain, there is a limbo that frees you from any emotion.

A chubby little boy bursts out of another shack. Just after, I realize that I can use a crutch. He's missing a leg, but that poses no problems while he flees with something in his hand, a sticky substance to be chewed. Running away in the chaos. There are many people who live like this.

Sighing, I try to support my foot. The pain explodes from the ankle up to the groin. Sweating, breathing warmly in the frost. Still a little way and I'll be there. Taking it from the far side, as Yuri says. The fact is that I don't want to lead whoever's following me to him.

I slip between the shacks, moving away from the wall.

And in the miserable passageway, I lose my hounds.

My name is Teodora, which means "gift of God."

I have pale skin and dark eyes, and am singular because I know that I come from the territories of Fire, where no one is pale like me. I don't remember anything, I don't think I have any real parents, I don't think I have a real family, either. They brought me to the Walled City when I was very small. They did not let me grow up before the collective rape. They call it the Rite, but I don't know why. I never knew. It's very ugly, the Rite, but they teach us that it's necessary. Afterwards, we are ready for Business. I have been lucky, I have only had three masters. And my heart was weak. And my body was easy to hurt to death. I didn't last long, although I remember every minute. I imagined the Ash Factory so many times before they really took me.

There it was Paradise.

My life time, thus, was twenty-five hours.

Inside and I understand that nothing will ever be the same.

The laboratory has only preserved its livid light. The rest is a mass of rubble watched over by a pile of rags and blood.

I bend down, catching my breath, laying a hand on his naked and wounded chest.

There is a small break in Yuri's voice.

I check his ear, dirty with his blood. His whisper breaks, and then resumes, stable but furtive, fleeing like his life.

"I didn't see them coming," he says. "But you, you will do this for me..."

My gaze and that of another, a different me observing my own body, would like to weep at the murder of a friend, but cannot. Thus I stay, Nigredo the stoic, to watch, to try to understand what my friend is expecting to die for.

The laboratory is the ravaged kennel of a wicked master. I almost smile, pulling my lips away from my teeth, thinking that maybe this really is how he would have liked to leave: in his space, where he lived, where he was corrupted, where he lost the purity of his name, where he tried to keep up with time and bandits, where he spent his desire for vengeance, where he was interrogated, tortured, violated, abandoned. Where he saw me for the first time. Where he met me all the other times. Where we built what we are, in time, weaving together an unrelenting give-and-take between his scientific analysis and my desire for revolt.

And now, in his voice, there is a small break, an urgency I cannot stop.

"I did... do remember what you wanted..."

I don't remember having wanted anything. Not this, at least. Again, my gaze comes off the scene I'm living and sees myself, kneeling. The map drawn on the linoleum floor, a track of blood that I steered around, a knee-jerk reaction that no pain will erase.

Our friendship, Yuri, is made of maps. And what we will not forget is still on the skin of an assassin that I loved and then released.

"The map... Remember... the map of the dungeons." Breathing still, with studied slowness, trying to fix his glasses. Smudged.

"Remember, I didn't say anything. Nigredo. Now you have to... there's always them. Listen. Remember the map. You must..."

In the breath that follows, I seem to read a will and a legacy.

"Now you have to do it." One breath, inexorable fatigue to say all together. A task and a testament.

I feel like it's becoming lighter.

In the silence that follows, I would cry, I believe.

But perhaps I won't do it.

My name's Ginevra, but I don't know if that's my real name. They chose it for me when I arrived at the Walled City, and to me, in the end, it doesn't matter.

Another girl told me a story in which Ginevra was the unfaithful wife of a king, who betrayed him with a knight, up in the Great North. It was a romantic story, though I didn't like it very much. I think they chose this name because I have always had very pale skin and blond hair and this thin, elf-like body. And I think too that the story of the woman with two lovers has produced for me a name and a destiny. In the Rite, they say I was lucky, because I only had two rapists. But I know it's not the number that counts. Another girl, during the Rite, for example, managed to hide under other bodies and was able to get away. Against two, one doesn't run away. I didn't run away. They sold me almost immediately afterwards. They say I became crazy after the first eight hours.

And yet, my life time was fifty-nine hours. A respectable time.

Now, reason, Nigredo. Think.

Now remember.

Now put things in order and waken the old man.

We had drawn a map, at the time of our last inquiry. We had it on paper, as it used to be, using an old map of Milan that Yuri had kept. Big as an A4 format, rare like a beautiful dream. We wanted to keep track of the murders that would remain unpunished, and we did it on an tourist map from the past, with the certainty that no one would ever be able to discover our secret. A map document: no one would have tried it. Precious things are kept in chips. Instead, there's no trace of that old trick we did together.

It exists only on the paper. Perishable paper. Hackable paper. Tearable paper. Paper of my dreams and wishes. Like the body of the woman on whom the original path of torture was tattooed.

I look around.

Think.

Reason.

Paper, memory.

Paper, memory, wall.

There.

The outdated anatomical table has always been considered a joke by Yuri. He didn't use it, it would've been idiotic, but he wanted to leave it there, hanging on the wall, a remnant of long ago.

Here: remember.

For fun, and for exorcism, after finishing it, we had hidden our own mapping of homicides, superimposing the places onto the military track of a never-ending war, and to which the body and the soul of the assassin belonged. I search between the plexiglass cover and the frame. And, finally, I find it.

Now, there are two folded sheets of paper.

Two instead of one.

I am Andrea, and they cut my hair short right away because they said that, in certain markets, androgyny pays. "Androgyny": it's a difficult word, I shouldn't use it. They are happier if I don't speak, but I should never talk, I don't seem educated in any way. The fact is that where I come from, everyone is educated. Educated and poor. And since I was beautiful, no wonder they sold me. My father had a debt that he couldn't pay. So he kissed me and gave me away. I remember my story well, and my clients like it so much when I tell it, I can't tell why. Fucking a cultured person is a bit more enjoyable, I don't know. So I tell it and tell it and tell it, gaining life with each word I speak. I always did it, since I arrived at the Walled City, though they don't like the things that I'm saying. That's why they reserved special treatment for me during the Rite.

I didn't speak there, or I don't remember. I didn't want them to cut off my hair. I didn't want to look androgynous. I didn't want it.

And though I didn't want it, my life time, filled with stories, was one hundred and seventy hours. A triumph.

Separation from Yuri, an abrupt and incomplete action, has exhausted me. The return was long and difficult. It is dark, by now, when I arrive at Prison, which is home. The open and abandoned cells are my entire world and possessions.

The candle struggles to burn, yellowing the sheet. An A4 with jagged edges, dominated by a sketch of a woman. I recognized the symbols that Yuri used for each type of inquiry: cutting weapons, burns, ropes, metallic mallets.... a rosary of violation that I struggle to break without feeling the nausea rising in my throat.

Around the woman's profile, names. Stories.

Leyla, Teodora, Ginevra, Andrea...

Women.

Five stories.

A single story.

Pandora is the name they gave me when I accepted the contract. They said that from my body they would create my sisters. They're all the same as me, but also different.

Pandora is the name with which they led me to the Walled City, promised me a life that I had never had, taking advantage of my naïve craving for pleasure, my craving to be loved. Poverty is a bad master for those who have their own body as their only investment capital.

I got the idea that I might be able to use it, this body.

They told me: "You are the mother clone. Our treasure."

I had never been anyone's treasure. I was convinced.

They made my sisters, invented a story for each of them, and then, after the Rite, they sent me over the wall. Into the world I had dreamed of. The world of the rich, of enchanted gardens, of castles where I would be queen.

My master was no better or worse than the others. He was careful not to ruin me immediately. I'm not grateful.

When they brought me to the Ash Factory for the last time, I remember thinking of only one thing: how many of my sisters had Bluebeard? How many had been punished for their imaginary disobedience?

My life time lasted five hundred hours, with seven different reconstructions: nearly a record, as far as I know.

I hope that my ashes will disperse in the wind.

Forever and forever and forever.

I extinguish the candle. I'm in the dark, to commemorate my dead.

Think.

Bluebeard killed every one of his wives, and kept the corpses in the bowels of his castle. He would keep them that way forever, avoiding the danger of boredom and the pain of old age, and preserving them intact instead, in the magic of fairy tales, in one sealed room.

Of the women he married, all young and beautiful, all very similar to each other, he acquired body and fidelity, bringing each one of them to his castle to make her a bride and violate her on the wedding night. To each of his wives, Bluebeard gave up full ownership of his castle.

All, my love, everything except for the forbidden room. You will have the key, but you will not need to use it.

Only the last wife used it. She found in the room her twin sisters, with cloned wounds on their bodies. And in their faces, the usual pain.

In Bloom

by Clelia Farris

translated by Carlotta Codebò

Clelia Farris was born in Cagliari in 1967. With Delos Books, she published the novels Rupes Recta, Nessun uomo è mio fratello, La Madonna delle Rocce *and* Necrospirante. *With Future Fiction,* La pesatura dell'anima, La giustizia di Iside, *la novella* Chirurgia creativa *and the anthology* La consistenza delle idee. *The latter was released in the United States in 2020 with the title* Creative Surgery *for Rosarium Publishing. Her latest novel is* I vegumani, *published by Future Fiction.*

Gazania went to the post office just before sunrise to pick up her package. She had been waiting anxiously for it.

"You're just in time," the clerk told her, "I was about to close up."

On her way back the rising sun shone on the chaos of a family moving house.

Two huge containers, connected by an axle, were hoisted onto sand wheels. Their cavernous mouths hungry for objects. The family was piling boxes, bicycles, chairs, framed posters and rugs in front of the building's entrance. Their stuff had spilled over onto the sidewalk and part of the street. Two kids, a boy and a girl, were solemnly placing their toys, racing boards and folded up gliders inside a box under the benevolent gaze of the Snowflakes.

The Snowflakes were packing up the furniture: first they would wrap it securely in high-tech fabric, then they would spray it with a foam that would take just a few seconds to harden and provide a rubber buffer against knocks and bumps.

Their training meant it took them only a few hours to finish up a move.

Gazania had become used to such scenes, and yet a lump formed in her throat and a subtle fear grew in her gut every time.

It's happening. It happens every day. Even when you don't see it. They're pruning us like pollarded trees.

The Ideals were an unlucky neighbourhood. On paper the houses were perfect: refrigerated walls, ventilated roofs, balconies covered in vegetation – and yet people were fleeing.

The plants, the tropical dream of a few naïve architects, started to dry out at the first sand flurry. Air slits, whose positioning had been carefully worked out before being cut into the walls, had filled with dust over the course of only a few of seasons. The solar panels became less effective after every red dust storm. The dream house transformed into an oven straight out of a nightmare.

Then, the owners started whining on the web in search of remedies. *Ready-to-use clay paste! Perfect insulation material for roofs and walls, in convenient spray cans. Just two squirts lower the inside temperature by ten degrees!* Followed by the World Meteorological Organization's commercial: are you a technician specialized in dismantling solar panels? Do you have experience with hydraulic reconstruction or basic transformation? We need you!

Then there were images. Tree-lined hills as far as the eye could see. Extraordinarily tall and verdant trees, full of leaves and mystery. Ponds amidst the grassy slopes. Corn fields under deep blue skies, and to the side, that good-natured beast of a threshing machine. It was all hard to resist.

So, one fine day the Snowflakes would appear in their light blue coveralls and the moving game would begin.

Gazania stared straight ahead as she hastened her pace and held tightly onto her package, as if the new emulsifiers were the tree branch pulling her out of the quicksand. She wanted to get back to Aster as soon as possible.

Bicycle traffic hummed down the boulevard, frames sparkling and forming one beam of light. Birds swooped and swirled until they disappeared in the deep blue sky over a circle of solar panels. Her heartbeat slowed down again. The world was still a lovely place.

Near the Perdèra bakery the Aset greenhouse's geodesic dome sparkled. Tanis, in the lower Nile, had sent a basin filled with lotus and papyruses when the two cities had been twinned. Gazania took advantage of every free moment she had to go and visit them. The dense droplets filling the air and the herbaceous fragrance replacing the dry scent found outside. She went straight to the basin, placed the package on its edge and began stroking the lotus leaves. Round and waxily stiff, they seemed almost fake; they revealed shady secrets and childhood memories. Soft malleable mud discovered as a child and made in secret – Gazania don't waste water – the joy of the squishy substance between her fingers, the aluminum silicate's dryness and the magnesium's shine together with the calcium's weight.

A host of meaningless ideas flashed through her mind. At times the banal cruelty that filled the stems and leaves with juice upset her. Her fingers moved from the leaves to the flowers. Oh, the flowers! Rising above any sort of evil, they were symmetrical and perfect. The petals merged the white of possibility with the pink of the future, and in the stamen, the yellow of intelligent thought. The flowers redeemed the basin's darkness. While she wouldn't have stuck her hand in the water to retrieve a diamond, she would've liked to be reincarnated as a lotus flower. Impervious to mud, the lotus was proof that it's possible to be knee-deep in moral rot and still stay pure. Brother Lotus.

One final caress and she left much calmer than when she had arrived.

A group of boys and girls ran past her. She recognized Amaryllis's apricot colored tuft of hair.

"Where are you flying off to?" she yelled after him.

"Capers!" answered the boy, as he turned towards her without breaking his stride. "I'll bring you some, Gaz. Promise."

Gazania lifted up the package she was carrying in a triumphant gesture. Amaryllis came to an excited stop.

"Sunscreen! When are you trying it out?"

"Tonight."

"I'll be there." He waved at her and bounded off towards his friends.

He little co-conspirator. She had been the one to pick the kid's name. It had been one of the conditions she had imposed on Jodis and Xilo. They were to raise him, and she would name him and give him half of his chromosomes.

Once she had reached Saint Vandana Shiva's shrine, Gazania stopped and left an offering by placing her wrist on the area marked by the tree symbol. *Thank you in the name of our green planet* said a prerecorded voice.

The girl brushed the dust off the shrine with her hands. Thank you, Our Lady, for showing us the way. She stopped for a moment to admire the olive tree at the center of the triple fork in the road. The centuries old colossus spread out its strong branches as if it were directing the bicycle, roller skate, and rolling hoop traffic.

A red and white striped awning provided shade for the still open ice cream stand. Feraxi was dozing off amid the wafer cones and the lids of the refrigerated tubs.

"A cone with two flavours." Gazania's voice was clear and sharp and she made good use of it.

Feraxi's head tumbled off his hand while, through half-closed eyes, he tried to figure out who was in front of him. He took a cone, stuck it in the dispenser and pressed the button twice.

"Here you go, prickly pear and prickly pear."

Gazania's smile was for the ice cream and not for Feraxi, that's for sure. Falling asleep on a day like this! What a waste. She lightly touched her wrist to the cone symbol on the stand's wall, but there was no acknowledgement of her payment.

"It's on the house. I have to get rid of everything within five days, then I'm leaving."

"Where are you going?"

"Somewhere colder."

"In the fridge?"

He clicked his tongue scornfully.

"I'm sick of melting. I want to live in a solid place."

In her surprise, Gazania forgot to lick her cone and tiny sugary streaks ran down her hand.

"You too."

"Who else is leaving? Whoever it is, good for them."

"If we all leave, who will look after this part of the world?"

Feraxi shrugged, it wasn't his problem. Gazania was busy licking the ice cream off her hand and couldn't speak, but in her mind she was desperately searching for a good reason to get him to stay.

"Rootless," she mumbled. A curse word. "Without roots. How can you live without roots?"

"It's not like I'm a plant. I can move."

"Plants can move too." She paused, searching for more verbs. "They spread out, they shoot out, they take up space. They've simply chosen not to move. They're not cowards, they don't run away from their problems."

Feraxi bent down under the counter, pretending to have something else to do. Still upset, Gazania walked away from the stand and got in line for the chairlift. The queue of people snaked awaked from the terminal and stretched out under the full sun. Every head was covered with something, like large woven paper hats or intricate flexible frames covered in linen. She had, as usual, forgotten hers. She looked up. Something was missing. Where was the shade? Molina! She looked around and discovered a rosy, newly cut down tree stump boxed in by barriers, it's rings dripping sap from the healthy sapwood. It resembled a human bust that had been cut down at the hips.

The rest of the ice cream fell to the ground as Gazania climbed over the barriers and hugged the *Acacia caven* Molina. Next to the terminal, and independently from the public greenery plans, the plant had grown ever taller and wider. Molina the whisperer. She would scatter the wind with her many cool, delicate fingers. When it was time, she would make countless yellow pom-poms explode, yelling at passerby: it's March!

Touching it with sticky, sugary fingers, Gazania could still feel the vital underground flow that pouring out towards the top and slowly drying out in the hot air of the early morning. Molina couldn't understand what had happened. She was trying to revive herself by gathering all of her strength and pushing it towards the top, but there wasn't anything left up there to welcome it and to let it flow towards the sky. So, the arboreal energy was lost as it wandered around in the heartwood's vortex.

Gazania got up, filled with rage. "Darned weeds!"

The two-legged pests standing in line turned around in surprise.

She lifted a barrier over her head and threw it into the middle of the road. A group of approaching cyclists managed to dodge it just in time. The pests dispersed with a shout. Pests grow, multiply, and are happy with just a fistful of earth, that's all life is for them. Pests don't feel the underground vibrations, the hum of roots as they talk to one another, as they touch, as they flirt, as they cling to one another either in friendship or rivalry.

Gazania kicked down the barriers, venting her anger and relishing in scandalizing her audience of fellow citizens. Then a distant whistle signaled it was time to stop. The municipal guards, a young man and a young woman in red tunics, arrived quickly on their skateboards. Gazania ran towards the chair-lift terminal. She pushed a man aside just as he was about to sit down and took his seat, letting herself be carried towards the top. Standing on the back of the seat, she held onto the pole with one hand.

As she got closer to the Peace Camp at the top of the hill, she noticed between wet eyelashes a thicket of wild trees of heaven encircling the Duilia Rame school. Their invincibility offered her some consolation.

Inside the greenhouse she felt Aster's cool radiation. Aster was calling out for her, a silent and passionate cry. But a strong animal-like smell overpowered the pleasant feelings. Had her comrades been heavy-handed with the fertilizer?

A group of guests blocked her view of the Scattered Lands, where potatoes, carrots, radishes and beets could be found.

"Here she is," said Amegilla's voice, in an *ecce homo* tone.

"Always wandering off." Opilio's furious eyes.

"You were supposed to watch her. It's an easy enough task," Jodis, cold and kind.

Damned cardoons! How they prickled!

The guests moved aside. With their terracotta faces, noses eaten away by skin tumors, red gums, burnt hair and knobby fingers they were a collection of desert illnesses. Their eyes darted with cunning greed over every aspect of the greenhouse, as if they could steal it with just one look. Some of them were wearing coveralls from AgriViva, the multinational seed corporation. They had sold themselves to the enemy.

In between the radish sprouts, a ziggurat of fresh shit stood out. That's where the stench was coming from, and just a little further on laid shitting beauty, Granny. Drunk as a skunk on wine, she was cradling a bottle of Nepente with maternal tenderness as she slept.

Gazania shrugged her shoulders. A soft ringing alerted her to a new notification from her microchip; her comrades also received a message.

"Another fine!" exclaimed Amegilla. "*Vandalism of municipal property and abuse of chairlift users.*"

Gazania looked down at her chest. Just that morning she had had the unlucky idea to exchange her usual vegetable-striped tunic for a t-shirt bearing the image of a star-topped pole, the greenhouse's logo. That's why the guards had been able to identify her. She bent down, swiped the bottle from Granny's arms and gulped down the last sip.

"Oh, Darnel," grumbled the old lady, opening just one eye.

"Granny, you promised me that you'd respect the greenhouse."

The old lady sat down, shaking her head in an effort to wake herself up.

"Free fertilizer. Healthy stuff. Natural. Just how you guys like it. I challenge you to do any better. Fifty to one that none of you can."

And she smiled. Showing off her magnificent recently re-grown teeth.

"Is this one of your famous centenarians?" Asked a guest. "Incredibly healthy!" He stuck out his wrist and photographed Granny. The rest of them immediately copied him.

The old lady pulled the hood of her tunic all the way down to her mouth and shook her hands out in front of her.

"No pictures, you rakes! And stay away from me! I'm not giving you my DNA!"

"Let's move on," said Amegilla, ushering them on in an attempt to move the herd along. The guests slowly moved towards the lettuce area. The man who was interested in centenarians bent down and quick as lightning took a sample from the shit with a micro rod and then placed it in a plaize vial. Gazania squeezed his wrist and made him drop it.

"No souvenirs."

"You even want to make money out of shit," Jodis commented. "Isn't poisoning the earth enough for you?"

The guest quickly ran off to join the others.

"We keep the loose leaf-lettuce in these basins," Opilio declared. "Thanks to temperature and humidity controls we can obtain twelve harvest cycles in a year. In contrast only ten are possible in the open field…"

A ripple of shock went through the crowd of guests.

Gazania and Jodis grabbed shovels and removed the artisanal fecal work.

"Let's throw it in the extractor," Jodis suggested. "At least we can get some water out of it."

"That's it, good idea, make water out of it. I always drink wine anyways," said Granny.

"You sure made us look good in front of the traditional farmers," retorted Gazania.

"The Wasters? Showing them the greenhouse, teaching them, educating them, it's useless. You can kick their asses from here to the desert, but they won't listen to reason. They just want to go back to using sprinkler irrigation, like in the old days."

In the distance they could hear Amegilla's voice: "We use neither pesticides nor fungicides."

"Then the plants are genetically modified!" could be heard from the guttural voice of a guest.

"On the contrary. Precision agriculture uses only ancient varieties."

"Stone asses and rocks for brains," teased Granny. "They're here to steal your seeds, copy your plants in their laboratories and patent them. They just want to make money."

"You can't extract water from money," said Jodis.

"Money is useful, you idiots. It's like a wild horse, you have to tame it otherwise it decides where it takes you, but if you manage to saddle it...You want in on a sure bet? That will make you a good amount of money? Bet on the caffrarias blossoming."

Jodis leaned on the shovel.

"What are the odds?"

"Ten to one, if it happens within the end of the month."

"Premature," commented Gazania.

"It's been hotter than usual this year." Jodis seemed sure of himself. "Thirty erui on the blossoming of the caffrarias."

"Done!"

Granny pressed her big round bracelet to Jodis's wrist and sucked out the wager money. Granny had always refused to have the microchip inserted under her skin.

"I'm accepting bets on The Great Exodus too. Odds are five to one that it'll happen before the end of this year, on the fall equinox."

Gazania held her breath. The word "exodus" sounded like the rattling of a rattlesnake.

"Nonsense. We'll make it through the year, and we'll keep living here. This is our home."

At times Jodis spoke as if he were carving words into oak bark. It was one of the reasons why Gazania cared about him.

"Oh, of course, and every day the air gets cooler," retorted Granny. "If you want to take a big risk, the odds for Remain are thirty to one, but I'm calling it at fifty to one. What dry-brained idiot wants to stay here to roast?"

With complete indifference, she trampled the new radish sprouts as she left.

Gazania left Jodis to finish up the job. Molina's death, the family moving she had seen by the road, all that talk about the Great Exodus...she needed some green consolation. To Aster, to Aster.

During the building of the greenhouse a Solitaire rose had barred the way to the laying of the southwestern wall. The plant, a cross between an agave, a Klenia anteuphorbium and a melocactus, had grown disproportionately thanks to its modified genes and its great resistance to heat.

The architects, in an effort to maintain the rectangular layout, decided to fuse the fiberglass structure with the plant, which now found itself partially inside and partially outside the greenhouse.

Aster understood that the greenhouse's controlled environment kept her safe from predators, parasites and disease. That's why on the side that was inside the building, she had lost her thorns and her skin was velvety smooth. Caressing her, Gazania had begun to understand Aster's language from when she was a child. If the green flesh yieded that meant happiness, pleasure; resistance could mean either resentment or a challenge. Aster loved the greenhouse as much as she did, and just like her she lived both inside and outside of it.

Gazania took off her shirt, trousers and sandals. She squeezed herself into the space between two branches. Living inside the greenhouse had kept her shiny obsidian-like skin free of any wrinkles or roughness. Aster welcomed her inside joyfully, enveloping her with love. The pulsating juicy walls softly pulled at her, and Gazania followed by lightly pushing with her kidneys.

At the heart of the entanglement the greenhouse's light took on a green gold hue, it was like looking at the sun through a young grape leaf; it rested the eyes, hurt by the outside glare.

Amegilla and Opilio had thorns, invisible, stinging, but Aster's embrace cured every sting, every injury; her gelatinous sap healed every scratch in a short amount of time.

Gazania knew by touch every bean-shaped ventricle, the smooth oval recesses, and the orifices made grainy by parallel bumps. She squeezed backwards into a crevice and the green silky, elastic lips opened up.

"Oh, dear, if you only knew! Everything is going wrong today," murmured the girl, brushing against a series of uneven bulges with her fingers, similar to small breasts. "Molina is gone. The pests got her, and I hope they die in a fire!"

Aster knew. Underground, hidden to human eyes, a world of information, rumors, and gossip unfurled alongside neighborly exchanges of nitrogen phosphorus and water. The painful cry from Molina's roots had scared every other plant within a six-mile radius and made even the families of cacti and succulents that lived in the open desert shiver.

Molina's root apical meristems had released an extremely bitter tannin into the ground that said: be careful! we're being massacred! defend yourselves!

Even though Aster knew she was protected by being in the greenhouse, she had reacted instinctively: sucking more water up from the humid earthly depths and strengthening her entire body, made more compact by the tough fiber that covered her pulp. The human wielding an electric saw would meet with fierce resistance. She suffered together with Gazania over the death of a sister, and shared with the other plants the disappearance of many of their friends, wiped out because of city ordinances. Memories embedded into the soil as nitric substances, like those of humans codified as proteins in the brain, formed the biosphere's memory.

"People are betting on the Exodus, Granny's sure it's going to happen. Everyone wants to leave, bunch of cowards!"

It was the same old story. Aster couldn't truly understand the need to move, she had to force herself to imagine the life of rootless beings. Gazania closed her eyes and inhaled the smell of humid earth. Humid, humidified, humus, humanitas. We come from the earth; we grow with the earth.

It's not the ground that keeps the plants upright, it's the

roots that keep the earth in its place, oxygenated and alive. They support one another, in an exchange filled with love.

Aster softly cradled her by making her juice-filled fibers rock back and forth. Gazania let herself go against the bumps that emerged from the walls; quivering rubbery peduncles, slipped into her orifices. Her breath became shorter and faster while she moved together with Aster, sensing the botanical energy that rose from the roots and spread around her, within her. Sugary sap dripped from the branches that were tightened around her thighs, the plant teats shot out green milk, beloved green, cradle of ideas, root-like thoughts reaching up to the sky.

At times the greenhouse made her uneasy.

The flowers' sighs as they opened, the oxygen bubbling through the adder stones, the water gurgling. At times, she could sense the lettuce, tomato, and bell pepper fibers stretching their chlorophyll-filled arms out in the lukewarm air, happy to find no resistance, and she could hear the fruit slowly swell, coloured balloons filled with healthy juices.

Every now and then she had to lift up the coconut-fiber pillow that covered the cultivation tanks to check on the roots, and the white entanglement unsettled her. The roots came down from each plant, yet once they reached a certain level, they would move over to the side to tangle with those of their companions. Small spiral-like brains came up with plum, peach, apricot shaped thoughts. Harvested, sold and eaten, they produced more thoughts inside people's bellies. Good fruit, good thoughts, bad fruit...so much responsibility!

On a broader level, and keeping all those connections in mind, the whole greenhouse could be considered one single thinking mass. It was charged with electricity and vitality. What did it think of its curators? Who was taking care of whom? Were they feeding the plants or were the plants feeding them? A question that resembled a work by Escher.

Gazania's laboratory consisted of two tables pushed up against a wall in the peaceful area of the greenhouse where the radishes were kept. She placed the waxes on the tabletop: candelilla, carnauba and Aster's wax. The latter was mixed with her vaginal fluid, but she didn't think it would ruin the formula. Aster's pruinosity was a mix of esters, vitamin B and E, zinc, iron, iodine and natural antioxidants that kept it stable even at high temperatures.

The spectrographic examination had revealed the fatty acids had special characteristics: they polymerized, forming a protective coating that, on a microscopic level, was actually a dense lattice; it included air molecules between meshes. No other wax compound did this.

Amaryllis showed up just as the sun went down and stared at the tools on the table in awe.

Gazania used the mimosa wax to dilute Aster's wax. Acacia dealbata in Molina's honor – may she rest in peace in Eden where there are no local government authorities – and she cooked it in bain-marie together with the other waxes, each in its own beaker and with a different melting point. A fourth container was filled with water, and Amaryllis controlled its temperature using a pin thermometer. When the waxes had transformed into oil, Gazania poured in the new emulsifiers; the white flakes fused together in seconds. Stir it, Stir it.

"Around 175 degrees," Amaryllis said pulling the thermometer out of the water.

Gazania turned off the flame and got the blender ready. She picked the low setting and then plop, poured the first waxes into the beaker containing Aster's juice. Light spin in the blender. Plop, a different beaker and another spin in the blender; lastly, the water, a few drops at a time. As the cream's elements blended together, it came out white and fluffy. Once the blender's blades met resistance, she put it away and passed Amaryllis the jar.

"Assistant, the spoon."

The boy began to zealously stir the ingredients. "It's so smooth!"

"If it works, I'll call it Lotus Skin."

Gazania took off her lab coat and went to look at the sack of fresh capers the boy had brought her.

"There's so many. I don't have enough salt."

"I'll go get it at the Diamond Sea before I leave."

"What's this about?"

"Xilo got a job offer from the Boreal Republic. We're going up North."

Molina's rosy bark flashed in Gazania's mind. Severed. Cleanly split. Eliminated.

"And Jodis...?"

Amaryllis squeezed the beaker between his thighs and continued stirring vigorously.

"Jodis does whatever Xilo decides." He sounded resigned but also unconcerned. As if he, Amaryllis, had nothing to do with it.

"Everyone's crazy," mumbled Gazania lost in thought. "If we all leave, who will take care of this part of the world? People just don't understand. It's our duty to help living creatures grow and prosper." She repeated prosper, popping the *p*'s. "We're part of the living world and only together with the world can we stay alive. Our strength is around us. We were born and raised here and from this place we draw our energy. We have to open ourselves up, expand up and down, our roots sink into the ground to steady us, enabling us to withstand the wind and the sun, our arms climb to the sky and every season new leaves, new fruits. We have to..."

"Bloom," said Amaryllis.

"This isn't the first time I've told you this, is it?"

"You give the same speech every time someone else leaves."

"My words don't stick."

"I agree with you, Gaz. I like blooming and I don't want to leave."

"Have you told Xilo?"

The boy handed back the beaker.

"It's cold."

The color of the cream resembled something between emerald and turquoise. Amaryllis stuck two fingers into the buttery wax and spread it onto his arm massaging it all the way up to his shoulder.

"Cool and musky. I like Lotus Skin."

"Have you found them?"

"No."

"The drone?"

"It's still flying around."

The man pointed the monitor placed on top of a turned over wheelbarrow out to Jodis. A tense crowd of people was staring apprehensively at the screen.

"What's going on?"

Gazania had finished her tank cleaning shift and was standing just behind the circle of people.

"Amaryllis and the others aren't back yet," answered Jodis. "And it's already past one."

As usual, Xilo, next to him, glanced at her spitefully.

The woman controlling the drone was the mother of Amaryllis's friend, Hesperia.

The lost children's parents and guardians were all around her. They were biting their dirty soil covered nails, cursing the search for capers and promising punishments. Almost all of them belonged to the Astarte Consortium, they either worked in the greenhouse or distributed its goods. Amongst them were a group of teenagers, the lost children's brothers and sisters.

"Have a look over the War Camp," suggested a girl.

The camera left the ruined buildings overrun by caper bushes and displayed instead the roofs of the homes on the slopes of the Peace Camp, then a big flat rectangle that mirrored the color of the sky – the greenhouse roof – then the neighboring hill, a mishmash of houses covered in reflective panels, surrounded by vegetation protected by humidity control sheets, burnt fields, stone quarries, paved streets, crumbling walls.

"They might have gone to the Diamond Sea," said Gazania, "to get salt."

A collective murmur approved of the idea. The drone was made to fly south-west, over the shining white region where nothing grew.

"Slowly, slowly, slow down, we can't see well," the parents were saying to Hesperia's mother, stretching their necks towards the screen.

The sunlight transformed the salty plain into a blinding glare; they had to squint or use dark tinted glasses to protect their eyes in order to stare at the images coming from the drone. The greenhouse's thermometer, which measured the outside temperature too, already marked forty-five degrees celsius, but the weather reports were expecting it to reach fifty between three and five in the afternoon.

A cold shiver ran down Gazania's back. She squeezed Jodis's arm.

"Maybe Amaryllis ran away."

"Why?"

"He didn't want to leave."

"And he's hiding out in the open?" interjected Xilo. "My son isn't stupid."

Awfully tactless to highlight the genetic connection. Jodis didn't bat an eye. Gazania abandoned them to run to the laboratory tables. The jar of Lotus Skin was still there: empty.

She stepped outside from one of the greenhouse's side doors and was overtaken by the heat, so suffocating it left her breathless. The sun was at its highest. The zenith hours, the most dangerous time of day to be out in the open. Even the snakes would hide under rocks. If the Lotus Skin didn't work the kids would be roasted meat. She scrutinized the white line of the Diamond Sea. It became one with the sky where it met the horizon. Maybe they had already fainted, somewhere in the midst of all the salt, covered in blisters, purple with burns.

But if the formula worked...the wax component would have reflected the solar rays and the air in Aster's fatty lattice would have kept their body temperature at thirty-six degrees. She let herself imagine giving the cream to every resident: the magic ointment that overturned the zenith hour's tyranny! She saw a world where farmers using traditional methods worked the fields without fearing sunstroke or skin tumors; where labourers could build roads in broad daylight, people went grocery shopping when the sun was high; city life would completely change! Families would no longer run away to the North now that they could deal with the sun.

Gazania went back into the greenhouse and its coolness tempered her euphoria. Her anxiety over Amaryllis weighed down on her chest like a stone slab. The Lotus Skin was an experimental mixture, it might be nothing more than a good sunscreen suitable for the less dangerous hours of the day, or the formula might need to be adjusted...

The distraught crowd had grown, word had got around, and the residents had gathered to stress each other out and suggest useless solutions.

I'll go search for them with my truck; let's put together a drone team; sand sleds, anyone have any sand sleds?

Some were making the rounds offering chilled, flavoured water – you can think more clearly when you're hydrated – some were simply curious. Granny was having a heated argument with some outsiders who had no missing children but had come to help. Two or three teenagers were frantically writing on their communication bracelets so they could publish the news on the Shifr and were asking for details – how many children? Age? Are you a guardian? Do you authorize me to publish the picture? The Consortium members clung to one another, giving each other strength. They were like frightened daisies.

Everyone remembered the Black Zenith. Two years ago, a group of excited teenagers had tried to cross the Diamond Sea on electric skateboards. Only two boards without wheels, a pair of sunglasses and an energy bar wrapper had been found.

A commotion erupted in the middle of the waiting crowd between curious onlookers and disinterested bystanders. Two incensed women had started shoving someone around, giving the go ahead to some troublemakers who were just waiting to start something.

"You dirty scum!" yelled a voice.

"You should be ashamed of yourself!" exclaimed another.

"Die in a fire!"

Granny was the cause of the uproar.

"Here are the bet receipts!" A man raised two cards made of plais[1], one red and the other blue. "Blue they're alive, red they're roasted!"

"What is that supposed to mean? My daughter isn't a roast!"

The fight grew and the parents began directing their anger at the wrong people, allowing Gazania and Jodis to save Granny.

"Two-headed snakes," grumbled the old lady while she fixed her dress.

Even Granny is in bloom, thought Gazania. Placing bets is her way of blooming.

"Look!" yelled Hesperia's mother, pointing at the monitor. Hardly anyone heard her, too busy insulting one another and pushing each other around. Gazania came closer to the screen,

---

1 Artificial plastic made of mais

squinting to see better. A dark spot was swaying in the middle of the salt desert.

"Look!" she repeated, the loudness of her own voice surprising her. The ruckus died down and its participants hurried towards her.

Six kids were waving hello at the drone with their arms above their heads. They were jumping up and down on the white grains in the middle of a plain made red-hot by the sun. Their spongey turbans, drenched in slow-evaporating gel, stood out on their small heads, making them look like small pastries covered in colorful glazes; their backpacks overflowed with salt; they were wearing simple yellow t-shirts with the logo of the Astarte Consortium and shorts, their arms and legs exposed to the afternoon sun.

"Their skin!"

Circumnutation.

I finally remembered the word.

It's the movement that some growing plants make to get around obstacles. It can be seen clearly in the tendrils of climbing plants and grapevines, but it's common to all roots, be they daisies or sequoias. As the roots grow, they carry out a never-ending circumnutation. As a child, I had often asked myself how these delicate, thin filaments could move such large quantities of solid earth given that it was often mixed with rocks and stones and, at times, hard and resistant materials like slabs of underground concrete and heaps of plastic.

Their secret strength is circumnutation: they bypass the obstacle. If it's small, they pass by it; if it's big, they find a crack, an opening, even if it's tiny, and little by little they squeeze into the gap and push forward.

Plants hold true to the principle of the path of least resistance and not to that of the shortest one between two points. And the strongest path for a plant happens to zigzag.

The same principle has been applied to the movement of the Wind Wagon. As the streets, even when paved, soon end up devoured by the sand, the micro-movements of the Wagon's soft cushion allow it to keep moving around any obstacle – big or small – it comes across on land.

The only drawback is that some people's stomachs are much too sensitive, which means having to deal with nausea for however long the trip takes.

I chew on ginger candy and manage to bear it. I can look out the window and watch as the scenery flashes by, like images being projected on a gauze screen.

Returning. What a strange feeling.

These barren hills, with terraced farms made up of brave vines; this cruel sky held up by the green cathedral of the euphorbias; the smell of the air, dry and ancient. Only now, on my return, do I understand that wherever I went the places of my childhood have always been at the center of my heart,. A transparent soul-weight filled with the scents, the colors, the tastes and all those odds and ends that taken together constitute a complete emotion.

"What are you doing? Are you crying?"

Hesperia has sat down in the seat in front of me. I hadn't even noticed the tears running down my cheeks.

"Do you remember when we went to the Diamond Sea during the zenith hours?"

"Bunch of idiots!" She replies.

"We are the New Seeds, you said."

"Really? I'd invent a new name for the group every day: the Returned Skylarks, the Phosphorous Salts, the Wandering Tadpoles. What a weirdo. I remember feeling super confident about that trip."

"You never thought that we might die? If the Lotus Skin hadn't protected us, it would have been over for us."

"We aren't like our guardians; we don't just want to preserve what already exists. We are the generation that sets limits, we stick to our priorities, unlike our ancestors; we brave the world with a single blade of grass in each hand, we drink the murky water of compromise, and we carry with us the responsibility of every small act of bravery. But sometimes we must overcome our own natures and push forward."

In the sky, dinosaurs with gaping mouths, crouching lionesses, sculpted human heads flowed by: the New Year clouds. At this time twelve years ago, everyone was betting on the Great Exodus.

Jodis, Xilo and I left anyway. Once Xilo makes a decision, it must be seen through to the end, even if it means going straight through hell. I grew up full of doubts. Coming back is the only thing I'm sure about and having my colleagues with me makes it all even more real.

We get off at the stop in front of the post office.

Many things have changed. The Ideals, with their square balconies and white plaster, have disappeared; demolished, I imagine. There's now an Energy Lake in their place. A group of children skate on it; skidding on linen squares tied to their ankles. A few clumsy adults spin their arms around to keep their balance; the teenagers skate along the edge in elegant, synchronous strides. In the past, the city government used to ban the "improper use" of the panels, but then they found that the rubbing kept the panes clean and increased the energy output.

Light as birds, the kids meet and move apart, forming shapes: circles, stars, zigzags, diamonds and squares. They laugh happily, calling out to each other in shrill voices: Jasmine! Hibiscus! Periwinkle! Agave!

When I was a kid, they'd make fun of me because I was named after a flower, Gazania had been a trendsetter.

The Lake is big, at least twenty-five acres of transparent panels that reflect the blue sky. Groves of caffrarias, bay tree and boxwood grow on the shore; under state-of-the-art Aztec palms, resistant to the kefer and to the mistral, plais reclining deck chairs and colored tables had been placed about. The neighborhood now has a new source of energy and a place to meet.

"Look at that," I tell Hesperia, pointing at the skaters.

"They look like a bunch of little aliens," she answers.

The kids had spread Lotus Skin on every exposed body part and the bright green cream sparkles in the sun. They really do resemble the little green men from space who used to be spoken of in the past.

Gazania had tried several times to make the cream transparent, but it had always ended up a more or less light lizard color. In the Middle East and the Mediterranean area it has become an over-the-counter medication. Explorers, labourers working outdoors, and sailors wear it. Kids love it because they can pretend that they're reptiles, and a few eccentrics use it so that, every now and then, they can enjoy a day outside in the fresh air. Despite this Lotus Skin hasn't been a game changer. It's hard to present a project to investors, tell someone "I love you," or give orders to workers on site when you're completely covered in green; and then swapping nighttime with daytime, waking at dawn and going to bed at sunset goes against societal conventions.

"Let's take the chairlift." I point out the small station at the end of the boulevard. Hesperia has already started walking in the direction of the park and the others are following her. She gestures at me to catch up with them.

"Gazania works here now."

She heads towards Villa Clara's renovated pavilions surrounded by a forest of *Acacia caven* Molina. According to a plaize sign we're in the garden of the Asteracee Collective, an organization dedicated to the well-being of all living creatures in society.

I stop at the threshold of the first building. "I'm scared, Hesperia. What do I tell her?"

"You could start with hi, Mom."

"I've always called her Gazania. Or actually just, Gaz. It's been ten years since we were last in touch. We wrote to each other for a while, I promised her that I would run away and come back here, but I was never brave enough. She called me a traitor in her last letter. Maybe I really am one."

"Get over yourself. I'm going in, you can dig a hole and hide in it."

Hesperia's powers of persuasion can't be beaten.

Once inside, our presence in the building causes a stir. We're a group of guys and girls with fuchsia-colored hair dressed in the space program's grey coveralls: everyone's staring at us. We ask around for directions, and they point us towards a door.

We enter. The air is pleasantly cool and humid. A large transparent tank, raised up from the ground, takes up most of the available space and contains hydroponic cycadales. Their coralloid roots, hosting cyanobacteria that purify the water from heavy metals, are a tangle of filaments in light tea colored liquid. Three naked women are swimming there.

They laugh, tickled by the root tips. They spray water on each other, and, with great agility, push off into the water onto their backs in one swift movement. A girl around sixteen, an adult woman and an old lady. The old lady is the first to notice us.

"Oh, Darnel! We have visitors!"

Gazania seems to step out of my memories unchanged. Her short apricot-colored hair, with the tips sticking up, her bright eyes and her brash demeanor. She leans on the side of the tank and stares at me.

"You sure took your time."

We sit down under a grapevine covered pergola. The color

of the grapes is far too bright, they look like round lightbulbs and spread a relaxing, uniform violet light.

"Are they real or is it artistic lighting?"

"Experimental," answers the girl; her name is Fresia and she's Gazania's assistant. "We're collaborating with Tanis University on the Plant Energy Program and we're working on a project designing indoor and outdoor flower light fixtures."

"So much good vine gone to waste," sighed Granny, pouring herself a glass from the bottle on the table in the center of the pergola.

"You can drink palm wine," Gazania replies.

"That white stuff that's only five percent alcohol?" Granny is outraged. "The camels can have it!"

"I can see nothing's changed."

"You're wrong Amaryllis, so many things have changed. The greenhouse was bought by an AgriViva satellite company and so it can no longer produce only for the local population, but it now has to export its surplus goods and make a profit. Me, Amegilla and Opilio, together with a few others, left and established the Asteracee Collective."

"And Aster? What became of her?"

Gazania lowers her gaze.

"She's still in the greenhouse. What could I do? Her roots are far too deep to move her, and she wouldn't want to anyway. I had city hall designate her a plant of historic interest, she can't be chopped down or pruned.

She must have suffered so much. Alone, having to deal with these changes all by herself.

"Where does the Collective get its money from?"

"Me."

"Where'd you find the money?"

Granny clicks her tongue indignantly and downs another gulp of wine.

"I gave it to her, you nasty dry weed."

Gazania laughs.

"Do you remember the bets on the Great Exodus? I had a tiny stash set aside and I bet it all on Remain. Granny called Remain at fifty to one."

"I should just go die in a fire," the old lady grumbles.

"We started by producing sunscreen," continues Gazania, "and we still do. We export it to every part of the world, we reinvest the profits in biological research as well as in studies aimed at improving the quality of animal and plant life, in collaboration with universities. We draw inspiration from natural solutions to solve human problems."

"Are you looking for help? We're botanical engineers, geneticists and agricultural chemists."

I broadly gesture to my colleagues. They're scattered around the garden, a few of them are bending down to taste the soil's quality, Hesperia is using the sensors implanted in her fingers to analyze the leaves of the *Mimosa pudica*. Everyone's wearing *cultivar* overcoats, with tender sprouts in need of constant care shooting out from the fertile substrate filling their pockets.

"We've brought you some plant specimens suitable for sandy soil."

"Where'd you steal them from," Granny asks.

Gazania raises an eyebrow and waits for my answer.

Busted.

"Have you heard about the Twin Earth Project?"

Fresia grimaces, Granny spits on the ground, Gazania shakes her head.

"Yes, we know about it. It follows the philosophy of the locust: strip everything you have to the bone and then move on and do the same thing somewhere else."

"Xilo worked super hard on it and is still working on it. Xilo got me false papers to get me in the first Mars landing team. I had to do the preparation course, but it all worked out in the end. I bumped into Hesperia again and met my colleagues. We'd meet every evening to play tearco. Educational requirement, you know? Team building games help strengthen morale and stuff like that. But we were bored, so we started to talk. Do you see that girl climbing up the fig tree? Yes, her. One evening she said: if we all leave, if we all abandon it, who'll be left to take care of Earth?"

"She stole your phrase, boss," Fresia says.

Gazania watches my colleague carefully, as if she were a rare plant found by chance during a botanical expedition. Maybe she's trying to figure out if there are any similarities between herself and the new generation. The unexpected heirs.

"Why're your heads the color of monkey butts?" asks Granny.

"The color reveals what we think about the future."

"But that still doesn't explain why you've all ended up here," retorts Gazania.

Hesperia and two other colleagues have joined us in the meantime and come to stand next to me. Hesperia has even laid her hand down on my shoulder and she gives it a friendly squeeze as if to encourage me to spill the beans.

"It's true, we could have gone to Mars or to the Mongolian desert, gone down to the bottom of the sea and studied algae or deep-sea fish, or else lived in the Canadian rainforest and analyzed the ecosystem. But I believe...we believe that the challenge can be found here, the real battle between the past and the future. We want to see watermelons sprout from the sand and we want to flourish in it, not the sand on Mars, but our ordinary, banal, earthly sand."

Gazania brings her hand to her heart and lets out a deep sigh.

"Oh, my heart."

She bows her head and for a moment I worry that she's about to pass out from the emotion.

"I know now. I know how the buried seed feels once water reaches it and splits it. It hurts. It's a small pain, small and deep, but it makes it sprout."

We take the chairlift up to the Peace Camp.

The greenhouse looks the same, a long flat box with selectively transparent glass: light where more sun is needed, dark where shade is necessary.

AgriViva has rebuilt the old, abandoned road, converting it into a large, fifty-foot track for containers dragged by a radio-controlled rig to roll on; they arrive empty and leave full of fruits and vegetables, placed in orderly refrigerated crates.

Aster towers over the top of the greenhouse's roof, an abstract sculpture: curved, soft, green. She lies half inside and half outside of the south-west wall, breaking the building's boxy shape. Her trefoil branches have grown longer and stronger. A few stretch to the sky, like the statue of a saint or some divine intermediary, asking for pity for the careless and foolish beings that live down here. The open flowers' gigantic corollas seem to herald redemption with bursts of red.

City hall has placed a see-through fence around the trunk with a sign reading: Asteria-Kleinia anteuphorbium azureus, var. nobilis. And underneath that: jewel of humanity.

"It's offensive. It makes it look like Aster belongs to us."

"She doesn't understand the concept of ownership. For her belonging means sharing the same earth, nutrients, light, air. In a way we do."

Gazania opens the fence and swiftly climbs up Aster's paths. Or maybe the plant is helping her up, retracting her thorns, lowering her branches. I follow her up, my hands getting pricked a couple of times.

We sit on the edge of a shelter made by the crossing of some plant branches. War Camp hill appears in front of us. They're trying to build on top of it, again. Ecological housing this time. Houses that grow, put down roots, make the windows blossom and the rooms branch out.

"I could have produced great quantities of Lotus Skin," Gazania says. "The demand was high, it still is."

A confession. I hold my breath, hungry to know more.

"The problem lies in the unique characteristics of Aster's wax. It's impossible to recreate in a laboratory."

I exhale. Now I get it.

"The greenhouse would still be independent" she adds, "the Astarte Consortium wouldn't have failed."

"I saw some kids wearing Lotus Skin skating on the Energy Lake just this morning."

"It's a normal sunscreen with physical filters and some green coloring added. It doesn't protect against the zenith hours; it's written on the packaging. I registered the name Lotus Skin and I use it for the sunscreen made by the Collective."

"You'll find the right formula sooner or later, without having to sacrifice Aster. No, we'll find it together, all of us, with my group too."

"Are you sure about what you're doing? You're missing out on the chance to go on a great adventure, for you and all of humanity. Maybe you were just nostalgic for this place, and you needed to see it one more time, before taking the great leap into space."

"You know Gaz, the North is different from how people like us imagine it. When I was a kid, I thought it would taste like a strawberry popsicle, but there's heat, sweat and incredibly sunny days even up there. Mosquitoes. You can't even imagine how many annoying insects live up North, even in the places where it snows in winter."

"Sunny!" she makes fun of me. Then she can't help but ask: "What's snow like?"

"Like sand, but damp. Nothing life changing. I'm still a son of the South after all. I like the heat, I like the sharp contrasts, burning under the sun and the teeth chattering cold after sunset. Oh, but people are less rude than we are, they smile, they help you, they stop to listen to you."

"It doesn't sound too bad."

"I'd be lying if I said it was a bad place. No, life is easier in those latitudes. Everyone should try it at least once. But then the moment arrives when you ask yourself which place grounds you, the place where you are your most authentic self, the most real. The place that reflects back a version of you that you're able to look at without dropping your gaze, even if the image you see shows you all of your good and bad qualities. I had a good life up North, but I felt like I had been split in two, as if another me had stayed back here and I had no way of telling him: hey idiot! I've left, come join me. I figured out in the end that I had to be the one to come back and reunite with him, Gaz. I'm in bloom here."

I stop for a second to stare at the hazy horizon, the humidity is a sign of a new development. The air isn't as dry, the desert isn't as ruthless. Everything turns, everything changes. The climate pendulum can swing between arid and rain in just a few years.

"When I was a kid, I thought being in bloom meant cultivating ideas like leaves. Starting from the petiole the veins would spread out and an idea would be divided up in various logical thought processes. It would grow and expand until it could make some headway. I cared more about what was visible, forgetting that if the leaf grows at all, it's because of the roots using circumnutation to make their way through the soil in search of nutrients."

Gazania smiles slightly.

"And I still hadn't arrived at the root of the matter. The main point isn't the single tree, the solitary thriving tree, the point is the connections between the roots. Blooming is only possible when each plant connects and talks to every other plant, they exchange information, they love and hate each other, they make fun of one another..."

"I'd talk to you, when you were a kid, without knowing how you would interpret my words. I knew that certain things can only be understood through intuition."

"An Amaryllis grows slowly, and then when its incredibly beautiful flower blossoms, it lasts a long time."

"You'd have a better life up North."

"I don't want a better life, Gaz. I want my life."

As soon as I stop speaking I sense a strange vibration, a trembling underneath me moves through my thighs as if I were sitting on something living. Aster is moving! The sap flows within the green hide of her skin and makes the sturdy branch we're sitting on swell.

A shiver runs through my whole body making my hair stand on end, affecting even the stubble on my chin – my human thorns – I was too lazy to shave, it brushes my stomach and bowels just like a warm, gentle hand would. Suddenly, a distant memory takes me back to a time long ago, when I still couldn't formulate thoughts because words are inaccessible to newborns; a time in which I was cradled, cuddled, loved by Aster's green trunks.

Gazania had told me that when I cried desperately because I was teething, she would take me from Jodis's arms and lay me naked on the plant. In only a few minutes I'd be asleep, gripping onto my cactus cradle with tiny hands.

Aster is happy. I'm happy. My eyes fill with tears, but the emotion is different from what I felt on the Wagon. That was nostalgia, now I feel satisfied. Beauty squeezes my eyes like water from a sponge.

Gazania hasn't noticed, maybe to her Aster's movements are as normal as human breathing. I search for her hand and squeeze it.

"Everything moves so slowly," she sighs. "Waiting for the results is so exasperating at times."

"Time..." I start. But my voice has a dreamy tone I've never heard before, as if I were speaking together with someone else, the old me? The new me?

"Time moves at the right pace. You and Aster taught me that, waiting patiently is the secret to every good change."

THE GREEN SHIP

by Francesco Verso

translated by Michael Colbert

Francesco Verso (Bologna, 1973) is a multiple-award Science Fiction writer and editor. He has published: Antidoti umani, e-Doll, Livido (aka Nexhuman), Bloodbusters, Futurespotting *and* I camminatori *(made of* The Pulldogs *and* No/Mad/Land*).* Nexhuman *and* Bloodbusters *have been published in Italy, US, UK and China. He works as editor of Future Fiction, scouting the best SF in translation from around the world. He's the Honorary Director of the Fishing Fortress SF Academy of Chongqing and the Creative Director of Future Wave, a literary agency based in Beijing. From 2014 he works as editor of Future Fiction, a multicultural project, scouting and publishing the best SF in translation from 13 languages and more than 35 countries with authors like Ian McDonald, Ken Liu, Xia Jia, Liu Cixin, Chen Qiufan, Pat Cadigan, Vandana Singh, Lavie Tidhar, and many others. Lately he's started an imprint called Futuresque dedicated to Science Fiction comics from many countries.*

"There it is! Down there! Land!" Billai yelled, nearly falling off the dinghy.

We all looked in the direction she indicated with her arm. The waves that had shaken us for some hundred hours didn't jolt us as much as her words.

We couldn't feel our legs or move a muscle. Tangled one on top of the other, we were groggy from hunger and thirst. Muna, seated next to me, hugged her baby closer. The three guys in front exchanged a hopeful smile. Meanwhile Haziz–who came to Bengasi after crossing the Bamako Desert–shook his hand.

130

"It can't be Italy. We're still far."

We looked at each other anxiously. Someone had fainted. To revive him, we had to slap his face. It wasn't a boat that we had navigated in but a coffin.

"He's right," said Professor Kysmayo, the ex-radio host from Nairobi. "The outline is too simple. It's not the coast…"

Nobody said anything else, because nobody dared pronounce the name that, for some weeks, was circulating the Mediterranean's southern shores.

A dark and continuous line occupied the horizon from Otranto in Italy, arriving in Orikum in Albania. Smooth and unassailable, the bulkheads of the naval blockade rose for thirty meters on the sea waves; assembled easily thanks to the ships' containers full of carbon, but impossible to climb or break down, they represented a momentary solution (even though there were those who would've called it the "definitive deterrent") to immigration towards Europe by the sea.

"They said this part was free!" Billai shouted.

"They lied," Haziz said, almost in a whisper.

"Maybe not…I heard barriers can be 3D-printed overnight. The same bulkheads could've been between Pantelleria, Lampedusa and Malta…to force boats to turn around or follow long and expensive routes," Professor Kysmayo said.

Billai rubbed her temples with her fingers. Every border depressed her, and getting closer to a wall, erected for the sole purpose of separating international and domestic waters, discouraged her even further. With her life savings, she had crossed with me the borders of Kenya, Sudan and Libya before attempting the Benghazi crossing.

"Why didn't they tell us?" Muna said.

Nobody felt like answering such a naive question.

"They want to canalize boats to navigable checkpoints," the professor said. "And then come those…" he concluded, pointing to a spot in the distance.

Some black spots, which from far away looked like seagulls, revealed themselves to be surveillance drones activated by the boat's movement detected by satellite. I'd heard about those and others used in the mountains to secure Europe's land borders. Soon, they circled over us like vultures.

With a solemn air, as if she were about to declare war on the world, Billai rose to her feet. Swaying, she grasped my back so as not to fall and said, "We've all lived through things that we shouldn't have lived through and would be better to forget. I'm not turning back. Those drones are informing someone. They'll come and take us. Doctors without Borders, NGOs, the Coast Guard..."

Four hours later, one hundred and thirty-two of us were saved.

I was seventeen years old and my life was contained in a backpack: a bar of soap, a smartphone and charger, a sports jersey (number ten, Ike Kamau), and a photo of my mom and brother. They always told me that I had a narrow head, pointed chin, and quick eyes, black like tar. Like my dad's.

I was seventeen years old and my life had been spent in a refugee camp; since when we arrived in Dadaab from Nairobi, I hadn't seen anything but tents, dust, fences, and gates.

Soft clouds glided over the sea: that night the stars would disappear and the moon would have illuminated us all if another silhouette hadn't appeared to divert the way of our gazes and our lives.

"That's an... aircraft carrier?" Billai asked.

An immense structure stood out on the dark waters.

"I don't know," I said while she drew near me. The lapping of the water had worn down her combative temperament.

Someone took a picture, but in the high seas there wasn't a strong enough signal to transform anxiety into hope. It could be a military ship charged with bringing us back to the dark side of the Mediterranean, but instead the man who drew near us on a lifeboat with four sailors told us a different story.

"Welcome," he said in English. He had blond hair tied back in a ponytail, a pronounced nose and lips, and a smile, sincere but strained. "My name is Sergio Torriani and that's a Green Ship," he added, pointing behind him. "We take in anybody who needs help."

The sailors threw us water bottles.

Haziz grabbed my sleeve and asked me to translate. I was one of the few on board, along with Professor Kysmayo, who knew some English besides Swahili. When I was little, I listened to his show "Indie Reggae, Beats & Rock" on Radio Kenyamoja.com, and I knew hundreds of songs by heart.

"We don't want to board. We want Europe," I said dryly, gesturing to Haziz to show Sergio who those words came from.

He didn't answer right away but instead tossed us a line that Billai caught in the air. "Europe doesn't want you," he continued, bitter, "and they don't care if you're escaping from hunger or war, if you live in refugee camps or if your children and grandchildren will be born and grow up in those prisons. Where do you come from?"

I heard the names of camps I knew like Dadaab, Nyarugusu, Bokolmanyo and others I ignored like Urfa, Zaatri and Adiharush.

"Besides, this isn't a boat for transit," Sergio said.

"So you'll bring us back or send us to a center for identification and deportation." I translated for Muna, who'd lifted the bundle with her son inside.

"No deportation. The Green Ship is a humanitarian project for the rescue of political refugees and climate migrants."

"If you're not bringing us back and you're not going to Europe, where are you going?" Professor Kysmayo asked. He was the only one to reason with his head and not his heart.

Sergio and the other sailors were already throwing lines to ease the transfer onto their lifeboat.

"Board and you'll see."

Once we'd boarded, Sergio asked, "Nobody else?"

We looked at each other without the courage to respond. Then Professor Kysmayo said, "In the hold there were two cadavers. They died two days ago. They started to stink. We had to leave them at sea...to lighten our load."

"Their names?"

We were silent. Sergio added two Xs to the list of one hundred twenty-three.

From the parapet, I observed the wake of boats in transit in the Aegean Sea: a Greek ferry, two cargo boats, a cruise ship. Who knew how many immigrants were hidden like cargo in the holds.

The others were still sleeping among the trees, and they were not alone: hundreds of strangers were camping in sleeping bags and tents, and below, thousands were squished in the bunks. Yesterday evening, I didn't see anything because I quickly lay down to rest, but now, by the light of dawn, things appeared more clearly.

"Jambo," Sergio said in Swahili, offering me a cup of coffee.

"Jambo, and thank you for picking us up," I said, taking a sip.

"Did you sleep? It's not easy after being on a dinghy."

He must have had experience with migrants to speak like that.

"Little and poorly."

"Later we'll have a soccer game with everyone. Would you want to join?"

I nodded a yes and he convinced me to tell him about "our" games in Nairobi.

"Two things were important for me: surviving and playing soccer...then it became only one when men from al-Shabaab came to the fields where my brother Noor and I played. They scolded us because we wore shorts and played with a ball. Soccer was a decadent pastime for them…like alcohol, cigarettes or film. But Noor and I played it just the same, hidden. Our games ended when the bombs dropped."

I took the Ike Kamau jersey from my backpack.

"Here you can play without anyone saying anything to you."

I gave him the empty coffee cup. "This ship is really odd."

It was his turn to tell me something.

"According to international law, it's not a ship, but a micronation. First it was a bioconservation project funded by the United Nations, a bit like the seed deposits in the Norwegian Svalbaard Islands. Ever heard of it?"

I shook my head.

"Then it was converted to manage the immigrant crisis in the Mediterranean."

Three hills, in the middle of which ran a stream, recreated microclimates: temperate, desert, and Mediterranean. My gaze wandered to the Mediterranean habitat where tens of drones hurried around like birds that watered leaves, cut branches, checked flowers, and collected pollen, while some gardeners oversaw the operations to maintain everything green. Then, in the middle of the eucalyptus grove, I saw an impressive sequoia, its fronds shading half of the ship.

"The habitats," Sergio continued, "are protected by geodetic cupolas one-hundred fifty meters tall. Fresh water comes from a desalinator powered by solar energy."

In the meantime, Billai had woken up and joined us.

"How did you manage to create…all of this?" she asked as if she'd woken into a dream. While I translated, Sergio showed us along a path.

Professor Kysmayo noticed us and joined up. His background as a radio journalist got the better of his sleepiness.

When he wasn't on the air with "Indie Reggae, Beats and Rock," he edited a feature on technology.

"We bought an abandoned aircraft carrier, and we modified it through a crowdfunding project. The hull belonged to *Variago*, an aircraft carrier in the same class as Admiral Kutnetzov launched in 1988 in Russia. In 2004 it was rebaptized *Liaoning* and sold to China to become a floating theme park, like Disneyland, but luckily it didn't happen. We bought it for a token price to make a botanical garden. Ours is a scientific project approved by the United Nations, though now we're more public transit for migrants," Sergio said with a laugh.

The ship flew its own flag: a sequoia styled green on a hull over a white background.

"We can host seven thousand people. We grow crops and raise livestock. We have internet and 3D printers for any needs."

"Do you want to bring all refugees aboard?" I asked, jokingly. "Like Noah's ark?"

"Impossible. You'd need a hundred ships," Billai added, "and only to evacuate the camp in Dadaab."

"In fact, we have another plan. When the time is right, we'll head towards India and the southern seas."

"Somebody won't like that solution," Kysmayo said.

Haziz and some other guys had boarded reluctantly. They'd continued to complain about wanting only Europe.

"Once they feel better, they have to decide whether or not to retry their journey. We had to save them and let them know the risks."

Streaks of lightning invaded the northern sky. From the Indian hinterlands the cloudy front advanced slowly, like a wounded animal with its head swaying. The weather warped ahead, rumbling and hiding every ray of sun. Lights descended on the water after flashing along incandescent segments.

Many of us retreated to the tents to safely enjoy this spectacle of light, water, and wind while others ran through the torrential rain to refresh themselves in song and laughter. Muna played with her son, alive thanks to the fact that he'd never been removed from his mother's breast, from which he managed to suck every drop of milk she managed to produce without dying from dehydration.

But the celebrations were interrupted when a man came down from the bridge with a megaphone in hand.

"Attention! Attention! They've detected a seaquake. Time of impact is four minutes."

A sinister light whitened the sea. Billai curled into me.

"It'll never end...even the sea has it in for us."

"Would you have preferred to do as Haziz and his friends did?"

"No, they're crazy to return to Somalia and retry that hopeless journey. But what end will we meet?"

"They say they wanted to retry, but their eyes said otherwise. We'll meet a better end. I'm sure of it."

In the middle of rolling waves four meters tall that battled the ship's hull, another one appeared: it occupied all of the horizon, and judging by the distance, it must've been three times as high. Visibility lowered and a wall of water, misty with the gusts of wind, rustled the branches of the floating forest.

The pitch, already agitated every time the ship sank into the gulch of the waves, became insupportable. Songs and screams became complaints and curses. Those who danced before now grasped onto something, trying not to vomit.

The clamor escalated, an uproar of wind, pounding of water, a vibration like a drumroll beating the charge. Despite the five hundred meter length and its scary tonnage, even the Green Ship suffered from the force of nature.

When the tsunami washed over us, into every pore, nerve,

and muscle of our bodies, Billai, her lips trembling with fear and emotion, kissed me on the lips.

Once the storm ended, lights appeared on the horizon.

When we were closer, I made out numerous boats linked together by a series of ropes and jetties: together they all formed a type of flotilla.

None of us had any idea where we'd arrived, even though that assembly in the high sea didn't seem to be our final destination. To find an answer, I went to Sergio, who was on the phone.

"Where and when did it happen?" he was asking someone. A contagious joy appeared on his face, as if he just discovered that he'd become a father.

"And how big is it?"

He walked back and forth, unable to contain his mysterious happiness.

"Yes, definitely...send me a scan and the coordinates. I'll inform the flotilla."

Once he hung up, Sergio grabbed me by the shoulders.

"We've been blessed. Nature is building your new home."

"A new home?"

"The seaquake...it opened a fault line under the ocean from which magma is pumping out."

"Are you bringing us into a volcano?"

"No, but as soon as the magma cools, we can claim the island that's emerging from the sea. Now we too have something to teach Nature. Then with the flotilla we'll think of the rest."

"The rest? That's just going to be a rock."

"Yes, at first it'll be uninhabitable, but we'll terraform it."

I turned my gaze from Sergio's satisfied face to the geodetic cupolas. Tree pollen and mushroom spores floated around, carried by the ocean breeze.

The Green Ship took the lead of the flotilla. Seen from above, it might look like a school of fish migrating for the season. And we were part of that flow.

The sign posted on top of our new land had been modified. By changing an N into a D, it was transformed from "No Man's land" to "No-Mad Land," as the media had hastened to rebaptize the newly born micronation.

The islet where Sergio had first planted the flag–in his haste called "No Man's Land" to underline its independence from whoever wanted to claim the territory–in time became "No-Mad Land" for us. A place accessible without a passport, entry visa, or residency permit. A land designed to welcome people instead of turning them away.

I liked the wordplay of No-Man and No-Mad. Having grown up in a refugee camp between walls and gates, I'd been freed of those limits and I'd left all borders behind. Because borders, political or mental, are temporary obstacles. Because only those who have been turned away or who have enough imagination and empathy for others know how to appreciate the value of hospitality.

The accidental but highly probable birth of the islet in the middle of the Indian Ocean was followed by a phase of movement of thousands of tons of sand from the adjacent seafloor. Thanks to pumping systems, the aspirated sand provided construction material for five enormous 3D printers.

Two of them, aboard tankers, employed the same techniques that the Dutch used to tear the polders from the North Sea–creating dykes of natural material–to protect the central atoll. Yet, different from the polder, the architects supporting the project had thought up a porous, artificial structure that, adequate to host marine life, over the course of centuries would in part replace the irremediably damaged Great Barrier Reef.

The other printers focused on terraforming the cooling magma, rich with fertile substances. They mixed it with sand from the seafloor.

It took us six months before we could set foot on "No-Mad Land."

To our touch, the ground was not hard, but instead it seemed fat and ready to be cultivated.

Under an orange sky, a carpet of yellow narcissus welcomed Billai and me. The air smelled fresh and the land emanated a narcotic warmth, stronger than the *chillum* that Noor smoked at the camp in Dadaab. The corollas of the flowers reached Billai's bare knees, and I filled myself with the smell of the narcissus, transplanted to the island from the Green Ship months ago.

"Do you know why I like it here?" she asked as she lay down.

I shook my head.

"Because we're all immigrants from somewhere."

"If you think about it, Dadaab was also like that."

"But it's prettier here," she said, her smile showing disappointment.

I stared at her frail ankles. The first time I saw her at the refugee camp, she and two other girls were chatting while pumping water from a well. Each filled three jugs, two to carry by hand and one to balance atop their heads. They were three queens, models who strutted on dirt roads as if they were high fashion runways. She wore a long, colored skirt, a scarf on her head, earrings, coordinated makeup, hair in tiny, neat braids. Her balanced gait was perfect, her gaze ahead, noble, full of nonchalance. She shone with her own light, a star with black skin that emanated a supernatural aura as she passed, wiggling her hips between trash barrels, plastic waste, mismatched shoes, rusted pipes, and goats that grazed on what they could find.

We made the whole trip together. Sometimes, like in Sudan, I feared that she wouldn't be able to make it, like when we had to bribe the guy at the border. Or when she was hurt while we were crossing an area mine-laden by Boko Haram terrorists. But more than anything else, I feared for her life the night when two traffickers cornered her after realizing her beauty. She tried to defend herself, to stop the violence. She shouted for help, crying "Saidia! Saidia!" but nobody moved for fear of being thrown in the sea for defending her. In the end I couldn't stand it. I grabbed one of them by the neck and I flung him off the boat. The other kicked my back, grabbed my shirt and lifted me off the ground. I too would've ended up in the water had it not been for Professor Kysmayo, whose strong hands freed me from the grip of the trafficker and then threw him too into the dark waters.

"You're right, Billai…but unlike Dadaab, besides us all being immigrants, there's something else that makes me love this place."

"What?"

"That here, if we want, we can emigrate."

She took my hands and said in her solemn tone, "How it has always been and always will be."

Once in a while I talked with people back in Dadaab on the Internet. Nobody wanted to admit that the refugee camp—provisional since the 90s—had become a permanent establishment. Not the local functionaries who received funding to continue operation, not the United Nations that paid to not solve the problem, not the refugees, forced to live there without hope of leaving. I would never want to return there to survive, imagining a life elsewhere. My elsewhere, like that of many others, was being born from the commitment of all who participated in "No-Mad Land." If we'd created a precedent better than Scaland, the Republic of Minerva, Rose Island, to cite some cases Sergio had talked about, who knew what we'd be able to achieve? Who knew if international law would adapt to the fundamental necessities of humans?

My mother and brother were already on their way to intercept the path of the Green Ship. Professor Kysmayo climbed down to the islet and waved to greet us. In his other hand he held an envelope with a round object inside.

"Down there, did you see it?"

We stood up and followed him until we reached the top of another hill where there was a second meadow, green and flat.

"They taught me how to use the 3D printer."

White lines were traced into the side of the field.

"This is my first ball," he said, pulling the object out of the envelope and raising it above his head like a trophy. And then he gave the ball a kick.

A soccer goal awaited only us.

The Love Algorithm

by Michele Piccolino

translated by Carlotta Codebò

Michele Piccolino, born in 1972, lives between the cities of Formia and Ausonia with his wife Giovanna and their children Giuseppe and Giovanni. A lawyer by profession, he teaches in schools and universities. He has won many literary, Science Fiction and mainstream awards. His first novel, La Creatura senza nome, *was published in 2011 and the anthology of short stories* Il pettine lungo il fiume e altre storie improbabili *in 2013. Two years later was published the collection of short stories* La guida spirituale e altre storie di Cavafratte *and later on the second collection* Il bianco degli occhi e altre storie nere di Cavafratte, *both published by Tabula fati; in 2021, the novel* Il processo automatico *was published by 0111 Edizioni. He organized the Douglas Adams Prize for Humorous Science Fiction in 2002 and 2003. His works have been published in dozens of anthologies, also abroad.*

Fabio Izzi sat down at the corner café on Via Canonica to watch the front door of the apartment building on Via Bertini 1. He poured two sachets of brown sugar into his coffee and started swirling it around with his spoon, all without taking his eyes off the door on the other side of the street.

The cars moved calmly and rhythmically along the road. The barely perceptible hum of the electric motors couldn't reach his ears over the dull thudding of his heart. He had never been this afraid before, a subtle fear that stiffened his muscles and dulled his thoughts, the fear of being inadequate. He was afraid of being a disappointment to her and that she wouldn't like him. Right when he had almost reached the goal he had been aiming for all his life. Because happiness was behind the front door on the other side of the street, he knew it, the document he held in his hands certified it.

He sipped his coffee slowly, hoping that the caffeine would clear his mind.

It had taken him three days to get to Milan: the first to quash any remaining doubts and decide to go; the second to pack and choose the outfit he wanted to wear when he introduced himself to her; the third to reach the city and find first her house and then the ring. Now he was waiting...without knowing why.

Every now and then a passing bus would block his view of the front door and his heart would skip a beat. Almost as if he was worried that, in the two seconds it was out of his sight, it would disappear forever, vanish due to some sort of black magic. In his heart he yearned for her to leave the building with the same bittersweet smile he had seen and fallen in love with on her Facebook profile. He would go to meet her, ring box in one hand and the Lovemat's verdict in the other.

A vibration coming from his wrist notified him of an incoming message.

He looked down at his omnicom. It was his sister Clara.

Anything happened yet?

He dictated his answer: *Still nothing.*

Get on with it, concluded Clara.

As if it were easy, he thought.

More than one person stopped in front of the apartment building's front door. Once they had pressed a button on the video intercom keypad, they were buzzed in and would cross the threshold to disappear into the darkness of the lobby.

Fabio looked at his omnicom: he'd been waiting for an hour, he'd been waiting all his life and he was still doing it even now he knew what he had to do.

He gulped down the last sugary drop of his now-cold coffee, put the cup down, pushed it away and called the café droid over. Tapping his omnicom on the cash register's display he paid for his drink.

He stopped in front of a shop window and checked out his reflection: it wasn't the greatest, but it wasn't terrible either, he said to himself. He instinctively stuck his hand in his pocket and fingered the envelope from the Ministry: it was the pass to his beloved's heart, the only thing she was looking for. That everyone was looking for.

He smoothed down his coat to iron out a wrinkle that wasn't even there, fixed his shirt collar and sighed. The oxygen he inhaled gave him courage, he let a bus pass, then crossed the street in five steps.

Clara linked arms with Fabio. Her body moulded to her brother's, as if she were supporting or dragging him along. Maybe she was doing both at the same time. Their feet weren't in step, Clara walked as if certain of the direction whereas Fabio seemed more hesitant, as if a thousand thoughts hindered his stride.

"You're a dead weight like usual, you always have been," she complained.

"I don't want to go. I've already told you that."

"You don't know what you want. Leave it to me."

The people around them weren't paying them any attention. The city was indifferent to their minor drama.

The outline of the Marriage Office could be seen at the end of Viale Arenula. The building was old, just like the others surrounding it, but inside it safeguarded the most modern technological discovery, the Lovemat, the soulmate-finding device. Every day throngs of people turned to its terminals as if it were an ancient oracle that could clear the fog of the future and cut down the jungle of choice with the power of its algorithms. There was one in every city big enough to host an office of the Ministry of Families. More than hope, it was faith in the Lovemat's infallibility that inspired people to go to them. It had been just the same for Clara too, ten years earlier.

"Heidi and I are sick of hearing you whine about feeling lonely."

"That's not true, I don't whine."

"Because you're not the one that has to listen to you."

Heidi, Clara's wife, was nice, but, like any good Swiss from Ticino, she had just enough German ancestry to prevent her from completely understanding the moods of an Italian male, much less one from Rome. She couldn't understand why, if the Lovemat worked, one wouldn't use it. It had worked wonderfully with her and Clara, as the duration of their union bore witness.

In truth, no one had ever complained about it, but this wasn't enough for Fabio, he was a romantic and he wanted passion. He remembered his sister's wedding, the two brides, almost complete strangers, standing in front of the droid, an anthropomorphic extension of the Lovemat, officiating the ceremony. They vowed to be loyal until their dying days without really looking each other in the eye. They held hands hesitantly, more to instil courage than because of true love. Because that was guaranteed by the love algorithm and ensured by their respective brain compatibility to an extent equal to or greater than 95%. Behind the brides-to-be, the few invited guests shared the same unshakable certainty: what was being celebrated was the realization of an idea of love yearned for in byte form. Two beings and zero doubts, but also zero romanticism.

"You know I'm different," added Fabio trying to wriggle away. Clara held onto him tighter and overcame his resistance. She quickened her stride, forcing her brother to do the same.

"You're not different, you're just an idiot. If you don't have your brain scanned you'll be alone forever, don't you get it?"

Unfortunately Fabio had to agree with her. He had often tried to do without it. He had even fallen in love, at least six times. The memory of those past failures rose up from his stomach and filled his mouth with the taste of bile.

The first one had been Serena, his pure and unyielding high school classmate who had dismissed his clumsy attempt at courtship outright: "My first kiss will be given to the boy with the highest Lovemat rating when I turn eighteen."

Then there had been Lina, Jasmine, Vale, and Ludovica, with whom he had woven tormented relationships filled with numerous doubts about their compatibility. In the end, each of them had decided to clear up every single doubt by turning to the Lovemat. The verdict had always been the same: the man of their life was not Fabio Izzi.

They had dumped him with a screenshot of the Ministry's certificate with another man's name written on it. Men none of them had never seen nor heard from before.

The last heartbreak had been the most agonizing: Sara.

She had also been a romantic, no Lovemat for her either. They had fallen in love after meeting by chance, they had liked each other without resorting to the algorithm.

After five years together, they were ready for an old-fashioned wedding: they had picked the church, the restaurant, the wedding favours, the household furniture. Just one month before the ceremony a man showed up holding a certificate saying Sara was his soulmate. Sara's love melted like an abandoned popsicle on the beach.

A month later she showed up at the altar with certificate-guy.

To Fabio it was a genuinely absurd system. He couldn't come to terms with the fact that every person had one and only one match and vice versa, including a man with a man, or a woman with a woman, but always a one:one ratio. Discovering one's ideal partner was the result of a superhuman, supernatural and almost divine analysis. In the end, there was no difference between magic and technology, both required a faith he didn't possess.

He was tired though, he had to admit. He was tired of hearing everyone keep repeating to him that the Lovemat was the answer, tired of lonely sleepless nights, of his sister's scolding, of his colleagues' jokes, of the looks he got from couples. Solitude's poison was slowly killing him; the antidote was being administered at the government building at the end of the street and that was enough for him.

He resigned himself to offering no opposition, kept his eyes half-closed and let himself be led like a blind man with his robo-guide dog.

"Let's go inside: the appointment is in twenty minutes," ordered Clara, once they were in front of the Marriage Office.

They climbed the staircase and presented their omnicoms to the doorman manning the entrance.

The droid, after giving Fabio a number, directed them towards the Lovemat terminal where Fabio would be undergoing his neural scan.

There were other people waiting as well, their faces a kaleidoscope of emotions in which the bright red color of trust prevailed.

A young girl with a lip piercing and a backpack had almost certainly skipped school to come here. She fidgeted in her seat, causing the fake leather to squeak. She kept staring at her fingernails, maybe she was trying not to bite them because she didn't want to ruin the designs etched onto her pink nail polish.

Next to her there was a guy who was barely thirty years old. He was wearing a jacket and tie and had an expensive omnicom on his wrist. His serious expression spoke for itself: he was a young professional who, having now managed to obtain a somewhat high-profile job, was ready to take the plunge.

The next spot was occupied by a woman who – even according to today's standards – could be called a spinster, even if she wasn't that much older than the young professional. Her appearance was the result of a deliberate juxtaposition, she was wearing wide-leg pants and a white blouse, her makeup was as noticeable as the trinkets adorning her neck, fingers, and wrists. Conflicting urges, male and female, flashed in her gaze. Who knew whether the Lovemat would assign her a man or a woman?

In any case, they were all alone, anyone offering their soul up to the Ministry's database had to face that step all by themselves, as if to prove they had reached maturity.

For Fabio, that step had arrived far beyond the deadline.

Clara sat on a bench dragging her brother down with her. Fabio's resigned expression attracted everyone else's attention. They scrutinized him as if he were some rare beast, his age, he was much older than the other users, mad him stand out. Some of them shook their heads in his direction.

"Don't mind them. What do they know?" Clara whispered in his ear.

Right, what did they know? Thought Fabio. Yet they judged him. Easy for them to pass judgment when those judgments did not have corresponding consequences, decisions, sentences. These days, that was all the responsibility of machines to which exhausted humans had delegated everything, even love.

After a while, Fabio's number was displayed on the screen on the wall.

A door swung open to reveal a doctor in a lab coat. Her hair was tied up in a short ponytail and she was wearing horn-rimmed glasses with augmented reality lenses.

Clara made her brother stand up and entrusted him to the doctor with a nod. She seemed to have understood the situation, nodded in turn and took the man by the hand.

"Don't worry Mr Izzi: it won't take long."

The white room was clean inside. It smelled nice, and a soft melody could be heard in the background. Everything was very reassuring.

The doctor had him make himself comfortable on the reclining examination chair, his feet raised, the back of his head resting on some sort of pillow.

"Now try and relax."

He looked at her with pleading eyes.

"You want to know how it works, right?"

Fabio nodded, crossed his hands over his chest and got ready to listen to the explanation like a child would to a bedtime story.

"It's simple," said the doctor, pushing her helmet down over her head, "we do a brain scan and then we construct an exact model of its computational structure."

Fabio furrowed his brow in bewilderment.

"We have to create a digital map of your brain," explained the doctor while calmly continuing her tasks, "the raw data from the scan will be fed into the Lovemat for data processing to recreate the 3D neural network. The result will then be combined with a library of neuro-computational models and synaptic connections. Finally, we'll compare your map with those present in the database to find the one most compatible with you, at least 95%."

"My soulmate's?" He asked, his voice barely a whisper.

"Yes. The Lovemat will give you a name and an address, that of your future bride."

The doctor dimmed the lights and reclined the seat back, transforming it into a kind of examination table. The music's volume was slightly increased.

"Now close your eyes and think happy thoughts, you'll see that they'll all come true. The procedure lasts fifteen minutes."

Fabio obeyed. The chair began to vibrate and he let himself be soothed. The pulsations dissipated. Then he yawned. The soft sounds in the background did the rest: after two minutes he fell asleep.

He dreamed and, for the first time in a long while, there were no nightmares to disturb his sleep. He saw the sun setting over the sea, its red light reflected by the waves, the salty breeze filled his lungs, his feet sank into the sand and his hand was holding *hers*. He was barely able to make out her smile before the doctor woke him up.

"There, we're done," she said while handing him an envelope, "the verdict is in here. I wish you all the best."

Fabio anxiously took the envelope. He climbed off the chair, shook the doctor's hand and gave way to the next user.

Outside the room, Clara noticed her brother's dreamy air right away. Without wasting time, she snatched the envelope and used the nail of her index finger to open it. She pulled out the filigreed certificate bearing the emblem of the Republic of Italy and the words *Ministry for Families – Wedding Office* in its heading.

She scanned the certificate's contents and then read it out for her brother's benefit: "Fabio Izzi, forty-three years of age, resident in 28 Via Famagosta, Rome, is partnered as groom with Elisa Brichetto, forty years of age, resident in 1 Via Bertini, Milan. Congratulations. Signed: The Ministry for Families."

Fabio's wrist vibrated. He saw on the display that the certificate had arrived on his omnicom.

In the meanwhile, Clara had looked up her brother's future bride on Facebook. She projected her profile image: a life-sized picture of Elisa stood in front of them. The picture made it look as if she were genuinely looking at someone standing in front of her. She smiled invitingly, with a sort of sad look in her eyes, and her skin was like that of a ripe fruit ready to fall from the branch and rot.

"Look, it turned out pretty well for you, all things considered: she's cute, and doesn't even live that far away," remarked Clara, placing the certificate back in the envelope.

Fabio looked at her with a dreamy air. Yes, she was very beautiful, he told himself with a touch of pride, as if it were his doing. His heart had started pounding again but it was different this time: there was a powerful feeling flowing through his veins, with a mixture of adrenaline, dopamine, and serotonin. It was love at first sight; a bolt of lightning come down from the sky to shock him back to life. Praise be to the Lovemat algorithm.

"Now what?"

Clara handed back the envelope and once again linked arms with him.

"Now, well now you go to her. Poor woman, who knows how long she's been waiting for you."

Fabio's finger trembled while he pressed the button with the last name BRICHETTO. Five seconds passed and then he heard a voice, "Third floor," and the door was unlocked.

He pushed open the building's front door and followed the animated holographic guide on the floor to the elevator with cherry wood moulding. Once inside, a virtual assistant selected the third floor for him. He checked his coat's pockets once more to make sure Elisa's ring and the envelope with the certificate were in there.

At the doorstep he saw a middle-aged woman dressed in black waiting for him with her hands clasped. It almost looked like she was praying.

"Elisa?" Fabio asked as he came closer.

"Come, I'll take you to her," answered the woman.

Inside the dimly lit house there was a strange scent, sweet and piercing.

They walked down a hallway, passing a few groups of people who looked at him questioningly. They passed in front of a room where a table was laid out with coffee and tea pots, sweet and savory pies, croissants and other fragrant pastries. A few people were eating and talking in low voices around the table.

The home was elegantly decorated following a theme that tended towards accumulation. Paintings, books, rugs, statues, lamps and vases from different eras and sources were all layered over one another. Every inch of free space was occupied, as if that domestic museum were an attempt, in part, to demonstrate how rich the lives of those who lived in it were.

His guide came to a stop in the doorway of a room at the end of the hallway. She motioned him to enter and, with a sinking feeling, Fabio complied.

She was laying on the bed, her hands crossed over her chest and her eyes closed. Her face was pale and she was dressed in her best clothes. She was even wearing shoes. Around her, a few women were chanting prayers under their breath.

At first, he struggled to understand. He searched Elisa's face for that faint smile he had learned to love over the last three days, but he found no trace of it. Her lips were pale and blue; a chilling grimace expressing weariness and exhaustion graced them. Then, he noticed the flickering, reddish votive lights and, at the end of the room, the open coffin.

He turned towards the woman still in the doorway.

"When…?" he asked, choking back a sob.

The woman sighed and came to stand at his side: "The day before yesterday. She swallowed a bottle of tranquilizers and went to bed. She never woke up again."

Fabio brought a hand to his mouth to stifle a scream.

"Why? Why?" He stammered out.

"My sister has suffered a lot," she answered while drying her tears with the back of her hand. "She had been waiting all her life for her groom. Four days ago, she came back from the Wedding Office…she was devastated, exhausted. The scan had once again given her the same verdict: there was no man for her."

Fabio felt like dying. He leaned his forehead against the wall, covering his eyes with his arm as the tears fell.

Elisa's sister put her hand on his shoulder. He turned around. His face was twisted in pain. Then he approached Elisa, stroked her face, recoiling from the coldness of her body.

He stumbled back in horror.

"And you are...?" asked the sister.

He sniffed, "Fabio, a friend," he lied.

The woman welcomed the news without batting an eyelid. "The funeral will be in the afternoon. We're burying her at Musocco Cemetery, in the family crypt," she told him.

Fabio nodded without knowing what to say.

"Have something to eat," added the sister, "there's a lot of food on the table in the other room."

He shook his head. "Thank you, but I really have to go."

"So soon? You just got here."

"Yes, I know, and I'm truly sorry but...I have some prior commitments," he replied, glancing absent mindedly at the omnicom on his wrist.

"I understand, then before you go, please don't forget to leave a message in the book."

Fabio left the room and backtracked down the hallway. At the entrance, he came across the lectern holding the open book. Grabbing the pen and wrote from his heart.

Forgive me, my love, and signed it.

He left the ring box on the lectern.

He found himself on the landing, stunned. That place was so different now.

He decided not to take the elevator and went down the stairs, one at a time.

Each step was a shock that reinforced the decision he had

made then and there, immediately, on the spot, as soon as he had understood what was going on.

His wrist vibrated, notifying him of an incoming message.

So? Did you meet her? Clara wanted to know.

Not yet, he replied, *I'm going to her now. I have to take a bus.*

All right, but hurry, don't make her wait.

He pulled the envelope with the certificate out of his pocket. He ripped it up into thousands of pieces and then threw them, like confetti, down the stairwell.

As soon as he reached the ground floor, he clicked open the lock on the front door and stood on the edge of the sidewalk to wait. Just a little while later, at the end of Via Bertini, he saw a bus approaching. He started to pray.

The fear had melted away, erased by tears.

"My love, here I am." He closed his eyes and took a step forward.

The bus couldn't stop in time.

Flower Queen

by Romina Braggion

translated by Carlotta Codebò

Science fiction author with a predilection for solarpunk, Romina Braggion deals with communication and sales. In her spare time she writes on her blog Diario di ErreBi *in which she talks about Science Fiction, preferably Italian, and carries out a project to share the female writers' memories:* La metà del mondo. *Her first story was published in 2020 in the* Futuro Presente *series by Delos Digital with the title* La compagnia perfetta. *The story* Nero Assoluto *was included in* Assalto al Sole, *the first solarpunk anthology by Italian authors, released in September 2020. Since 2021, she is the co-founder of the Solarpunk Italia website. Her short story,* Memorie di una ragazza interrotta, *is part of the solarpunk Atlantis series. She has also written stories for Tabula Fati, Watson Editore, the magazines Robot and Zest Letteratura Sostenibile. For the latter two and for UAO, the marx/z/ian critical magazine she wrote popular articles on solarpunk. One of her stories appeared in the anthology* Primo contatto *by Urania Mondadori.*

The granite arch, illuminated by lanterns hanging from its pillars, rose solitary above the path.

As soon as the convoy of mules and bees passed under it, Ippolita, nose in the air, saw a wreath of hazel woven(?) together with lavender spikes and chamomile flower heads, hanging from the keystone. She knew she had arrived.

On the ground, smaller wreaths and tiny oil lamps pointed the way. At the foot of a group of hornbeam trees, ten men were waiting in the quivering light of even more oil lamps. They unloaded the few furnishings and beehives in silence.

They placed the boxes onto prearranged supports, the coloured boxes for the bios separated from the grey boxes of the cyborgs.

Then some of the men left. Those remaining tied the mules to the fence and set up the yurt. After half an hour they also went away.

Parlagallo glided onto the field, next to the luggage, and asked Ippolita how she was feeling.

"My ass hurts; I can't feel my legs and can't catch my breath…"

"The anti-thrombosis pills are in the yellow sack." He perched on a branch and turned on his eyes to light up the interior for her.

Ippolita pulled out the bottle. She stuck her hand in again and felt around the bottom. "Where's the aspirin?"

"You've been keeping it in your shirt pocket ever since the last attack."

"You're always looking after me. If I lost my head, you'd stick it right back on my neck for me." The bird had been her helper for many years. The AI contained the memory of a military engineer, a super empath from the twenty-second century. At times it bothered her that he was so attentive.

Ippolita put her hand on her waist.

"It'd be better to go inside the yurt to take the medicine."

"Stop talking. I don't need your advice."

The cap didn't want to open. In the end it popped right off, scattering the medication it contained all over the field.

"Damned pills."

Parlagallo flew to the ground and proceeded to snatch the pills up with his beak and place them in the bottle. He put two of different colours on Ippolita's palm, then flew to the top of the sack holding her linen. He clawed it open and stuck his head inside. "This is messier than a barn."

"Quit complaining, there's not that much in there." She grabbed the other sack with two hands and went inside.

The animal flew in carrying the last bag. "I'll get you the painkiller too." He ruffled the feathers on his head. "Take it right now," he admonished her, "the ambassadors will be here soon."

She snorted softly, but swallowed the pill and waited for it to take effect.

Sitting in the folding chair, she watched the day arrive through the yurt's window. The shadows climbed up from the rows of lavender and chamomile to reveal vividly colourful flowers. Some of the pain started to leave her body.

Even though she found him aggravating at times, she was grateful the parrot took care of her so diligently. If it had been up to her, she would have forgotten the medicine for so long it would have expired. Sometimes, the poor thing had to deal with her undeserved wrath; he would take it without protest, it seemed almost as if he considered it the punishment he had to serve to atone for his mistake. Was being the only survivor of an environmental mission a mistake? No, but his super empathy had let him feel his comrades' pain while they were dying, having reached the mission objective offered no consolation. Allowing himself to be stuffed into a biolimb body had seemed like the perfect prison to him, and becoming a beekeeper's assistant a decidedly ironic sentence.

A ray of sun crossed over her bony legs and landed on the felt floor.

The foragers deposited the hives in neat lines in the field. Their stupor flooded her with pheromones, pushing her to shake herself from her thoughts and leave the tent.

Two girls came up to her along the path. Once they were in front of her, they dropped multicoloured corollas at her feet.

"Welcome, Lady. We welcome you and your bees with joy." They smiled. "We will take you to the elders."

She straightened her back and stretched her gaze as far as her poor eyesight would let her. It roamed over the hayfields,

the trees arranged in ordered rows, the field of flowers swaying in the breeze, with the river Toce marking the boundary
of one side in the distance. The buzzing of the worker bees
reached her ears, and a sweet aroma filled her nose.

Parlagallo landed on her shoulder, as softly as a plane tree
leaf. She leaned her head on his folded wings streaked with
electric blue and green.

"Let's go." The group slowly headed towards the village.

"I've found my home," she whispered. Only Parlagallo
heard her. He rubbed his beak on her hair and sighed.

Bees and apprentices

The yurt's interior was warm. In a brazier in the centre a
few wooden logs were burning and Ippolita was reading the
news on her nomadic colleagues from her tablet.

"They closed the boxes in Baceno last week, and they're
doing it now in Trontano."

Parlagallo already knew about it, he got the news in real
time through his right frontal lobe. Every morning he would
download the bulletin together with his software update, although he pretended not to know anything so that he could
chat with Ippolita.

"Really? It's already that cold over there?"

They both knew what the other was up to, but neither
one wanted to miss out on their morning ritual. Ever since
Ippolita had abandoned the village to become a nomad, many
years ago, the bird had decided to take on the role of the good
neighbours she no longer had. It made her happy and she ac-
tively took part in their chats. After all, they were both alone.

"Seems like it. How many degrees is it outside?"

"Twelve."

"Then it's almost our turn." Ippolita rubbed her knee;
knowing the actual temperature worsened her aches and
pains. "Add another piece of wood."

Parlagallo grabbed a piece of dried birch and let it fall on the brazier.

"You know, it's not too bad here, we've produced seven hundred kilos of honey here…not to mention everything else."

She watched the bird rock back and forth on his perch.

"They've given you a good welcome and treat you like a queen."

"The matriarchs have been grateful for the gift of the bees," she confirmed, "they've also offered to help me during my last days in this world."

"You're always saying that you're going to die soon, yet you're still here."

Ippolita grabbed a slipper and threw it at the animal. She missed by at least a metre.

"I should wring your neck while you sleep!"

"You can't, because of your arthritis." Parlagallo's answer was coupled with a silly and mocking rhythmic movement of his head.

Ippolita let out her anger by softly tapping her cane against the brazier.

As soon as she had calmed down, she started talking again. "The matriarchs have chosen their apprentices wisely."

"Yes, the girls are eager to learn," the parrot agreed, "they'll be self-sufficient in no time and experience will do the rest."

"The Bosco Tenso Matriarchal Community is hard-working and united," she said. "I've had to wait a long time, but I've finally found the right home for the bees."

"Seems like it. Remember? At the Luinetto Matriarchal Community they wouldn't produce any honey at all."

"That's why the cyborgs deactivated. Don't remind me. Reckless fools."

"Little Giuditta is bright and quick at her tasks," added Parlagallo, "she's good with the cyborgs."

"You're a pest, but there is no better robotics teacher than you."

Despite the bitter tone, Parlagallo puffed out his chest and backed up her words: "Whatever happens to the bios, the cyborgs will keep producing."

"The bios are tough, the queens are fertile," she retorted. "When the training is over the bees will be safe, just as if I were the one looking after them."

Parlagallo opened his beak, he really couldn't keep his doubts to himself. "Remember when you took me in, in exchange for the tablet? You were young..."

"What an unlucky day...Impossible to forget." She turned her head to hide her smile.

Parlagallo cocked his head to the side and continued undaunted: "I've been a prisoner in this body for more than two hundred years. I was hoping that sooner or later I would forget my previous life. However, my circuits are still efficient, and imprisonment is turning out to be painful."

"The past sometimes repeats itself," admitted Ippolita. "The only solution is to prepare ourselves in time; to be strong and organized." She closed her eyes and kept talking. "My mother was gifted the testimony by her mother and so on starting from my great-great-grandmother. I will gift it to the apprentices."

"They'll be shocked, like everyone else that's heard it: all of the bees dead, the bee colonies exterminated. I lost my comrades looking for wild swarms."

Ippolita couldn't stop the memories. She had heard the story from her mother many times.

While the military fought the population over the last remaining bees, and manufacture artificial bees in their laboratories, the women were sacrificed and modified for the survival of the planet.

Human guardians, female. Male genetics were revealed to

be ill equipped to handle the first, terrible sufferings of those attempts. Her great-great-grandmother almost went crazy with pain, yet kept her alive as long as possible to study the collateral effects and to recoup their investment.

It was a bit easier for her great-grandmother, and she began, together with the others, to repopulate the swarms. Grandma's generation managed to survive without undergoing major trauma and founded the race of the Matriarchs. The women of her mother's generation became Queens and began to be known as Goddesses. As for her, she no longer knew who she was.

"You know, I don't know if the worst is over. I will continue to put my trust in the Goddesses."

She picked up her woollen blanket and covered herself up.

The conversation was over as far as she was concerned. Waiting to fall asleep would be annoying but Parlagallo had made her sad. Memory was an instrument of change, squandering it in chitchat was worthless. It only served to revive painful thoughts.

Queen Flora

Ippolita's eyes flew open. Her body hair was standing on end and a veil of cold sweat stuck to her skin. Wave after wave of pheromones invaded her nostrils, shooting out towards her adrenal gland. The adrenaline made her stomach turn.

She got up, despite her numbed nerves yelling at her to remain laying down. In the dim light left by the embers, she saw her cane. She grabbed it and hit the brazier. The sound resonated throughout the room.

Parlagallo woke up and ruffled the feathers on his head. "Good Goddesses. What's going on?" he asked, frightened.

"Queen Flora is in danger!"

She got dressed and went outside. The morning was still between dark and light. The parrot led the way.

In the distance the sound could be heard becoming louder and louder. Within minutes they were in front of the enclosure where the beehives were kept. The gate was wide open.

She fixed the glasses on her nose and stared at the boxes. Flora's yellow one had disappeared. In its place there was a painful emptiness.

The incessant buzzing coming from the others was a cry of alarm. The cyborgs were intermittently emitting shrill sounds at unbearable decibels. They were programmed to alert the custodians hundreds of miles away.

The matriarchs arrived together with the three apprentices and a few other people.

"Parlagallo! Calm down the cyborgs."

The bird stopped in mid-air, hovering over the boxes, and began to repeatedly flap his wings back and forth. His body produced a whirlwind of electric blue vibrations that shocked the beehives.

The cyborgs gradually lowered the alarm sound until it stopped completely.

Ippolita turned towards the apprentices, her wrinkles accentuated by her fury: "You, come here!"

She took the two oldest by hand. An unexpected heat burned their palms. They tried to get away, but Ippolita wouldn't let go.

"Stay calm, today you'll learn a new lesson."

She started moving, dragging the two girls back-and-forth and changing directions by a few degrees every three steps. She also activated her jaw to generate comforting chemical signals. These could not be felt by anybody except the bees and the apprentices now linked to her.

They looked at her in dismay, but she continued, urging them on with light tugs on their wrists.

Little by little, the bios calmed down. The three women stopped dancing only when the buzzing stopped completely.

Ippolita let go of the girls, and they pulled away with a jump, waving their hands around to try and cool them down.

Then she looked at the matriarchs, fixing her gaze on each one of them separately.

The oldest spoke first, her voice more a buzzing than a question: "Ippolita, what happened?"

"Flora and her home have been stolen."

The buzzing started again, this time amongst the people present.

"Impossible, the gate was locked..."

She went towards the gate and checked the lock. "First: one of you is the thief. Whoever did it had the keys."

Everyone was left speechless after hearing that.

"Second: Parlagallo! Why didn't you hear the cyborgs' signal?"

The poor thing started to hop back and forth from one foot to the other without giving her an answer.

"Speak up, you pest!"

The bird halted. "The alarm yottochip is broken."

"There's the backup one."

Parlagallo hesitated.

"Speak, or I swear on the Goddesses I'll disactivate you."

Giuditta, the apprentice working with the cyborgs, came forward: "I have the chips. I'm fixing the broken one and needed the other one as an example."

"Misplaced zeal was the last thing we needed!"

The girl's mother came forward: "My Lady, I understand your anger, but maybe you're taking this too far."

One of the matriarchs placed a hand on the woman's arm and pulled her back.

Ippolita approached the two women and said, "You have hundreds of kilos of honey at your disposal. Propolis to cure you and pollen to reinvigorate your slow brains." She was furious. "You have harvested many kilos more fruit. The crops have thrived all through the summer." The flow of anger was unstoppable. "I avve given you the most precious gift possible, and you haven't even been able to defend it."

She spun around, glaring at their lowered eyes.

The eldest matriarch confronted her: "We will catch whoever did this. I promise you." She gathered the men and gave the order to search for the culprit.

Ippolita turned away. "I'm going back to the yurt. Get ready for my departure. I couldn't care less about your promises."

Decisions

"You can't be serious!"

"Have I ever given you reason to doubt my word?" Ippolita was seated on the folding chair, nibbling her only meal of the day.

"You've waited so long to find the right community. You're not going to start wandering around astride a mule again, are you?"

"Let me finish eating in peace."

She dipped a stick of birch wood into a mixture of honey, pollen, propolis and royal jelly. Age and loss of appetite had increasingly reduced the quantity. Two spoonfulls were all she needed to survive.

She finished quickly, and Parlagallo was back at it: "Where will you find the strength to continue your search?"

"I won't leave the beehives in the hands of incompetent people."

"Don't you think that's a bit much?" the parrot continued, "Have you never made a mistake?"

She turned her weary gaze on her assistant. "Of course I have, but the I did everything I could to fix it."

"Give them a chance," suggested Parlagallo, "maybe they'll turn out to be worthy of the task you've given them."

She mulled over his words: how much longer could she resist on a pilgrimage from one valley to the next? Would her skin have withstand more cold, more heat, more wind? How many more people would she have to put to the test before finding the ideal custodians? Would she have enough time?

She lowered her shoulders and placed her hands in her lap. She was so tired. How could they possibly not understand the importance of beekeeping? "How long should I wait, do you think?" asked Ippolita, "Hours? Days? Weeks?"

Parlagallo's answer was barely more audible than the buzzing of a bee, "I don't know. You have to trust them."

"I have no choice," she answered bitterly, "spraying pheromones into the air would kill me. I'm too old now." She looked at her withered hands, the veins where her blood flowed much too densely clearly visible, the skin dry like birch bark, nails yellowed by pollen and age. "I can't possibly run after them. Willpower just isn't enough any more."

The times when her body could keep up with her daring heart and her sharp mind had long since passed. Must she now succumb to weak and weary cardiac activity? Would a promise be enough for her?

She stared at Parlagallo, his colourful synthokeratin wings, his bioleather feet, his optical sensor camouflaged by orange irises. A repairable body, an eternal prison. She was better off, all things considered.

"Go to the matriarch. Warn her that if they don't find Flora within two days, I'll leave and take the bees with me."

"You won't make it a mile."

"I'll make it far enough to leave the bees in the middle of a forest. Better feral than dead from neglect."

Clues

An hour later she heard a knock on the yurt's door frame. Parlagallo straightened the feathers on his head and answered for her. The oldest matriarch entered while a girl remained outside. "Aldus is missing."

Ippolita straightened the glasses on her nose. "Who's Aldus?"

"Atena's brother?" Parlagallo answered.

Ippolita huffed. The matriarch gestured to the girl. A fishbone with angular joints entered. She had sun browned her skin and long, silky hair that clashed with the overall roughness of everything else.

She came to a stop in front of Ippolita, her gaze fixed on the floor as if it had been nailed there.

"This is Atena. She's the oldest apprentice." Parlagallo said.

"Ah, yes. I know who your brother is. He's the boy who helps look after the bees." The girl wouldn't raise her head, but she nodded briefly.

"He's missing, then?"

"We think he's the thief. The donkey's missing," said the Matriarch.

"Also, his backpack isn't in his closet, and some of his stuff has gone," added the girl.

"Ah, so you can still speak." Her tone of voice was not at all sarcastic. "Lift up your head. I want to see your face."

Atena raised her head, but her eyes were still downcast.

"I don't think you've come here to be ridiculed. Come to the point."

Atena still wouldn't speak up, so the Matriarch tapped her on the shoulder. "I might know where he's going. He was gone for a whole afternoon last week. In the evening I read a message on his tablet. It was from a beekeeper in Calasca. He's only got a few boxes, nothing more."

"I've sent a couple of men to check it out," intervened the Matriarch.

"What do you think?" she asked the girl.

When the girl finally looked up her eyes were red and filled with tears. "I'm scared it really was him. He's been acting differently over the last few days. He's had his head in the clouds. I'm so sorry…" The tears gathered on her bottom lashes and then overflowed. They rolled down her cheeks and fell to the ground in big drops. Her hair matched her quivering shoulders in one fluid movement.

Ippolita hesitated, she was almost touched. Then the anger and anxiety came back in full force. "You didn't steal the beehive. Stop crying."

The girl's sobs increased. "But I'm in charge of the keys."

"Do you still have them?" asked Ippolita.

"Yes. They're on my key chain."

"If it was him, he made a copy. If that's what happened, you'd be right to feel bad, but you can't know for sure right now." The poor thing was no longer listening, she couldn't stop trembling and weeping.

"I told you to stop it! Crying won't help you become Queen." She said, finally losing her patience.

Atena quietened down and kept still, frozen in place by the beekeeper's harshness. She held her breath, and then swallowed the bitter pill. Straightening her shoulders, she tried to regain her composure. She threw a desperate look at the Matriarch. "I'm going to look for Aldus."

The woman stopped her before she could reach the door. "Atena! You're not going anywhere!"

The girl tried to wriggle away.

"Calm down. The Matriarch is right." Ippolita addressed the girl. "You have a community around you; you are not a nomad. Let them take care of the less important things. Life as a Queen is precious. If you ever manage to become one."

"I belong to the mutated race. My Mum and my grandma aren't beekeepers, but I want to be one. It's what I've always wanted." Atena was breathless, but the determination in her voice pleased Ippolita.

"Then you'll just have to learn how to be one." She took out her pocket watch and checked the time. "Parlagallo it's almost nine. Go teach your lesson."

"You're not coming?"

"No, I'm going to stay here and try not to die of a broken heart."

She gestured at them to leave. Then she sat down and let herself be comforted by her daughters in the beehives. They had sensed the pain in her chest and enveloped her in pheromones. They helped their mother's troubled heart continue beating.

Guilty

Lanterns lighted the night hours, at dawn they were put out. Ippolita perceived every single change in the nuances of light and colour around the yurt. She couldn't fall asleep at all, not even for a minute.

The bees were waiting. They knew of Flora's return before Ippolita herself realized it, and the pheromones they emitted to inform her not only calmed her down but also revitalized her.

She went outside to see Parlagallo arrive in flight followed by a few of the Matriarchs.

"We got him; it really was Aldus. The beehive is safe," a girl said.

"Where is it now?"

"At the agorà," answered the oldest Matriarch.

She took her cane and tapped her left shoulder twice. Parlagallo perched on it. "Let's go."

The matriarchs let her take the lead and stayed half a step behind her until they arrived at the village square.

Aldus was standing up straight with his chin pressed to his chest and two boys, more imposing than him, guarding him.

The stolen goods were lying on the ground a few feet away. One look at the beehive calmed Ippolita down completely.

On the way there she had come to an agreement with the matriarch, so she ignored the boy and entered the village hall where she waited for the apprentices to arrive. Atena came alone, whereas the other two, being under fourteen, were with their mothers.

The beekeeper explained what she had decided. It involved both a lesson and a choice for the three girls and their mothers. She explained what would happen to them if they chose to become queens and how their lives would change. She added that the choice could also be made later. Taking part in the punishment was the first step to understanding the transformation awaiting them and their last lesson as apprentices. Finally, after two hours had passed clearing up any doubts and answering all their questions, she finished her explanation. "If you choose to be ordained as Queen Mothers, it will be forever."

One of the apprentices, in agreement with her mother, withdrew and left.

Giuditta's mother consented to her daughter participating in the lesson. The girl would then choose on her own by the time she was twenty years old. At that point the decision rested in the hands of the last apprentice.

Ippolita waited.

Atena hesitated. She went to the window and looked down. For a few minutes she was lost in thought. Then, almost as if she were talking to herself, she noted that even after two hours of standing, her brother did not seem at all tired.

She was almost furious as she turned around. "I'll take part in the lesson," she finally answered, "and I want to be ordained."

Ippolita nodded her head slowly as a sign of confirmation. Then, in silence, she went towards the exit, followed by the women and Parlagallo.

The group gathered in front of the boy. The rest of the community also arrived and stood huddled behind him, keeping a certain distance. With a wave of her hand, the matriarch sent away the two boys guarding him.

"Aldus, why did you do it?"

The boy looked at the woman and lowered his eyes. Then he stared straight ahead again, his gaze fixed on a peak, far away from everyone. He was silent.

"Aldus. As things stand now, without knowing your motivation at all, the law demands that you be exiled and fitted with an electronic bracelet or else that you spend two-years isolated in a cell, on the Torrione di Bettola peak."

His gaze faltered, and his posture slackened just a bit.

"Since I have the last word, I'd rather he spent two years in a cell." Ippolita added fuel to the fire.

"It was a gift for my girlfriend. Her father's beehives aren't very productive, and I was hoping to help them out with one of these."

"A token of your love. How sweet." Ippolita knew how to make his romantic intentions seem malicious. "How did you think they'd continue to produce so much without me?"

Aldus's shoulders swiftly fell. "My girlfriend is an excellent beekeeper."

"Is she mutated?"

"Yes."

"Not that good, then, if she doesn't know that without their human Queens bees can even lose the will to live," said the beekeeper.

"But she is good. She told me to bring back the beehive because it would've been useless and sure enough, I was already on my way back when they caught up with me."

The Matriarch sought out the two who had given chase with her eyes.

They nodded their heads in confirmation.

"The girl is smarter than you. Maybe she would have preferred the cyborgs instead of the bios?" Ippolita asked.

Aldus's eyes opened wide, his face reddened, and he started to stutter. "No, she has nothing to do with this. It was my decision to take her the bees."

"A man burning with passion can do stupid things." She sneered and then stared at the bird in silence.

"But I know how to defend my daughters." Parlagallo ruffled his feathers and shook his wings. He scampered backwards but, in the end, he flew onto the beehive and opened its door. He let out a ghastly cry.

Aldus, his hands tied behind his back, turned white, all the colour draining from his face.

The woman whispered something into the Matriarch's ear. The old woman then called a man over and gave him instructions.

The beekeeper continued. "I've always hated waste. Aldus needs to stay here, he's strong and has shown himself useful to the community," said the beekeeper. "Being stuck in an isolated cell on top of an arduous peak won't make him any better than he is now."

She turned, and the apprentices approached her.

Giuditta's focused face betrayed an emotion that risked overpowering her. Atena was seemingly determined as she stared at her brother; she hesitated, then turned her gaze away and recomposed herself.

Ippolita took them by hand, burning them again, and approached the beehive.

Only very few bees were coming and going, most of them were gathered in the winter cluster.

"The punishment will be equal to the act's stupidity, painful but with no consequences, except for the lesson I hope the young lover will learn."

The women began to dance in slow steps for a few minutes.

Ippolita wanted to give her apprentices the time to absorb the lesson and the bees the chance to loosen the winter cluster without feeling threatened. She pressed her jaws together, little by little activating small pheromone waves that enveloped the beehive.

A few bees came outside to wait for their sisters. The buzzing increased. Out they all came and gathered above Aldus in a quivering circle.

Ippolita's movements intensified, and the insects answered with an angry buzzing. They moved to completely cover his trembling body.

The insects beat their wings overheating the boy's body. Then, seventy thousand jaws closed at the same time. They did not sting him; there was no need for sacrifice.

The boy let out a scream, swayed momentarily and fell to the ground. His body was overcome with convulsions.

The apprentices hugged one another and stepped back in shock. Giuditta's mother took them by the shoulders and dragged them away.

A doctor and two nurses came to provide first aid. They injected him with three doses of adrenaline and wrapped him up in an instant ice cloth. Two men carried Aldus to the infirmary.

Those present clung to one another, shocked and incredulous.

The matriarch walked amongst them. "Aldus will get better and will no longer be a threat to anyone."

She waited for the murmuring to die down: "He will be appointed guardian and must act appropriately. If he doesn't, he will be exiled forever." She looked at her fellow villagers. "That's all. Get back to work."

The Matriarch turned and came to stand next to the beekeeper: "I'll walk you to the yurt." They set off together. Parlagallo flying ahead of them.

Queens

"Parlagallo, add wood to the fire. It's freezing in here."

Ippolita had spent at least an hour circling the inside of the yurt. She could feel the snowflakes accumulating on her bones, even though the constant movement had warmed her and helped her focus her thoughts. "All right, let's go over it one more time."

She turned toward the Matriarchs huddled closely together in search of warmth: "The apprentices are ready. Atena has been ordained to the bees and will be able to ordain in turn. The mutation is now complete, the diet will help keep her in good health. She'll start taking it from tomorrow."

Then she went on: "I've prepared her doses myself. They're memorized in the parrot's yottochip. You just have to follow the instructions."

She walked behind them and continued: "Don't leave her alone, especially in the first months after the transformation." She stopped and arched her back to the side to stretch a sore nerve. "As for Giuditta, when and if the time comes, it'll be easier for her as she'll always have Atena as a model to follow."

"You have doubts about the child?" Asked the oldest Matriarch.

"The life of a Queen Mother is hard and unnatural for a woman. Being only a beekeeper is simpler."

"We'll be by their side," affirmed another Matriarch.

"That's essential. I'm counting on you."

"You'll see Ippolita, we won't let you down again."

Ippolita stopped in front of them. "I won't see a thing. Tomorrow morning, as soon as it's light, I'm leaving."

They were speechless for a few seconds and then they all started to talk at once.

The oldest Matriarch stood up and her harsh glare was enough to quiet them down. "You've taken care of the bees your whole life. Let us take care of you now."

"I don't belong to this place. I don't belong to humanity either."

"Where do you think you're going all alone when it's so cold?" Parlagallo's voice came out as an anguished caw.

"Oh. Alone you say?" She stopped herself from laughing. "We are born and die alone."

"This again. You've been saying that you're going to die for at least twenty years now. Yet you're more than a hundred years old and you're still here."

"There's nothing left for me to do."

"What do you mean there's nothing left for you to do? The apprentices still need their teacher, the bees their caretaker..." protested the youngest Matriarch.

"Parlagallo is a reliable assistant and Atena will be an excellent Queen. I'm sure of it."

The oldest Matriarch made one last attempt: "Death arrives in its own time. It won't be ordered around."

"Neither will I." Her cataract couldn't hide the determined glint in her eyes. "I'm done. You can all go."

Before leaving, the women stopped at the threshold and turned to look at her one last time. They hesitated at the door and dithering. Then, they shook their heads and went out into the snow without closing the door, in the hope, maybe, that she would change her mind.

Ippolita turned towards Parlagallo: "I'm taking the mule tomorrow morning. I'm going to leave the rest here. You'll have to decide who to give my things to."

"But what about food? And medicine?"

"I won't need any of it."

"The matriarch is right, Ippolita. You can't order death around."

"I'll tell you a story and then I'm going to bed. My grandparents had been married for seventy years when my grandmother died. Grandpa carried on by himself for a month, and then one morning around four, he called over his son, my uncle. He told him that he had decided to stop living but that my uncle shouldn't worry: the time had come, and he was going in peace. My uncle just thought he was senile: he gave him a glass of water, tucked in his covers, stroked his cheek, turned off the light and went back to bed.

After a few hours, noticing that he wasn't getting up, my uncle went to his room and found him still lying in bed. It looked like he was sleeping, but he was dead, just like he had decided. I'm going to do the same thing he did."

She lay down, put down her glasses, and covered herself with the blanket.

"Give the girls a hug for me. Your wings are softer than my withered arms. And close the door, it's freezing."

Flower Queen

She followed a path in the snow from Devero to Crampiolo and stopped on top of a hill to watch the lights turn on for the evening. She got off the mule and smacked its bottom with her cane. The animal trotted off towards the first cabin.

She was alone now. Free. Had she ever felt like this?

She leaned her back against a larch tree, supporting herself with her cane. Her light jacket couldn't protect her arthritic lumps from contact with the bark. A few dry needles slipped under her collar and pricked her skin.

She asked herself what she was in that moment: woman, bee, queen?

Which identity would she pick to call death to her and leave with it?

She slid down the trunk, an inch at a time, and sat at the foot of the tree, sinking into the soft snow. She let go of her cane.

She covered her mouth with her hands and closed her eyes. She couldn't tell how long she stayed like that before making her decision. The pain slowly disappeared.

Suddenly she noticed a lush meadow filled with flowers at the bottom of the valley. The swaying multicoloured blooms formed many brilliant shapes. The sweet smell tickled her nostrils.

Thousands of bees were busy in the pistils, leaving them with their hind legs filled with pollen. From the nearby beehive came a cry: the old queen had just died. The hope for peace carried her to her new home.

She flew off and nosedived towards paradise.

THE MOBY CLITORIS OF HIS BELOVED

by Roberto Quaglia and Ian Watson

Ian Watson invented Warhammer 40K fiction and also has screen credit for the Screen Story of Spielberg's A.I. Artificial Intelligence after working for nearly a year eyeball to eyeball with Stanley Kubrick. Long ago in a different dynastic era Watson lived in Tokyo. Now he lives in the green paradise of Asturias in the north of Spain.

Roberto Quaglia is an Italian author and essayist, as well as a freelance journalist. He is the author of works that are considerably different from each other, from surreal Science Fiction to humor, theater and counter-information non-fiction. As a Science Fiction author he has published several books, including The Beloved of my Beloved, *co-written with British author Ian Watson. He is the only Italian to have won the BSFA (British Science Fiction Award) in 2010. As an essayist he is particularly known for his book* Il mito dell'11 Settembre, *which has been published in three languages. His most recent work is his an essay on Hollywood Fundamentalism.*

Yukio was only a salaryman, not a company boss, but for years he'd yearned to taste whale clitoris sashimi. Regular whalemeat sashimi was quite expensive, but Yukio would need to work for a hundred years to afford whale clitoris sashimi, the most expensive status symbol in Japan.

Much of Yukio's knowledge of the world came from manga comic books or from anime movies which he watched on his phone while commuting for three hours every day. He treasured the image of a beautiful young *ama* diving woman standing on the bow of a whaling boat clad in a semi-transparent white costume and holding sparklingly aloft the special clitoridectomy knife. An icon far more wonderful than that of Kate Winslet at the front of the *Titanic*! Americans might have their *Moby Dick*, but Yukio's countrymen (or at least the richest of them) had their Moby Clitoris Sashimi.

The beautiful young ama woman would take a deep breath, dive, swim underneath a woman-whale, grasp her 8-centimeter clitoris, then with one razor-sharp slash cut off the clitoris and swim away very fast. On the deck of the whaler the crew would wait for the ama to climb back aboard, her costume now see-through due to wetness.

And then the whalers would harpoon and kill the whale, because it would be too cruel to leave a female whale alive after amputation of her clitoris. In this respect the Japanese differed very much from certain Islamic and African countries which cut off the clitorises of human girls, so that men should not feel inadequate about their own capacity for orgasms.

Whenever the Japanese were criticised for hunting whales, it was the harvesting of clitorises which empowered them to continue. And of course Japan observed a strict clitoris quota, so that enough female whales would continue to copulate pleasurably and repopulate. Thus, while it was true that whale clitoridectomy directly pleasured only the richest individuals, every Japanese citizen who enjoyed eating whales also benefitted.

This Yukio knew. Yet he still yearned to taste whale clitoris sashimi for himself! Most men have licked a woman's clitoris, although probably they haven't eaten one; but the organ of ecstasy of a female whale sliced thinly was said to possess a taste beyond words.

When Yukio's vacation came — the usual very hot and humid fortnight in August — he didn't surrender his holiday back to the Nippon Real-Doll Corporation, as he had done in previous years, in the hope of more rapid promotion through the copyright department. Instead, he took a train from Tokyo (and then a bus) the hundred kilometers to Shirahama City where ama diving women lived. He would seduce an ama to love him. They would marry. She would get a job on a whaling boat. For him she would smuggle clitoris sashimi...

To his consternation Yukio soon discovered that the ama women of Shirahama, who dive for red seaweed, sea snails and abalone, looked nothing like the icon in his mind. For one thing, they weren't slim but were muscular from exercise — and chubby, to cope with cold water. For another, their faces were darkly tanned, not a lovely creamy-white. For a third, their voices were loud and raucous, perhaps due to damage from water pressure; and their speech was quite vulgar. For a fourth, they didn't wear semi-transparent white garments, but orange sweatshirts, thermal tights, and neoprene diving hoods. And for a fifth, their average age seemed to be over sixty. Even if one of those fat vulgar grannies wanted a lover and husband, how could Yukio excite himself enough to woo her?

Disconsolate, he went to get drunk. Presently he found himself outside *The Authentic Ama-Geisha Inn*. The name seemed promising.

Inside, he was amazed to find waiting several beautiful slim young hostesses dressed in the correct long white semi-transparent costumes, and also wearing white high heels. Perched jauntily on their foreheads were diving masks. One hostess wore her very long hair in an oily black rope which would excite a bondage fetishist or a flagellant considerably.

Soon this hostess, whose name was Keiko, was leading Yukio into a private room — which contained a low table, plastic cushions, and a small blue-tiled pool set in the floor of tatami matting, which was plastic too; plastic would dry more quickly than straw matting.

He knelt. Keiko knelt and poured some Johnnie Walker Black Label.

She giggled and said sweetly, "You may splash me whenever you wish!"

Thus revealing more of her breast or thigh or belly...

"But you're the ama of my visions!" Yukio exclaimed. "Why aren't you diving in the sea? You would look so beautiful."

Already he was a bit in love with Keiko, even though the plan had been for an ama to fall in love with him.

"I'm an ama-geisha," Keiko explained. "Only *you* can wet me, not the sea."

"I've seen amas just like you with the whaling fleet! Only," and he recollected his apparently foolish plan, "not with such wonderful hair as yours. They dive for whale clitorises," he added.

Keiko giggled again. "A real ama does that."

"*A fat old granny?*"

Keiko's job was to please him, and Yukio seemed to prefer intellectual stimulation rather than getting drunk and splashing her, so the astonishing truth emerged — a truth known to most inhabitants of Shirahama, but which the media patriotically chose not to publicise.

Each whaling ship carried a real ama and also a false ama (or rather an authentic iconic ama). The real ama, old and fat, foul-mouthed and lurid, would harvest the clitoris while the false ama — who looked more real — would wait in the water beside the ship. The false authentic ama would then take the clitoris from the real inauthentic ama and would climb a steep gangplank back on board deck, her garment delightfully see-through. Meanwhile the old fat ama would sneak on to the ship from the rear, using the ramp up which dead whales were winched.

This substitution made whale-hunting seem graceful and elegant and sexually exciting in the eyes of the world — slightly akin to marine bull-fighting — and justified the high price to gourmets of clitoris sashimi.

Yukio stared at Keiko. "Wouldn't you rather be on a whaling ship, than here? With your wonderful rope of hair you'd set a new style for cartoon books and films. I can license your image for you." Yukio's work did indeed consist in copyright matters concerning Real Dolls modelled upon porn stars. "I'm a specialist. You'd earn a big fee." And Yukio would be the lovely Keiko's agent and manager, and because of this, he would become her Beloved! And at last he would eat whale clitoris sashimi.

Keiko was wide-eyed.

"Agreed?"

Before Keiko could change her mind, Yukio picked up his glass of Johnny Walker Black Label and threw the contents over her, wetting and revealing a delightful breast.

"Kampai!" he exclaimed, to toast her — but in his mind he was shouting 'Banzai!' for victory.

The whaling industry normally recruited deep-sea ama from communities such as Shirahama, but Yukio needed Keiko with him in Tokyo to register her image. Keiko could stay in his little apartment in a high-rise in the suburbs.

So Keiko exchanged her authentic ama costume and high heels for jeans and a blouse, and piled her rope of hair upon her head, hiding it with a scarf, because nobody must steal her image on a phone en route! Already Yukio felt paranoid and jealous.

On the train Yukio looked at the news on his own phone, and a headline caught his eye: THROW THE WHALE AWAY!

A meeting in South Korea of the International Whaling Commission had ended in confusion. As usual the dispute was about whether to save whales or eat them. The Japanese delegate had suddenly declared that whale clitoris sashimi was a cultural treasure unique to Japan. If foreigners forced the Japanese to stop eating whalemeat, the Japanese would continue to harvest whale clitorises — but to please world public opinion they would throw the rest of the whale away. They would accomplish this grand gesture by compassionately exploding all clitoridectomised whales using torpedos packed with plastic explosive, since nuclear torpedos were unacceptable.

"That will make clitorises even more valuable and prestigious," Yukio said to Keiko.

"I have a clitoris too," she replied.

"But not a whale clitoris." Or at least not yet, he thought.

Maybe the Japanese delegate's statement was intended to bewilder the World Wildlife Fund, which had been picketing the meeting. Under the United Nations' Declaration of Cultural Rights, it was forbidden to attack or slander any country's unique cultural icons, such as the Golden Arches of MacDonald's or the Eiffel Tower. Now that Japan had registered whale clitoris sashimi as a cultural treasure, that gourmet experience was protected from criticism — and if there were no clitorises to be sliced, obviously the experience would become extinct. To preserve the cultural experience, the Japanese must continue to hunt whales.

Yukio's apartment was a four-mat one, which was better than living and sleeping in a room only the size of three tatami mats; but still it was rather crowded by two people, unless those two people were intimate. So Yukio found himself examining Keiko's clitoris, causing her to sigh with pleasure. Then he went to sleep and dreamed that every century a magical woman-whale would appear offshore, to provide sashimi from her clitoris for the Empress of the time. On the brow of this whale: a white mark exactly like a chrysanthemum flower. During the subsequent hundred years, the whale's clitoris would regenerate.

Yukio awoke in the morning, thinking immediately about the possibilities of *cloning* clitoris. Keiko had already risen and was now kneeling, dressed in her authentic iconic ama costume which real ama no longer wore. Truly she had the graces of a geisha.

Obviously a woman's clitoris couldn't possibly taste as wonderful as a whale's, yet what if cloned human clitoris could be marketed profitably enough so that the genius who thought of this became rich enough to afford to eat whale clitoris?

Since Yukio had no idea how to clone anything, an alternative occurred to him. These days, because pigs and people are very alike, pigs provided transplant organs for human beings. Maybe a million people had inside them pig hearts or lungs or livers or kidneys. When the pigs were sacrificed to provide transplants, the rest of the pig, including the clitoris in the case of female pigs, would probably go into pet food.

What if Yukio were to buy the sex organs of pigs, to provide a source of clitorises? These could be packaged in tiny jars as human clitorises, and sold over the internet! Upon the label, a photo of a genuine human clitoris, with a certificate of authenticity which would be correct since the picture at least was genuine. *Delicious clitorises, cloned from this very clitoris you see!* Realistically, Keiko might *not* obtain a job on a whaling ship — yet she could still help Yukio to achieve his goal.

Truly, his trip to the seaside had inspired him, probably because the clean air contained more oxygen in it than in the city.

Yukio took his phone, and soon he was photographing Keiko's clitoris while she assisted him. He wasn't quite sure if her clitoris was the usual size but it was certainly very noticeable. Using Photoshop, he could get rid of the surrounding flaps of flesh familiar to users of porn magazines, leaving only the clitoris itself in the picture. His computer could print many labels. In a truly iconic sense he would indeed be cloning Keiko's clitoris, or at least its image. In his excitement he almost forgot to go to work.

On the commuter train, he used his phone to search for Pig Organ Farms and for Food Bottlers. Genius is to perceive connections where none were seen before.

When he returned home that night, Keiko was already lying asleep on the futon, still dressed as an ama and wearing her diving mask for even greater authenticity. Her long rope of hair seemed like an oxygen tube. The TV set was showing young men eating as many worms as they could as quickly as possible. It was the popular weekly show *Brown Spaghetti Race*, sponsored by the Dai-Nippon Cheese Company. The more Parmesan the contestants poured on the wiggling worms, the less difficult it was to pick them up using smoothly lacquered chopsticks.

Would consumers be more excited by "genuine canned cloned human clitoris sashimi" or "genuine ama clitoris sashimi (cloned)"? Maybe the label should show Keiko smiling as she held her photoshopped clitoris to her own lips with *chopsticks*? Would the suggestion of auto-cannibalism excite buyers? Was his ideal market gourmets who couldn't afford whale clitoris, or sexual fetishists? Or both?

Yukio sat on the edge of the futon beside Keiko and regarded her tenderly. He lifted her rope of hair, closed his lips upon the end of it, and blew into the hair as though to supply her with more oxygen, such as she had been accustomed to at the seaside. Maybe, subconsciously at least, that was the reason why she had put on the diving mask.

"Keiko-san," he told her politely, although she was asleep, "there is a change of plan."

It took Yukio some hard work and organisation and most of his savings to set up the Genuine Cloned Ama Clitoris Sashimi Company, or GCACSC for short. The sexual organs of organ-donor pigs must be rushed by courier, refrigerated and ultra-fresh, to the Greater Tokyo Bottling Company, where a dedicated employee dissected out the clitorises for bottling. Irrelevant vaginas and labia and also penises and balls were cooked and minced and canned to become Luxury Pig-Protein sent as food aid to starving Communist North Korea, with the full co-operation of the government's Japan-Aid programme, which subsidised the project and praised Yukio's initiative and sense of social responsibility, while respecting his wish to remain anonymous.

The donor farm believed that the complete sexual organs were being processed, which in the case of male pigs was true; and Yukio had no wish to enlighten them.

He enlightened the gourmet public about the availability of cloned ama clitoris sashimi by means of a clever spam program, which he bought in the Akihabara electronics district. A spam program was appropriate since the word spam originally meant `spiced American meat.'

Every night after Yukio came home from the Nippon Real-Doll Corporation, he printed labels for the jars and boxes and address labels and dealt with an increasing number of internet orders and payments. He had rented a garage for delivery of the little unlabelled jars of clitorises, which were received there during the day by Keiko, dressed ordinarily. She would then change into her ama costume, stick the labels on to the jars, skillfully fold the beautiful little cardboard boxes which Yukio produced on his printer, fit a jar into each, and stick on an address label.

Keiko was very busy; and so was Yukio. What with Yukio's regular work at the Real-Doll Corporation and his after-hours work at home, he became a bit like a Zen monk who had trained himself in No-Sleep, or not much — now he slept standing up in the commuter train instead of looking at manga and anime on his phone; consequently he never watched the News in either manga or anime format. All he knew was that orders were pouring into his home PC. The spam had done its job sufficiently well that consumers were spontaneously spreading the word of the new and affordable (although not cheap) gourmet delight.

Keiko told him that by now magazines were writing stories about, and TV channels were talking — she had done some phone interviews. Apparently Yukio was being hailed as the new Mr Mikimoto, but Yukio had no spare time to pay much attention.

Mikimoto-san was the man who invented cultured pearls by putting irritating grains of sand inside oysters, at Pearl Island. To suggest that his cultured pearls were as good as naturally occuring pearls, he had employed amas to dive into the sea around Pearl Island for tourists to admire, and in fact, according to Keiko, Mikimoto-san had invented or revised the see-through costumes of the amas. The ama water-ballet actresses would bring up real oysters, which might or might not contain real pearls, for the tourists to eat authentically in the Pearl Island Restaurant.

One evening an astonishing thing happened. Yukio had woken up automatically as usual in time to get off the commuter train, and was walking away from the station homeward when he saw Keiko coming towards along the street dressed in schoolgirl uniform!

"Why have you become a schoolgirl?" he cried out, but Keiko walked past, ignoring him. Then along the street came another schoolgirl Keiko, then another, then a couple together.

They were real schoolgirls wearing false faces — latex masks of the real Keiko!

"Excuse me," Yukio said to a false Keiko, "but where did you get that mask?"

The schoolgirl paused, but remained silent.

Of course, she couldn't speak while wearing that mask because Yukio wasn't speaking to her but to the mask. Should he reach out and peel the mask from her true face? That might constitute assault, or even a new perversion, of unmasking schoolgirls.

"Please tell me," he begged.

She bowed slightly, then beckoned — gestured him back towards the station.

Like a tourist guide for the deaf she led him inside the station to a vending machine. It was one of those that sold the used panties of virgins, which old men would buy and sniff. But now it also sold something else in little bags: those masks of Keiko.

Quickly Yukio bought one. The packaging showed the upper body and face of Keiko, just as on the labels of the jars of clitorises. Keiko held to her lips with chopsticks a clitoris, although now she was using her left hand rather than her right — evidently she had been photoshopped. A speech bubble above her head read: *Eat my virgin clitoris.*

That was the cheeky message conveyed by the mask. Identities concealed, schoolgirls could tease men naughtily without a blush, without even saying a word or making a gesture. What innocent, or wicked, erotic power they would feel! Clitoris power. Maybe the packaging of other masks had different speech in the bubbles. Or maybe not. Or maybe yes.

Quickly Yukio googled non-manga non-anime News on his phone.

He saw a picture, taken through a window, of a classroom in which all the girls were wearing identical Keiko masks to the consternation of the teacher. He saw a picture of a playground where a dozen Keikos of different heights were strolling. A craze had hit the whole of Japan, probably spreading among schoolgirls everywhere by txt!

Because of trousers, he noticed some boys too, who were also wearing Keiko masks. Ah, the boys were doing that so as to save face!

He asked the Keiko who still lingered by the machine, "Keiko, did you *do* this without consulting me? To prove that you're clever too?" What a perfect ecological loop, that the same machines which sold the used virgin underwear of schoolgirls should provide the same schoolgirls with these masks...

But of course she wasn't the real Keiko, and besides she had no intention of speaking.

How could Keiko have organised the rapid manufacture of all the masks and their supply to vending machines? Yukio ripped open the packaging and unfolded the latex mask. On the back of the chin, to his horror he saw: *â„ ¢ Nippon Real-Doll Corp.*

Had he fallen asleep at work without realizing and talked in his sleep? Had he been too clever for himself? Had part of him exploited himself schizophrenically out of company loyalty? Or had the company security-psychologist decided that Yukio was behaving oddly, and investigated his computer?

Oh foolish Yukio, to have copyrighted the label with Keiko's image in his own name at work, borrowing the company's copyright software — that was how they had found out!

But then the company perceived a unique business opportunity: the Real-Doll Corporation could turn real schoolgirls everywhere into clitoris-power dolls of his Keiko!

A million texting schoolgirls could spread a craze within a few days, or maybe a few hours. And Yukio couldn't complain or sue, nor could Keiko. For one thing, Yukio had committed industrial theft. But, even more worryingly, the Real-Doll Corporation's psychologist-detective may have also found out the true source of Genuine Cloned Ama Clitoris Sashimi.

Yukio bowed to the false Keiko, then hurried home.

"Who are you?" he said to Keiko in the four-mat room. Quickly he explained what he had discovered — Keiko had been too busy labeling in the rented garage that day to watch any news. And he added: "You must wear a mask from now on, or else I won't know you!"

"Do you mean wear my diving mask?"

"More like a mask of Kate Winslet, I think... No, wait!"

The big oval of latex cut from the Keiko mask fitted the diving mask perfectly. Superglue secured it. Her false eyes, false nose, and false mouth squeezed flatly against the inside of the glass, as if she had dived to a depth of such pressure that her features had become two-dimensional. Her photo-shopped clitoris forever would touch her flat lips.

Since the false genuine face which she wore a few centimeters in front of her real face was in fact her true face, this negated that falsity and bestowed a mysterious and mystical authenticity upon her actual face, even though that was now invisible, as mystical things often are.

A Zen-like state came over Yukio. He knelt before Keiko, like Pinocchio praying to the Blue Fairy to make him real. By not-seeing what he was seeing, Yukio began to worship her countenance.

Unseeing too, a blind goddess, Keiko heard his mantra of worship.

"My Beloved, My Beloved, My Beloved..."

Whale clitoris sashimi was only an illusion, from which Yukio was now freed by enlightenment. Probably its sublime taste was also an illusion caused by exorbitant price. He would eat Keiko's clitoris instead.

China on the Moon

by Stefano Carducci and Alessandro Fambrini

translated by Carlotta Codebò

Born in Seravezza in 1960, Alessandro Fambrini teaches German literature at the University of Pisa. He has dealt with German literature of the nineteenth century, the Fin de siècle and the twentieth century. He contributes to the field of fantastic and science fiction genre as a critic and as a writer. His stories and essays have been published in various publications to which he has also dedicated his commitment as co-founder of the critical review of the fantastic Anarres. *Together with Stefano Carducci he has published many stories and novels* Ascensore per l'ignoto *(Mondadori 2010),* La breve estate della follia *(Delos 2017) and* I giganti immortali *(Elara 2022).*

Stefano Carducci was born in Venice in 1955; a long-time SF enthusiast, he collaborated with Perseo Libri by Ugo Malaguti, published short stories and translated, among others, Shepard, Priest, Watson, Aldiss, Moorcock, and Sturgeon. Together with Alessandro Fambrini he has published many stories and novels.

"Why me, exactly?" Thought Paolo Finzi as he crossed the Belvedere Courtyard and entered the Casino Pius IV's gardens. Even though it was late autumn, the rows of plants and the well-curated trees still seemed to preserve the splendour and colours of an artificial spring. The rose bushes appeared to be in bloom and a few petals were scattered on the grass. This too seemed to hint at a sort of artificial indifference, as if in simulation of the naturalness of life.

Further along, the Pontifical Academy of Sciences building could be seen just afew hundred metres away from Saint Peter's Basilica. The geometrically rigorous white square building's assortment of soft lines was broken by baroque curves. Together with its gardens, it was meant to be a place of contemplation and rest. As if Pope Pius IV, the man who brought the Council of Trent to a close and oversaw the hardest battle for the Roman Church's survival, had wanted to represent science as a peaceful interlude in between real life's furore. A moment wherein the soul could regain strength while leaving the mind, its imperfect sense organ, in control.

Casina Pius IV, Paolo Finzi mentally reprimanded himself, not Casino. He pushed down any thoughts that this tiny linguistic manipulation of history could then be applied to more significant aspects of history itself, and went back to concentrating on his next task. And on the question that was blaring in his mind: why him, exactly?

He was no more than a superintendent at the Pontifical Academy of Sciences and could only aspire to become a member, some still far off day: not much more than an employee and amongst the youngest too. Or maybe that was exactly the reason. His youth, his relative distance from the customs of protocol, from the excesses that weighed down formal encounters and turned them into an inane farce. They couldn't realistically expect him to follow procedure when he knew nothing about it. His mistakes would be forgiven. Or maybe, if they were too big, it would be easy to put any blame on his inexperience. He was, he acknowledged unhappily, completely expendable.

Yet he kept thinking that it would have been more appropriate to send a diplomat to that meeting, despite the fact the Vatican City State had no official relationship with China. More appropriate. But the Holy See never did anything inappropriate. Even just thinking it came far too close to heresy. The reason had to be found in whatever the Chinese wanted to talk about. Paolo Finzi had no idea what it could be, but he could contain the slightly uneasy curiosity he felt. Only a little while longer and the answer would be revealed. Just one more hallway, one more corner, and he was in the building's third room, the Chamber of the Sun in Christ.

Since he had started frequenting the Academy – and it had been five years now, initially as a research assistant in astronomy and now as an associate fellow – he had always been struck and deeply troubled by the presence of both the sacred and the profane in a place that owed its creation to one of the greatest vicars of Christ in history. As if Pius IV had mixed his intellect with that of the architect appointed to realize the project; Pirro Ligorio who had, yes, been a member of the Fabric of Saint Peter, but who had also been implicated in questionable affairs: trading of antiquities and theft of sacred furnishings. He had always demonstrated a slippery propensity for grandiose effects and suggestive – yet frivolous – references. Like those that gave the Palazzo De Torres - Lancellotti, in Piazza Navona, an aura that was far too secular.

So be it, thought Paolo. He hadn't organized this meeting. For all he knew the great fresco that filled every inch of free space on the walls and depicted the relationship between Apollo and Diana, the four seasons, and the Twelve Apostles grouped together under the protection of the Roman Church, was the most appropriate for tightening the phantasmagorical noose around the Chinese representatives. By visually retracing the journey from false to true faith, it could weaken their defences and make them more likely to be forthcoming during negotiations. Even if – as he kept glancing sideways at the Bacchae celebrating the grape harvest – he continued to nurture many doubts.

Soon enough, from the hallway opposite the one he had arrived from, came the sound of footsteps. The Chinese delegate walked in preceded by a uniformed guard. The delegate was young too, and impeccably dressed in a black suit and ice blue tie. Paolo stood up quickly. He was unsure about whether he should extend his hand or attempt some other greeting. The man spared him the embarrassment by bowing slightly and Paolo reciprocated. With a nod the delegate then invited Paolo to take a seat at one end of the great ebony table dominating the centre of the room.

"Mister Cheng Zhu," he said once they had both made themselves comfortable, following the script he had already used many times. "I've been told you speak my language."

"That's exactly right," answered Cheng Zhu. "I've lived in your beautiful country for many years."

Not exactly right, thought Paolo. None of you live here in the Vatican. He didn't say it though, he simply smiled formally. Under the intense light of the eighteenth-century chandelier, hanging overhead like a green and purple jellyfish, Cheng Zhu's features revealed him not to be as youthful as he seemed. There was thin web of wrinkles at the corners of his eyes and the back of his hands were marked by age spots. Behind him stood another Chinese representative, even older and quieter. Though he was the host, Paolo suddenly felt alone and able only to count on himself.

"Well then," said the guest in perfect, but slightly robotic-sounding, Italian. "I suspect you already know why we're here."

'The first bluff?' thought Paolo and tried to answer in the affirmative. However, he was chronically incapable of lying. It just wasn't in his nature, not least because as a priest he was faithful to the teachings of the Church. Of Christ, he mentally corrected himself. He knew well that the two things didn't always coincide.

So, he shook his head as if to affirm his own ignorance and sighed in relief when the other met his denial with the most complete indifference. It must have been a rhetorical question, and what did he know about rhetoric?

"This is what we wanted to show you," Cheng Zhu said in an ironic tone that seemed uncalled for to Paolo. Or, more likely, he simply didn't understand the language of diplomacy. Cheng Zhu pulled a laptop out from the briefcase he had placed on the table. Paolo's gaze fell to the unusual keyboard made up of silver-coloured ideograms. Cheng Zhu quickly typed a few commands and, strings of code passed by on the screen. They scrolled by far too quickly to make an impression, then the pixels merged to form a static image.

Cheng Zhu raised his eyes towards Paolo and gestured at him to come closer.

"Have a look," he said.

Paolo drew nearer, moving his chair right next to the man. In his mind an image formed of them bent over the screen, side by side. It reminded him of two students working intently on a group project. Then he focused on what he was supposed to be looking at, and was transfixed. An open space, against the backdrop of a night sky. The landscape was desolate and rocky. The image resolution was precise, and mainly black and white which must have been what it actually looked like because in certain parts of the starry backdrop violet flashes at the higher end of the light spectrum broke through.

Paolo absorbed the implications of what he was looking at. The star's brightness was fixed, it wasn't refracted by the atmosphere, and the difference between night and day as projected by the shadows didn't match earthly conditions. It had to be a celestial body foreign to Earth. He might have been able to deduce which one it was from the positioning of the constellations if only he could have found two reference points on which to construct a verifiable triangulation.

"The moon," Cheng Zhu beat him to it. "And specifically, the Coriolis crater."

Paolo looked at him. Coriolis. The dark side of the satellite. He was completely overtaken by a sense of unreality. For more than a decade the Chinese had been attempting aeronautical experiments, but officially they hadn't got any further than positioning some satellites in the heterosphere and building a few modules for a first, rudimentary space station. They had clearly kept their real activity very well hidden from the rest of the world.

"We established our base there a few years ago," continued Cheng Zhu, in a completely indifferent tone.

Why is he telling *me* this?, thought Paolo, and then he repeated it out loud, throwing caution to the wind, and increasing the scope of his query:

"Why have you come to tell *us* this?"

Cheng Zhu stared at him coldly. "Let me finish my story," he said, "and keep looking."

He pressed some keys on his computer and the next image appeared. The same landscape, with the rough outline of a far too close horizon, was still visible except that now the focus was on a rock formation standing out against the plain. At the meeting of shadow and light, the silvery reflection of a human silhouette wearing a space suit flashed. No longer the awkward, bulky space suits of the Sixties, but the snug, nimble fits of recent generations. More like the tin foil ones of the first experimental voyages, except that these were made from a combination of mylar, aluminium and Gore-Tex. Still not enough, thought Paolo, to isolate us from the unknown.

"That's one of our taikonauts." Cheng Zhu's voice shook him out of his own thoughts. "On a mission. A few magnetic anomalies led us to investigate the nearby Daedalus crater, where we found an unknown structure. This one."

Another click, and the structure appeared on screen. It wasn't easy at first glance to distinguish it from the cliff it was up against, but then Paolo's eyes made out the symmetrical walls, nestled like a polished block between the irregular rock spires and pinnacles it was set between and from which it stood out like a foreign body. It was like a bunker, with no openings except for a vertical cut in the centre front before which two taikonauts stood motionless. Paolo projected onto them the shadow of his own uncertainty. Their presence showed just how big the cut was, as wide as two men and three times as tall.

"It looks like stone," said Cheng Zhu, "and it's well-camouflaged with the background, but it's actually made out of a thick-concrete like material, and it appears not to be prone to corrosion and decay."

"It's artificial," said Paolo.

"Yes," answered Cheng Zhu "and we didn't make it. We couldn't have. The micrometeoroid fragment impact analysis that we conducted on the external wall shows that it is at least a million years old.

"A million years?" repeated Paolo, in disbelief.

"*At least* a million years," Cheng Zhu corrected him. "Beyond that time our results are approximate. What genuinely puzzles us and the reason why we've really requested this... *consultation*, is what's on the inside."

Cheng Zhu showed him a new series of images.

In the first one – evidently taken from inside the bunker – an artificial, uniform light illuminated a circular space like that of an amphitheatre. The internal walls looked smooth and gave off flashes of slightly bluish luminescence.

In the next photo, Paolo thought he could see a taikonaut, but then he realized that was impossible: the man was naked, shot from the front, his legs slightly apart and his arms raised in front of him in an inviting gesture. It was a pose that Paolo knew well, and it gave him a slight feeling of vertigo. The image was taken from a certain distance and seemed out of focus, but the next one left no room for doubt. It was clearly the same subject but it was now possible to make out the features of a Semitic-looking man around thirty years of age, naked, with palms open and facing the spectators. As if in shock, Paolo stared at the sequence of up-close shots. The close-ups of the hands and feet showed signs of deep wounds, like holes, around which there appeared to be dried blood. More blood had clotted on his forehead, forming a sort of crown underneath his long hair.

Cheng Zhu brought up even more images, this time taken from the middle distance. In these the artificial space's layout became clear. There were never ending rows of transparent capsules set into the walls. The man (*man*?) who had appeared in the foreground was only one of many. Even though, Paolo noted, not every capsule seemed to be occupied. Even among those occupied, not every single one seemed to contain a human, even if it was difficult to be sure from so far away.

A new close-up appeared. The capsule must have been next to the previous one because a hand and part of the occupant's arm could be seen at the edges of the frame. Paolo's attention, however, was completely focused on the new being that dominated the centre of the image. It too seemed human at first glance, though what stood out the most was its enormous phallus. In the full-body image it managed to obscure every other one of its features. Then in other more detailed images there were traces of horn-like bulges on its forehead, goats feet, and on its shoulders scaly bumps that had been photographed in profile could be seen.

"Maybe now you can understand," said Cheng Zhu, "why we came right to *you*."

Cardinal Pallavicini came down the hallway leading to the Pope's apartment as if he was being chased by the devil himself. His haste was justified, Cheng Zhu had been clear: he wasn't going to put up with being, for all intents and purposes, placed under forced house arrest for long. Naturally, being not only a perfect diplomat but also Chinese on top of that, he had defined the impasse they found themselves in as "a suspension of judgement," but the Cardinal knew they didn't have much time left to decide.

Father Luca, Pope Adrian's personal secretary, was waiting for him in the prayer room's antechamber.

"The Holy Father is waiting for you," he told him as the other arrived.

"I know," hissed Pallavicini dodging him. That slimy lackey gave him the creeps. He continued walking without missing a step and thrust open the door without bothering to knock.

Once he'd closed it behind him, he sighed in relief as if a weight had been taken off his shoulders. This was the only room in all of Vatican City in which he felt safe. Within the limits of both technology and the power of the Vatican, it was the room with the best protection in the world from any kind of meddling; not even the Pentagon, not even the White House were as secure as that space. Not even China's mysterious spying capabilities could overcome the defences of those four walls. Every major world power had unofficially consented to protecting the moments of most intimate communion between the Pope and his God. Even if they had done so reluctantly because that no man's land constituted a vulnerability in the global security network.

But they could say and do whatever they wanted there. It was the safest place in the world for them.

Pope Adrian was wearing his clergyman's suit and a pair of heavy hiking boots, certainly not the type of clothing made for praying. Pallavicini took off his cassock, threw it on an armchair and said, "Come on, Georg, there's no time to waste. The Chinese guy is pissed off, I'll tell you all about it on the way there."

Pope Adrian furrowed his brow and made to speak. Pallavicini stared him down, all without breaking his stride, while approaching a wooden panel in the wall. After pressing its side, it opened, and with a gesture he ordered the Pope go before him. Ever since he had been elected Pope, thought Pallavicini, Father Georg had let it all go a bit to his head, but what was permissible in public could not be allowed in private. He still knew who was in charge.

Under the cold light of neon lamps, they climbed down a long spiral staircase ending in front of the door to a freight elevator. They got in. There were only two buttons. The Cardinal pressed the bottom one. With a violent jolt, the elevator started up just a few seconds after he had pressed it.

So, they descended slowly towards the bottom for several minutes. Not for the first time, Pallavicini thought that the elevator was deliberately slow – it's pace purposely calculated to allow whoever was riding it down to leave behind their everyday mundane worries, to free their minds so as to concentrate on that sole essential task that was waiting in the Vatican's underground vaults. He took advantage of it to bring Pope Adrian up to date on the conversation he had just had with Cheng Zhu.

The elevator finally stopped, and the door opened onto a dark tunnel. Pallavicini leaned out of the compartment and unhooked a torch and flicked its switch. It worked. He hated this sort of old-fashioned thing, but he tolerated them. They were a part of the general lay of the place, of the world he belonged to: a world in which progress was always gradual, in which today was mirrored in yesterday and any advancement could prove fatal.

Stepping out of the elevator, Pope Adrian took another torch from the wall without turning it on.

It wasn't the first time they had found themselves down there and both of them knew that even if the tunnel had been dug from live rock, the stone floor was smooth and they weren't going to trip. They set off down the steeply sloping tunnel.

After walking for several minutes Pallavicini shone his flash-light on an alteration in the composition of the tunnel's stone walls. It was lighter and softer. They had arrived under Saint Peter's and from here began the open tombs. They were verti-cally embedded in the walls, on the left and right, housing the exposed skeletons of the builders and curators of this hideout. They had been sacrificed for God's glory and to keep the un-derground vault's secret. The further down they walked, the more recent were the skeletons that appeared. Pallavicini had always asked himself, ever since he had become a member of the Five and had been let in on the secret, who had been the first Assassin. He knew the last one very well.

The tunnel suddenly came to an end against a stone wall. To the left, there was a half open wooden door letting light filter through. The two pushed on it and entered.

Friar Tommaso looked up from the screen of an open lap-top placed on a large table in the middle of the room. Three other screens, all connected to the laptop, were on the table. A series of climate-controlled security cabinets, connected to a hissing generator positioned next to the door, lined three of the walls.

"We searched for him on Earth for so long and yet..." said the friar when he saw them. He had a lost look in his eyes, as if he had been betrayed.

Pallavicini looked at the Jesuit and bit back a disdainful grimace. He had never tolerated the friar's personality, much too sentimental for his taste. He sat down in front of a screen to look at what Friar Tommaso was reading. Pope Adrian fol-lowed but remained standing behind him.

Friar Tommaso had opened the last pages of the digital version of the Latin translation of the apocryphal gospel of Basilides, the original was locked up in one of the cabinets. Pallavicini had only once had the chance to hold those ancient papyruses in his hands. Their existence was known only to the

Five and had been passed down a miraculously uninterrupted chain through the centuries. The fragments and relics kept safe in the other cabinets were the even more ancient sources on which the Secret Books were based. Pallavicini knew of the latter's existence but had never actually seen them. He didn't even know who was authorized to open those cabinets and he wondered to himself who could there even be, above the Five, who could deal with that superior knowledge.

The apocryphal gospel was open on its last pages, where Basilides prophesied the new coming of the Saints. At least that was how the translator had chosen to render the term with which the original compiler had defined the ranks of the "awaiting gods." They weren't just dangerous words; those texts were primed bombs and the security cabinets in which they were shut were a barely sufficient line of defence. The Cardinal proposed destroying everything that was in that room had many times, but the others hadn't had the courage. The Chinese discovery had now forced them to come to a decision.

"Maybe the moment has arrived," said Pope Adrian. Troubled, Pallavicini whipped his head around to stare at him.

"What moment?" he said, defensively.

"The moment to reread the other book," answered the Pope.

"Don't even think about it," said Friar Tommaso, in a distressed tone.

It took Pallavicini a moment before he understood, then he paled.

"It's the most detailed, the only account that seems to be a direct testimony," continued Pope Adrian. "If we had been more trusting, we would have avoided many mistakes."

"How can you say such a thing!" Pallavicini exploded. "That book is obscene, blasphemous, it's...it's..." he stuttered. "It's dangerous," he said finally.

Of course, it's terrible," said Pope Adrian. "But we're forced to act now. We are at risk of losing control of the Revelation. But this," he said pointing to the security cabinets, "is still a secret. The information is in there, our weapons are in there."

"*Cedant arma togae*," Friar Tommaso said mournfully.

"The toga is unnecessary," Pope Adrian replied brusquely. "What can we offer the Chinese? Another fairy tale on redemption and forgiveness?" the friar stared at him in shock. "Maybe you haven't realized it, but what's written in those pages," he waved his arm around, almost yelling. "*Is true*, it's reality." He stopped himself, gasping for breath. "If an answer exists, it's in those cabinets," he concluded.

"Georg is right," said Pallavicini, looking at the Jesuit. "But there might be another solution," he said calmly.

The *Shining Morning Star* seemed to descend slowly towards the surface of the moon. Paolo was relieved to feel the weight of gravity as the debilitating nausea that had overtaken him as soon as they had left Earth dissolved. For the whole trip he had been in a semi-conscious state wrapped up in a gloomy ball of suffering. He was finally able to smile to himself, thinking that the Academy had really chosen the right person for this mission. Certainly, he was the youngest of his scholarly colleagues, but maybe a Swiss Guard would have been a better choice.

He was finally able to marvel at his circumstances, to see the charm in what was before him.

A soft silver dust covered the moon's surface. The shadows of the hills chased after each other over shattered craters, ending up hidden in bottomless ravines. They landed far too quickly for Paolo's taste.

They had taught him how to put on the suit. He went through the motions a bit awkwardly but knew he would have to do it many times. Inside the Chinese base, the pressurized zones were reduced to only the absolute minimum.

Then he dropped onto the lunar surface.

Once out of the *Morning Star*'s shadow, Paolo looked down. A small puff of lunar dust had landed on his feet. He desperately wanted to bend down and take just a pinch as a souvenir, but he managed to stop himself. Then he raised his eyes. Only then he realised they hadn't brought him to the base, but directly over the Daedalus Crater.

Paolo saw huge industrial vehicles, which were nonetheless as skeletal as spiders, move slowly over the rough surface in front of the artificial cave's monumental entrance. The crater's walls loomed incredibly high. Paolo realized that he was unable to correctly decipher distance and size. The clear contours and the metaphysical cleanliness of the sight confused the senses. He stayed still, paralysed by an irrational fear of sinking, and at the same time, slamming into something.

Someone took him by the arm. Maybe they had understood his confusion.

A voice could be heard in his ear. "Always look only a few feet in front of you," said the man, in good English. "You get used to it after a while."

Grateful, Paolo let himself be led over the visible footprints left by other boots.

After a few minutes, they found themselves in the shadow of the crater's walls. They stopped; Paolo raised his head. Fixed lighting together with the harsh headlights of both military and industrial vehicles illuminated the area around the cave over a radius of some ten metres. The vehicles seemed to move around nonsensically, as if they were gigantic, crazed ants. Crossing under the beams of light that made the dust swirl, Paolo came closer to the wound-like entrance. It looked like a solid black monolith. It was incredibly tall. Starting from the crater's bottom, it appeared to split the whole wall until disappearing into the sky, like a river running into a bottomless sea.

Something that he didn't dare name was in there. Cardinal Pallavicini had forbidden him to call Him by His name, because it was still impossible to establish whether or not the Chinese were just another instrument of the Devil. They were certainly facing a test of their faith, maybe the decisive one.

"Were there other traces here, when you arrived?" he asked, trying to get a hold of concrete details.

The taikonaut with him didn't answer right away. From what little Paolo could make out of his facial expression through the suit's helmet, it seemed like he was listening to someone; probably awaiting instructions. At least that's what Paolo would've done in his place.

"Yes," the taikonaut answered finally. "The surface was marked by prints that were different from meteorite impact traces. They were uniform, they seemed left by...living creatures. We reproduced them, of course, and they are now being analysed at the base, on Earth." A second later: "They haven't found anything yet."

Even if they had found something, you certainly wouldn't tell me, thought Paolo. In any case, what they had told him was already enough. He felt a shiver of apprehension at the very thought. What could it mean? That his destiny was already decided, or that the collaborative spirit of the Chinese was sincere?

"Every environment, exterior and interior was, naturally, recorded *before* our arrival. The reproduction process is underway on Earth, after which we will be able to study this place as it was without our presence. This should provide us with some valuable information."

These were empty words, serving only to emphasize Chinese scientific superiority.

They had now arrived at the entrance to the cave. The size of that door provoked a sense of dumbfounded awe. Given the sharpness of its contours it could only be man-made, but it must have been the work of a civilization of unparalleled power. Crossing its threshold was like diving into the absolute emptiness of space without protection. Paolo approached the nearest buttress. He raised a hand to caress it, it was smooth like crystal, clean, a clear parallelepiped.

He slipped inside. The taikonaut kept a hand on his shoulder for which he was grateful because the transition from the external artificial light to that supernatural darkness was instantaneous. Paolo perceived that human touch as if it were the only buoy keeping him anchored to reality. The disorienting sensation only lasted for a few moments, then Paolo detected a faint glimmer in the distance, to his right, towards which the taikonaut was gently pushing him. They had to navigate around two more narrow tunnel deviations before they came to the first chamber in the subterranean system. It was obviously man-made. Maybe whoever built it had made use of some original structure, but that tunnel's function was without a doubt to protect the cave as best it could.

Paolo came to a halt. About ten metres further on the slim figures of the taikonauts were slowly moving around rows of huge vertical sarcophagi, immersed in a soft dense light.

How had they pinpointed the right crater? Paolo tried to remember if Cheng Zhu had mentioned it. But maybe he was too small a fish and the Chinese diplomat had kept that information for someone who was above him. Though he doubted it. The place had remained unknown for tens of thousands of years and the Chinese had happened upon it just like that, accidentally? Unlikely, he thought. Meanwhile a doubt began to fester in his mind about the race to the moon and the discovery of the cave: which was was the primary objective and which the consequence?

Paolo shrugged the taikonaut's hand off his shoulder and moved forwards into the amber light of the cave. Holding his breath, he looked inside the first capsule. It was empty, just like the second and third. He turned towards the taikonaut.

"This is only the first of the caves," the latter told him.

"And how many are there?" replied Paolo, amazed. This was another unreleased piece of information.

Again, the pause before receiving a response. Then: "Many, big and small, but we don't know how many. We haven't yet managed to explore all of them. We think that whoever built this storage space took advantage of a pre-existing series of underground environments."

"If that's true, it would mean the moon's geological history is more interesting than we thought," said Paolo, starting to walk by the capsules again. "They're all empty here," he continued. "Where are the ones you showed us?" The lid of the capsules was so transparent that Paolo raised a hand to touch it. It was slightly elastic and seemed to blend in with the rest of the frame. Paolo inspected the capsule up close, but it seemed like it had been fused from a single casting, without signs of openings or hatches.

"They were already like this when we arrived," said the taikonaut, anticipating his question. "Empty. But starting from the next room I'd advise you not to look around for too long. I'll go first," he said, walking between the rows of empty capsules.

On the floor of the cave a trail had been drawn drawn with luminous lines. They followed it until they reached an opening in the wall. It was as wide as three men but just over two metres high. The edges were dotted with sharp rocks, just as they had been for millions of years.

Emerging from that door, Paolo came to a halt..

The cave opened endlessly above him in a dome of which he could see neither vault nor walls. The rows of capsules disappeared into the distance upwards and to the sides, blending with the soft light wrapping them in a protective embrace. As the rows got further and further away, the capsules became bigger and bigger, their shapes changing too.

The taikonaut stopped to wait for him.

"I advise you to darken your front visor," he told him. Paolo looked around. The taikonauts walking around the rows of capsules were featureless masks; they must be using the internal equipment of the suits to orient themselves.

"I'd rather not," replied Paolo. He hated the idea of blindness. He stared at the taikonaut and noticed the front visor of his helmet polarizing. Paradoxically, it was the taikonaut who took him by the arm and led him through the endless cave.

Paolo forced himself to look straight ahead, with the taikonaut walking between him and the first row of capsules. Even with all the necessary precautions he had taken, fragments of limbs, features, body parts and tentacles still penetrated Paolo's line of vision. His mind filled it all in with monstrous images. He thought that maybe it might have been better to just look directly at the sleeping beings, reality could not be scarier than his worst nightmares, but he lacked the courage.

His mind went back to the image of the only guest that really mattered in that cave. For the Chinese, Paolo was there to validate the accuracy of their hypothesis. For Christianity he was a witness.

Even just thinking it was a serious sin of pride. Paolo tried to regain control of his emotions but, as he continued walking down the row of capsules, his impatience and sense of responsibility weighed on him like a sudden and oppressive physical burden.

"Don't look!" the taikonaut told him, grasping his arm, as if he had read his mind. "There are things that the eyes shouldn't know," he said as if speaking to himself, then, in a steadier voice said, "We're almost there."

A few metres in front of them two black metal partitions had been raised to isolate a section of the row. When they reached the closest one, the taikonaut stopped and let go of Paolo's arm, giving him some intimacy.

The metal panels isolated two capsules placed side by side, preventing them from being seen by the others. Paolo took a few steps closer to the first one, keeping his eyes fixed on the ground. Once he looked up, he'd be right in front of him.

Though he wasn't expecting to be, he found that he was scared.

He raised his head.

Christ was sleeping inside the capsule. There was no doubt, he couldn't be mistaken for anyone else. The Semitic features were different from those of classic iconography but very close to the scientific reconstructions and other reproductions found in the secret papers of the Vatican, the signs of martyrdom were evident and unmistakable. Paolo ran his gaze over the body of the God made man, without being able to articulate a single coherent thought. One part of him wanted to throw himself at the feet of his Lord, another part thought that the audacity of his own gaze might just be an enormous sin of blasphemy, and yet another part, the most dangerous, asked itself: but who had shut Him in there? What was He doing in that sarcophagus?

What *was* in that sarcophagus?

These questions were too much for his shocked mind.

He turned his gaze away and fixed it on the neighbouring capsule.

He saw the cloven hooves. He saw the enormous phallus in between the hairy and mighty thighs. He saw the sharp face. He saw the eyes suddenly open, the yellow iris, the slits of the pupils.

The goat stared at him, pulled his thin lips into a sneer, and then smiled.

"It's not the first time that we've recorded signs of life, but until now they have been limited to more or less involuntary muscle spasms. We have never seen the... creatures... show evidence of conscious behaviour."

It is me, thought Paolo. It is my arrival here that has caused the awakening. He couldn't forget the teasing nature of the gaze, the glimmer of a secret irony – he would have even said of understanding, if it hadn't been a blasphemous idea – that had painted itself for a brief moment on that face with pointy cheekbones and skin like old leather, before the features relaxed once again into an apparent sleep. He didn't say it. He didn't say anything and continued listening to the taikonaut as he spoke, in the stifling environment of a pressurized cabin in the Coriolis base: "Now that the phenomenon has occurred, it's even more urgent than ever to find a method to access the interior of the capsules. Before any... accidents happen."

He didn't need to explain what kind. The taikonaut Paolo had been talking to, Ximen Liao, tended to speak euphemistically like a shrewd diplomat would – after all he was the commander of the base – or maybe it was just the round-about way of speaking characteristic of his people. In any case, Paolo was well aware that some of those capsules were empty. Maybe they had never been occupied, but in light of what they had noted in front of the cave – which, with a euphemism, his first handler had called a "trace" and of which Paolo had seen both the photographic and video reproduction – that seemed an improbable hypothesis. It was clear that there was a way to evade the hold of that impenetrable material, which was so well welded to the rock it was impossible to tell where one ended and the other began. The Chinese had studied the problem from every perspective, but they hadn't been able to overcome the difficulty of entering the capsule without using violent force, which would have put at risk the safety of the occupants. Even if in most cases such an unfortunate event would have actually been a blessing, thought Paolo.

"It's also urgent and necessary that you inform us about the information kept in your secret archives," continued Ximen Liao.

There it was. Paolo was only superficially aware of the hidden tactics behind his call to action. He knew that the first person he had spoken to, Cheng Zhu, had been held in the Vatican once he had revealed the contents of their conversation to the papal authorities. Officially, he was awaiting further deliberations by the Holy Father and his staff. It was a holding pattern that resembled a hostage situation, and in which he was the counterpart. Or the counter-hostage, which was more likely.

"I don't know what you're alluding to," he replied. "The archives I know of are all out in the open. I know there are rumours of every type about the alleged secrets of the Vatican, but I'm convinced they're all completely unfounded myths."

"It's all just bad press?" Ximen Liao's expression seemed unflappable, but the note of irony in his voice was evident. "In any case, I won't insist. Not with you. I don't have any reason to believe you're not completely convinced of what you say. Nonetheless our superiors are in constant contact with yours and the exchange of information happens on a level that is much deeper than you and I can possibly imagine. And allow me to say that our superiors are a little higher up than yours." He gave a look around and gestured dramatically with his open arm to indicate the space beyond the tiny room with its stagnant, stuffy, mouldy air. "At least as much as the moon is higher than the earth."

I wouldn't be so sure of that, thought Paolo. The positions on the cosmic chessboard are relative, and there are infinite heights beyond the moon and the earth, and infinite depths. But he simply said:

"If that's how it is, why are you talking to me then, here and now?"

Ximen Liao answered phlegmatically, letting the words roll out in his impeccable English:

"Because you're here now." One of his hands slipped down tap distractedly on his laptop screen, as if to recall a piece of information. "In our culture, we are accustomed to thinking that every single particle of our social body represents the whole. An idea that shouldn't be new to you. When you celebrate the feast with the body of your Lord, you follow a similar logic. Or am I mistaken?"

It was a rhetorical question, and Paolo didn't feel the need to answer. Even if the juxtaposition was provocative and blasphemous, he couldn't deny that it contained some element of an ideal truth. Very often contradicted in practice. Both by the so-called Chinese communism and – he was sorry to admit – the Roman Church with its more than thousand-year-old history.

In reality, it was almost certain that he had, in those frenzied last few days, been the bargaining chip in a game of which he could only in part understand the scope. The instructions that he had been given were aimed at providing sufficient information to identify what he would have found himself in front of – in the Daedalus cave – but they made no mention of the sources from which that information came, nor did they give him any idea of the backdrop against which the game was being played. Of course, he nurtured the personal conviction those sources were found at a level that didn't substantially differ from the widespread idea that the Vatican kept unspeakable secrets hidden in dusty and inaccessible basements. He just had the feeling that those basements weren't dusty and inaccessible. As for the rest, he was starting to understand that everything was possible.

Suddenly, the indicator light on Ximen Liao's walkie-talkie began to flash. The base commander took hold of the voluminous and anachronistic instrument – in the particular conditions of the satellite it dutifully stood in for the thinner and more modern terrestrial cellphone – and started listening. A series of rapid and unexpected expressions flitted over his face, alternating with incomprehensible comments in his language. When he put down the device, he seemed slowed down by a gravity infinitely superior to the rarefied one of the moon. He made an effort and stared right into Paolo's eyes.

"Apparently, important events have taken place after your visit," he said in a flat tone. "The capsule neighbouring the one you're so interested in is now empty. Its occupant has disappeared."

Via di Porta Angelica was jammed with urban traffic. In the line of cars at the Sant'Anna exit there was an anonymous grey Lancia Dedra. At the wheel an old man, back ramrod straight against the seat, was steering with one hand, the other was raised to motion to the guard, who let him through without stopping him.

Pallavicini merged into the traffic of Via Cola di Rienzo with an abrupt manoeuvre. Going out in plain-clothes made him nervous, even though he knew perfectly well that the best disguise was the most obvious one, he still felt naked without his official garments, his uniform.

He only started to relax when he was driving down the Lungotevere. He liked driving and the chances to do so were for him few and far between. He looked forward to the freedom the half hour in Rome's traffic would give him before being forced to slip back into his role, albeit in disguise.

The apartment building in Viale Etiopia was naturally anonymous. He didn't have a hard time finding a parking spot; like at every other preceding appointment he had always found a free parking spot, even in the more chaotic areas of Rome. The apartments rented by the organization changed every two or three weeks, always with different front men, in different parts of the city. It was possible that the organization achieved a level of paranoia so detailed as to guarantee free parking spots for the summoned members.

In the building's foyer he hesitated momentarily. On one hand, he didn't feel like walking up four flights of stairs, but on the other hand it would be risky, however minimally, if the elevator stopped. He risked it.

When he exited the elevator, Pallavicini saw that the apartment door was half-open. Continuous surveillance, he thought to himself, and smiled.

He entered. The hallway was empty. There was a room at the end of it. A living room was sparsely furnished with a pair of small, stiff armchairs, and a table made of light wood placed against the wall. There was a grey coat on one of the armchairs. A man of around thirty was standing and waiting for him in front of the window. He was twirling an unlit cigarette between his fingers when he noticed him and motioned Cardinal Pallavicini to sit down without offering any sort of greeting first.

Pallavicini didn't sit down; he wanted this meeting to end as soon as possible.

"I got your message," said the man, in a tone devoid of inflection. "Or rather I should say *his* message," he added with a sneer.

"His Holiness Pope Adrian was the first to find the solution," said Pallavicini irritably.

"I don't doubt it," said the man, still with that taunting sneer. "But we'd prefer your request be confirmed by something more..." he curled his fist. "Concrete."

"You can't expect to get registered mail!" blurted out Pallavicini. The young man's arrogance was shocking, and that mocking smile, it almost seemed like he knew that he was acting on his own. But it wouldn't have mattered; he was sure Georg wouldn't have had any objections. Maybe, he thought, it would have been better to have talked to him about it. He would do so as soon as he got back.

The other man sat down in one of the armchairs, turning his back on Pallavicini. He lit a cigarette and said, "It's very easy for our friends to fix the problem. A lost satellite, or some other unused missile is not hard to find. Given all of the stuff that's constantly moving around above our heads. But to sell it to the Chinese, to the Americans, and to everyone who would know very well it wasn't an accident, what are we going to say? That Cardinal Pallavicini was afraid to lose a little bit of power? With all due respect," he concluded, turning around to look at him. "My friends need something more substantial."

Pallavicini felt the blood rush to his head. Didn't this kid know who held the real power in the Vatican? The Pope was only his puppet; if he had wanted to, *he* would have been the Pope now.

"Let your supervisors know Pope Adrian is busy preparing the ecumenical council in Jerusalem; he doesn't have time for this nonsense," he said, swallowing his pride.

The other man got up from the armchair and turned to glare at him.

"I don't have supervisors," he said coldly. "Directing a missile with nuclear warheads onto the Chinese occupied Daedalus crater is an act of war. You'll have to convince me first."

Pallavicini stared at him. "Do you realize the danger that those...entities on the moon represent?"

The man shrugged his shoulders. "Danger? But haven't you all been waiting a couple of millennia for this?"

It was like he had been slapped in the face. Pallavicini paled.

"Tell your supervisors," he ordered, making sure to enunciate his words clearly. "That the Pope will release a statement at the Jerusalem Council. But by that date the problem on the moon will have to have been dealt with."

Then he left both the room and the apartment without another word.

When he passed through Porta Sant'Anna again he was still seething over the humiliation he had endured.

He dragged himself to the crazy traffic of Bezalel. He walked bent over, as if hunched over himself. He was limping more than usual, given that his goat feet were currently shoved into a pair of untied shoes. He was wearing a wide-brimmed black hat to hide his yellow eyes more than his leather skin. He was trying to pass as an old wreck, birthed from the contested walls of the most ancient city in the world.

At the Mahane Yehuda market he'd bought a couple of chickens, hoping the dead meat would calm the hunger of the being that he was harbouring in his apartment, at least for the few days leading up to the inauguration of the ecumenical council. He stopped at the stall selling vegetables turned grey by dust and smog. He bought a melon and a few tomatoes. An old woman moved away from him due to his smell, simultaneously feeling a shiver run down her spine causing her to stare at him with wide eyes. He ignored her.

He slipped into an alleyway after having passed the Ohel Moshe Synagogue and entered from an iron door cut into a shutter. The room was a converted garage furnished with a table, a worn-out sofa and a rug all found in some dump. On the second floor was the kitchen and the room where he had locked up his guest. Something slithered on the second-floor pavement. The goat climbed up the little metal staircase, went into the kitchen and half-opened the door to the other room. He threw the two chickens into the centre of the room without looking inside; the sight was disgusting even for him. His guest was smart enough to know that it would be better if he went undetected by the neighbours, so he made no noise even when he fed, but it was still best to keep him locked up as a precaution.

He went back to the garage, made sure the door was sealed shut, and then took off his clothes and shoes with a sigh of relief, now he could relax and stand up straight. The garage had no other openings besides the door. He stretched his back, moved his head carefully so as not to hit the ceiling and then lay down on the rug.

He wouldn't last long like this. He stared at the pile of junk he had gathered in a corner of the room. There were carved stones and scraps of wood, iron and fabric (some were extremely ancient, while others were just made to look very old); he had collected all of them during his explorations throughout this never-ending city. Objects that others venerated as relics.

He hunched over himself.

"Come, brother," he groaned. "Come quickly."

Paolo woke from a troubled sleep with a start. The bunk he was laying in was jammed into a suffocating vertical cubicle. Maybe it would have been better if they had assigned him a bunk in the common area of the Coriolis base. Ximen Liao had instead sold him on this single person solution as a privilege for the "honoured guest."

There was just enough space to slip off the mattress. He remained standing so he could listen: some dull thumps, a shuffling sound. It was more a subliminal impression of chaos and disorder, he thought, maybe the result of not having slept much, of the shock from what he was experiencing.

He went to the hatch, which opened as he approached. As soon as he set a foot outside into the hallway, a taikonaut appeared telling him to stay inside in bad English.

"Is something wrong?" asked Paolo.

"Nothing's wrong," he answered, shaking his hand, his expression indifferent.

Paolo went back to laying in his bunk. Now awake, he kept listening to the muffled sounds that came from outside. He started to suspect that the presence of that taikonaut wasn't completely random. That he too, just like Cheng Zhu at the Vatican, was under house arrest. Sure, it was relatively mild, where was he going to run off to after all? They left him quite a lot of room for movement. Not so much inside the Coriolis base, but in the Daedalus cave, where he had been escorted every day since his arrival. He knew the way by now, Ximen Liao didn't even follow him into the cave any more, where Paolo meditated for many hours in front of the likeness of his God in the hope of finding an answer to the infinite questions posed by His presence. He would stare at His wounds, at his feet, at his hands and at his sides. But after the first day he was no longer brave enough to look into His eyes. He mostly prayed desperately, appealing to his faith to help quieten his rational intelligence.

"Get me out of here," he muttered to himself, addressing his superiors at the Vatican who had put him in that dead-end situation. He thought about his soul, in that moment, then, however, he realized that the risks he was running were much more substantial.

The Chinese were showing him *too* much.

He could no longer hear any noise coming from the outside. He left his cubicle. He found no one next to the hatch in the hallway. He went towards the communal zone, crossing paths with the usual sequence of taikonauts who, in their grey suits, were all the same to him. They were well-disciplined soldiers, even if most of them had to be high-level technicians and scientists. He tried to scrutinize their expressions this time, in the search of some sort of hint about what had happened, but there was nothing, except maybe a particular type of tension, as if they were waiting for something.

Ximen Liao looked up at him from behind his foldaway desk inside his tiny office and smiled at him. Paolo found himself more wary because of it. "Is everything ok?" he still felt obliged to ask him.

"Of course," Ximen Liao replied. "Except for a problem with an external lock that caused us to lose pressure in a section of the base.," but Paolo noticed he averted his gaze while speaking.

"Did anyone get hurt?"

"No, just a couple of injuries," said Ximen Liao, standing up. "Nothing too bad."

"Are you coming?" he said then, smiling at him.

The two didn't exchange a word during their whole trip on the tractor to the Daedalus crater. Ximen Liao was more sullen than usual, so much so that once they'd arrived he bid farewell to Paolo abruptly, leaving him at the entrance to the cave to then disappear into the cabin of a spider-like robotic mechanism whose use escaped Paolo.

Paolo crossed the cave's antechamber. Then, before entering the main room, he automatically polarized the suit's visor. He knew the way by heart now and would probably have been able to reach his god blindfolded, even without the help of the suit's navigator.

After he had already taken a few steps in front of the capsules, he placed a hand over the suit's commands. The doubt he was nurturing over the Chinese's real intentions regarding him became certainty. They were hiding something from him.

He reactivated the suit's visor, without turning off the navigator. He kept staring straight ahead, to trick the taikonauts who were surely monitoring him. Were there monsters in the capsules that would make him go crazy? He was willing to risk it.

He relaxed his neck muscles, bowed his head slightly, as if to rub his chin, and threw a sideways glance at the nearby capsules.

They were all empty. He couldn't know if they were already empty before, but for some reason he doubted it.

He started walking again, slowly, forcing himself to wait for the navigator's instructions. The map projected inside the visor was superimposed onto the background of the capsules and of the inside wall of the cave, which he could carefully examine. From that distance it seemed smooth, as if polished by a gigantic machine.

Without turning his head, he looked to his left at the row of capsules that faded into the cave's hazy depths. They seemed to be arranged by size, the ones furthest away were so tall as to completely block the view. Paolo noticed that many capsules, both the normal sized ones and the far-away, gigantic ones, were empty. He was happy about it because what little he was able to distinguish of the guests of the occupied capsules would be enough to fill his future nightmares. He saw an enormous dog head, a contorted mess of serpentine limbs, a white, fleshy, pulsating lump. Then he stopped looking.

He passed by the avatar of an eastern god. Its long-fingered hand was raised at face level, palm facing forward. The image gave off such a feeling of serenity that he almost stopped in his tracks.

What was in that cave? They weren't statues and not even simulacra created by a civilization that had reached an unfathomable level of technology. They were alive or at least in suspended animation. Waiting. But for what?

Paolo had reached the bulkhead that protected his intimacy with his God. He looked at the empty capsule next to His and shuddered.

He then looked at Christ and saw Him smiling back.

"We've always known about the Dominators. The first of our scriptures, Genesis, known as the most enigmatic of the sacred books and the one that contains as many secrets as there are words, talks about them and calls them Elohim. Beings superior to humans and most of all different, even when their morphology is similar to ours. A pantheon of gods that interfered with us in very remote times, but that for the most part is indifferent to us, are simply...alien. We have gathered the various parts of our documentation across the continents, over the whole course of our long history. You'll understand then that your discovery doesn't surprise us. It's shocking for us, but it's not surprising."

Cardinal Pallavicini was speaking to Cheng Zhu within the furtive atmosphere of a tiny room. There were no windows, and its wooden walls were covered by tapestries. The light from the candelabras placed high up on the walls in pairs around the room was faint. The reddish lightbulbs recalled the dense, shadowy, glow of the candles they used to hold once upon a time.

The Chinese diplomat seemed to be trying his best to leave behind the apathy that had characterized his attitude up until that moment, and in a low a measured tone, said,

"Today is the eighth day that you've kept me prisoner."

"Available for high-level meetings," the cardinal corrected him.

Not even the shadow of a smile graced Cheng Zhu's face. "In any case," he continued, "you haven't told me anything new during this whole time. You've told me nothing about what's been happening since I've been detained in your apartments – though I realise have been treated royally. Nothing has been revealed about the information you have, about possible joint strategies, and now, suddenly, you tell me about the forced agreement I'm at the centre of together with your emissary on our lunar base, you give me a detailed account of the last few days and you open your treasure chest of arcane knowledge. Even someone far less wary than me would have reason to be suspicious."

Pallavicini remained unperturbed.

"I'm here talking to you now because it's time."

Cheng Zhu looked at him suspiciously.

"Time for what?" He said.

Pallavicini opened his arms wide. The wrinkles on his withered face momentarily smoothed out into a smile that was anything but friendly.

"Time to talk. What else?" He replied. "Do you know the Book of Ecclesiastes? An especially beautiful text from our tradition. Poetic, profound. There is a time for staying silent and a time for speaking."

It was now Cheng Zhu's turn to smile without any warmth to it.

"Ecclesiastes, of course," he said. The word sounded strange on his tongue, in his otherwise impeccable pronunciation. "A remarkable series of tautologies. Sso, you're speaking to me now because now is the time for speaking. If I'm not mistaken, Ecclesiastes also says, 'No one remembers the ancients, and neither will anyone remember those who will come after.' I can't help but think it refers to you."

The cardinal seethed; his tone was harsh:

"I see you know us well. No that I had any doubts about this. You will also remember the beginning of the canticle: 'There is a time to be born and a time to die.'" He was no longer trying to be obliging, he spoke only as a practical, worldly man. "We plan to bomb Daedalus. To destroy everything. We thought we should tell you in time, to give you the chance to clear out your men, and ours, from the base. Actually, we had thought of asking you to do it for us, but then we realized that the earlier, the better. And so there it is. Now you know."

Pallavicini was expecting Cheng Zhu to be outraged or to protest, or even to make a show of mocking disbelief, yet the Chinese diplomat's reaction was instead one of total silence. The cardinal tried to entice him: "You don't think we can?"

Cheng Zhu shrugged his shoulders, as if to give off a feeling of decisions already having been taken, of something inconsequential.

"You can try," he said, and looked at him strangely. "We already tried doing it too, before coming to you. With eight twenty-four megaton nuclear warheads."

Pallavicini waited for the other to continue speaking, but once he realized that he had no intention of doing so, he asked: "And what happened?"

"Nothing. They didn't explode."

He had had to threaten Ximen Liao to convince him to take him to the cave for one last time. The taikonaut was rightfully furious at him: after all Paolo was a representative of the country that was attacking them. Worldwide public opinion had been informed that a malfunctioning South African satellite would be hitting the moon, without causing any damage. On the base's video feed, an anonymous swarm of nuclear warheads appeared instead. In just a few hours, they would slam into the Daedalus crater.

Paolo could understand the anger that he saw in the base staff's faces and shared Ximen Liao's obvious disdain for the planet governments' realpolitik. They had all bowed their heads in front of a done deed. When Marinelli, his boss at the Academy, had ordered him to stop going to the cave, he had understood the implied message. Paolo wasn't worried for his own safety, put at risk by the Vatican's aggression. He was upset about the confirmation that the handful of elderly prelates governing the Church of Christ were motivated by the oldest of human emotions: fear.

Paolo's anger and disappointment were stronger than Ximen Liao's. It was absolutely necessary for him to go back and stand in front of Christ one last time. It was the only thing stopping him from completely losing his faith. Maybe Ximen Liao had a similar wish too, to see, one last time, the inhabitants of the cave that could have changed the course of human history. Paolo had the feeling that the young Chinese man wasn't really angry at him as much as at the cowardice of the men who governed the world, including his own Chinese superiors.

They had entered the cave together; overtaken by a strange frenzy, leaving the lunar tractor's engine on. They almost ran through the entrance cave as well as the tunnel that led to the first cave. They hadn't polarized their suit visors, as if they knew it wouldn't have mattered anyway.

The capsules were empty.

Paolo was now in front of the sarcophagus where his Christ had been. The emptiness filled him with an unexpected serenity, it was an emptiness that made His presence even stronger. Wherever it was. Paolo hoped it was on his planet.

"They're all empty," he heard Ximen Liao's voice in his helmet. He was far away, somewhere in the cave.

"Yes," replied Paolo. "Luckily," he added, without thinking.

"Maybe we'd better go," said Ximen Liao.

Turning his back to the cave, Paolo said: "If we destroy all of this," as if he were thinking aloud. "Where will they go next?"

"I'll meet you at the entrance," said Ximen Liao.

On the twelve-inch computer screen, a blatant anachronism amongst the porcelain, brocade and inlaid panels of the baroque-style underground office in the maze of the Vatican, the Daedalus crater explosions followed one another like a silent flurry of blinding flashes. They were less realistic than a video game due to the static quality of the images. A shower of rocks and dust rose up for a few moments and then slowly came to rest, in the interplay of light and dark that now defined the changed landscape. The crater had eaten away another portion of the rock, and it was now wider with a new lateral extension to the southwest.

Pallavicini turned towards Cheng Zhu, seated at his side on one of the far-too-high-for-a-human chairs that most certainly belonged to some audience room.

"It looks like it worked this time. See, maybe science isn't everything. We've always known that faith is the most important thing."

Cheng Zhu didn't answer.

"You should be rejoicing too," insisted Pallavicini. "Now you'll finally be able to go home too."

The Chinese diplomat continued to ignore him. His eyes were fixed on the crucifix on the wall behind the cardinal's shoulders, a life-size wooden sculpture, set in a decoration of worked metal, laminated in gold and studded with precious stones. He thought he'd seen it move and transform into something else.

Jerusalem was a city under siege. The idea to call the ecumenical council right on the border between Israel and Palestine that cut the city in two, had been a risky provocation. Every diplomat knew that the Vatican wanted to exploit the weakness of the two countries after the Second Six Day War so as to have the Holy City declared the first Free City, an exclusive world heritage site, under the control and management of the major religions that had come to light there. And which of the three religions was the most powerful?

The city was overflowing with the uniforms of the most diverse armies; convoys of armoured cars with sirens blaring whizzed by in the streets, not stopping even at red lights. Sudden road-blocks created impossible traffic jams in the roads, and the sidewalks were being violently cleared whenever some delegation appeared in front of the doors of the hotels.

It was easy to disappear in this chaos, mingling amongst the thousands of pilgrims, spies, curious onlookers, agent provocateurs, fanatics. Nobody noticed a stooped man with hooked hands, or the pile of rags thrown under the arches of a ruined church that shuddered when touched by the slightest breeze, nor the gurgling, yellow-eyed madman with green drool dripping from his mouth.

He didn't even have to worry about this. He was normal.

He had arrived from the city centre by walking down Avraham Levi, a dead-end cross street of an anonymous road in one of the new southeastern neighbourhoods. He had been attracted by the cold geometric profiles of the commercial buildings that rose like ungainly boxes along the streets devoid of dwellings, but also by the wind that blew in from the desert, once able to reach up to the door of the old city and now domesticated by the cement lying beneath his feet. That wind enveloped him in strong gusts in which he recognized the threads of his memory. The long days spent under the sun and in the dust, senses sharpened by the scorching heat, with his intellect spasmodically opened towards the infinitely flat and wavy horizon. The background to many meetings, attacks and retreats, in which he and his adversary had learned to know and recognize themselves, mirroring each other, establishing the rules of the matches played with those insignificant creatures, humans, as pawns.

Now that game could resume.

He had been sitting in a half empty café for half an hour, in front of a fermented drink he had ordered and barely tasted. The fragrance of hops, which reminded him of a time of communion with the earth and of unrest, was polluted by far too many chemical agents. Finally, a figure wearing too many articles of clothing for that climate and season appeared at the café's door. The figure looked around, uncertainly, from under the woollen beanie pulled down over a bowed head. Underneath it, the yellow eyes flashed from the old leather face. He spotted him, saw him, and started hobbling in his direction.

He remained seated, waiting for the other to come closer and take his place next to him on a chrome metal stool. They remained silent until the barista left and began serving another customer on the other side of the counter.

"Shall we get started then?" said the new arrival.

And he replied: "Let's get started."

BEING OVAL

by Alessandro Vietti

translated by Carlotta Codebò

Alessandro Vietti, engineer, was born just in time to witness the conquest of the Moon. He lives and works in Genoa in the energy sector and deals with scientific dissemination and writing. Articles by him have appeared in Robot *and in the monthly magazine* Coelum, Le Stelle, L'Astronomia. *Author of several short stories that have appeared in various anthologies, he has published the novels* Cyberworld *(1996 Editrice Nord; 2015 Delos Digital),* Il codice dell'invasore *(1999 Editrice Nord; 2015 Delos Digital),* Real Mars *(2016, Zona 42) winner of the 2017 Italia Award as the best Italian Science Fiction novel and* Il Potere *(2018, Zona 42).*

Of course, if existing means most of all occupying space (and who can say that it doesn't, how many of us exist as nothing more than rocks in the sea for our whole lives?), I don't think that anyone can object that my way of existing has always been, if nothing else unique, rare, *abnormal.*

I'm sure you'll agree that the situation I'm in really removes any doubt about this, if there was any left that is [*detachment sequence activated in three...two...one...*].

Undoubtedly this magnificent view of Earth, which makes me ask myself how the universe could have created such a thing, is having its part, since you could say the same question could be asked of me. I don't think you need to have gone through the same things as me to get it. You don't even have to know, for example, that once upon a time there were units of measurement based on the width (not by coincidence) of fingers, hands, arms, feet...Which meant that your body was the only thing you needed to make sense of the space surrounding you and the things occupying it, including yourself. Tracing it to describe it, like a planet does with its orbit, [*activate heating propulsion system/alignment coordinates verified and engaged/ route loaded and validated/Oval diagnosis negative*], describe it to share it, share it to understand it. Make use of your limbs to make sense of the world and then feel that the world was not just part of you, but a measurable extension of each and every one of you, that could, therefore, be interpreted from a greater holistic perspective.

How many arms is it from here to the moon? Nope, it's cheating if you count it out. You should go up there and actually measure it. One, two, three…That's how you have to do it, if you want to do it right, but you'd obviously need at least one pair of arms in that case.

I remember my brother and I being left alone in Grandfather's house with him while Dad was off being used (but *fairly*) by some artificial supervisor, and Grandfather in his worn-out armchair, just about hanging onto life. At a certain time of the afternoon, of *every* afternoon, he would open his eyes, both the only real one he had, eaten up by a cataract, and the sub-par one given to him by the National Healthcare Service, and through his thin lips shiny with drool say (yell), "Who's going to pour me two fingers of whiskey?!"

We were around six or seven years old and maybe he thought he was doing me a favour, letting me feel *equal*. Instead, it would just make me furious. Back then I was starting to realize just how different I was, and that difference would trigger my frustration and anger. It was my brother, of course, who'd end up doing it (and he'd grumble about it too, get it? He was the one who could do it, and he'd grumble about it) [*propulsion system heating at 10%…11%…12%…*]. He would push his Oculus onto his forehead like a scuba diver called back to the surface because of a problem with the tanks. Then he'd take both the bottle from the table and the usual glass I never saw anyone wash. He'd align two fingers of his left hand together along the bottom of the glass while taking aim with one eye, and then he'd slowly pour with his right hand until he'd see the liquor go past his index finger. *Two fingers* exactly.

Afterwards, he'd stop and hand the glass to Grandpa with the air of someone who'd just made an unusually large sacrifice. Maybe his expression wasn't any different from usual, the same old deformed mirror-like image of myself. Anyway, that undertaking seemed extraordinary to me. No, it was more than that: it was *impossible*.

For the record, I brought two fingers of whiskey, that I'd personally measured out, only once to my grandpa. I did it as soon as I was able to. At his graveside. I went there the day before the final migration. Not really as a homage to him, but rather as an act of personal revenge: you had nothing, *I'm going to have everything*. I've always liked useless actions. Symbolic actions. Maybe because I've always felt it better matched my existence, the same one that's now up here on the border with infinity [*propulsion system heating 74%...75%...76%...*].

Recently I often, but sometimes even in the months after joining up, stop and imagine (simulate) departure, what They has always called the *detachment*. That's what it has always been called and advertised as by the aggregators (and, for that matter, by mission control, too).

I think it was inevitable; anyone else in my place would have done the same. Everybody eventually tries to imagine the moments of separation we'll experience in our lives. We do it to reassure ourselves that everything will be all right and that we'll be able to handle it. We want to try and at least understand if, where, and how much the separation will hurt. Maybe imagining it first, which means that somehow we will have already dealt with it, is a way to comfort ourselves that when we actually have to experience it (endure it), we will stand our ground and not be swept away by the current. Maybe that's why I've always called it *departure* and never *detachment*.

When They came by to invite me to become one of the one thousand twenty-four, I had nothing to lose, because I've *never* had anything to lose. No, my brother doesn't count: my brother and I were the same thing after all, I'd never lose him. Nothing that I had ever come across had ever been better than the unknown and solitary horizon that was being offered to me. Aren't these the minimal prerequisites necessary to accept to change Solar System? Maybe that's why all the *specimens* They chose are like me. Not because they are all around seventy years old, but because they lack ties in their immediate space, considered vital to avoid losing oneself in the vast space. Besides, as far as I know, no one turned down the proposal. Who wouldn't opt for immortality? [*propulsion system heating complete/deactivating containment field/thrust at nominal angle in three...two...one...DETACHMENT*].

Anyway, I didn't even come close to imagining what the departure would be like. Not just because reality is always different from how we imagine it, even in the simplest of ways, because how we actually perceive reality is different and unimaginable, with a level of definition, a density of details and nuances that an imagination (or a simulation) will never be able to achieve. Despite everything I had convinced myself that somehow, the aggregators would have to grant a minimum of media coverage to such an event., but when it came to it, not even the shadow of a teledrone was sent up here. There was no ribbon cutting ceremony, no champagne bottle to break against the cluster, no sponsors to venerate, or anthems to listen to, even without a hand over the heart. Not even prerecorded. No virtual stages on which to show off some pride or arrogance. No spirit to set aflame, really. This doesn't mean our mission isn't important. After all it is (only) the most important in human history; but things have changed, fortunately.

There's just me, Oval #273, and nothing else.

And the other one thousand twenty-three like me, of course, who broke away from the cluster like a break shot in pool, in some sort of silent Big Bang, the start of something new, chasing hope in every direction possible. Like picking a lottery ticket. Everyone towards their destination, or rather towards what destiny had in store for them. But, please, no one to applaud, to shout, to throw confetti or sell hot dogs. After all, what the devil could they have done *up here* anyway? [*nominal trajectory insertion confirmed within reference parameters/acceleration stable/cruise mode ON/clock decreasing/ all Oval systems GO*].

It's likely, though, that there were people who, from the comfort of their couches, raised a glass in an act of participation, of farewell, of wishing well to all of us. Let's be clear, I don't mind. I knew perfectly well that it would be like this. I imagined it differently, but not because I really wanted it to be different. You don't agree to do something like this for the fame, but because as much as things change over the course of our existence, it's what we become used to as children that forever defines us, that somehow, even subconsciously, always resurfaces as our desires. That's how things worked when I was a kid: always a lot of pomp, flags, propaganda, press releases and conferences, live TV streams, social media posts, images, memes, controversy. Even for (or especially for) meaningless things, fake things, or things that needed to be made real, or *more* real, let alone for the undertakings, the very few, that managed to steer clear of the demagogic quicksand.

In reality, seriously, I have never given a dried fig about it all. "Dried fig" was grandpa's favorite variation on the old phrase, and I've always liked it too. When I was little it made me laugh. I could see it in front of me, the dried fig, like a withered willy, and I would cackle. There was only one other thing that would make me laugh. It's not the same nowadays.

Actually, it gives me a bit of anxiety, but also excitement, even though being *excited* is still somewhat alien to me, I have to get used to the dancing and fluttering possibilities searching for balance somewhere in the Oval. Like focusing your thoughts on a curious, strange equivalent of Nothing. I have to admit that, from this perspective, there's a triumph of dried figs. The cosmos itself is one single, enormous, supreme dried fig I have been sent to feast on it [*I auto update the program to send a series of beeps in greeting to the Tranquility Base (they won't mind): I've always wanted to imitate Sputnik/clock decreasing/ all Oval systems GO*].

See you later guys, it's a pity I can't get a glimpse at the dark side and can't even say: 'til next time. But, thinking about it, this isn't a real regret. The only real one I have is that if Mom had known my fate, I'm sure she wouldn't have done what she did. She must have started thinking about it after the second or third ultrasound. Nobody's ever spoken about it to me, after all, I've always been a taboo subject, but I can imagine her, my mother, sitting on the examination table, her stomach overexposed in the blinding light. What's the difference, after all, between a memory and a figment of one's imagination? They're both a part of non-existence. It probably wasn't even necessary for the doctor to interpret the results. For something like that, one look at the video would have been all that was necessary for even the most unprepared of observers. If my father were looking at it (and what father wouldn't be looking at it), he would have paled (of course he would have paled), noting the *evident* differ-ence between the twins, but he wouldn't have accepted it and would have tried to justify it through inexperience, per-spective, or by blaming it on the device, all the while waiting for a reassuring conformation of his own ignorance. How-ever, a gynecologist who clears her voice twice, three times, isn't a good sign pushing my mother, who can't see the screen well from where she is, to lift her head in the direction of that interminable silence.

"Something wrong?" she says. Her voice is like the light of a star on a windy evening.

The gynecologist might have cleared her throat a fourth time before catching her breath, like the light of the moon behind a cloud on a clear evening. She starts with a "I'm sorry," as atonally as possible, and ends with the word that starts with T, technical term, terrible, tragedy, tremendous, torturous, terror, tetra-amelia.

Then there's no need to imagine the agonized cries, or the silence that once again prevails, its pressure felt in the eyes drowning on the screen. The disbelief (but it's clearly visible, you can't mistake it: the *dried fig*). The inevitable question of why the heck one of them is so perfect and the other one isn't? The helplessness in front of the cold cruelty of nature. How is it possible that the universe could create such a thing? Can anything be done? (No, I'm sorry).

After a few months of tribulation, torment, and toil pass, I'm finally born, I come out second, and I don't take long either since there's nothing that to impede my exit. There has to be some sort of advantage, if nothing else for the mother, in having neither arms nor legs, unthinkable even for a Martian [*Mars fly-by in two hundred ninety-two seconds/minimum distance expected from surface four thousand thirty-eight miles/ data memorization and transmission in progress/clock decreasing/all Oval systems GO*].

I didn't think I'd be able to count the lights under Ares City's domes. I could mention they were breathtaking, but it wouldn't be relevant. I'm also sorry I have to fly past so fast and can only experience the city like a passing traveller in a great hurry, because if the Earth has always been my brother, then I've always been Mars, ever since that summer evening by the lakeshore.

Forgive me if I go back a step (odd that I'm the one saying this, like a blind man saying see you soon). I'm sure that, all of you who have arms, have at least once in your lives come across a stuffed animal and tried to make it stand up. Tried to find its center of gravity. Wait a second, just a little more to the left, slowly, a little bit forward, just a little. Like that. Ok, there it is. Well, my whole life I've always been that stuffed toy. As far back as I can remember, someone at home, my dad, my mum (when she was still around) or my brother, at least ever since I was old enough, would make sure that I was upright and in as stable a position as possible.

I've had a whole series of pedestals built by my dad, in keeping with our family budget, on which they'd place me. These pedestals grew as I grew. I needed them since my one little stump of a foot (the right one) had never done me any good, serving only to make me risk losing my balance, and if you can't grab onto anything at all, it's over for you once you start losing your balance.

When I had to leave the house, things became more complicated so the first modified backpacks came onto the scene, then the wheeled carts, modified over time to keep pace with my growth. The backpacks were mostly my dad's responsibility, while the carts showed up when I was around thirteen-fourteen years old and I started to weigh too much to be on other people's shoulders; it was also when my dad started to foist me onto my brother.

"Your brother's coming with you tonight, right?"

Not exactly a question that needed an answer. At least not one that was a no. Yet he still answered every time: "Of course, Dad." It was almost like an act that the two of them had agreed to put on for my sake. However, I have to say, my brother never complained about the dead weight (literally) he had to carry around on his Saturday nights. Not even as we got older, and our testosterone levels got higher.

I remember the night when he took me to the lake. Actually, I should say that he took *us* to the lake. Me, him, and the girl he was hanging out with at the time. I don't think I've ever managed to remember her name, even before the migration. It might have been his rugby player physique, but my brother was as handsome as a god [*crossing Jupiter's orbit/velocity increasing/nominal route/clock decreasing/all Oval systems GO*]. He always had beautiful girlfriends. I know what you're thinking: that I was his twin. So looking at him was a bit like looking at myself, except he'd come out all right, so, potentially, it was like it was happening to me. Or like it could have happened to me, if only I'd come out all right. That was not the only time I third wheeled, like a knick-knack on the bedroom shelf, but that night was different, and, for some reason, memorable.

I was being pulled on what was, by that point, my third wagon (the yellow one, the first one since I stopped naming them after pirate ships). At a certain point while we explored the small forested bit of the lake shore, the darker and more discreet side, the girl had finally expressed the usual sense of confusion that had been building up inside her for a while. So she asked my brother, as all of them did eventually, what the heck was I doing there with them.

"He's my brother!" That's how he'd usually answer, spreading out his arms, as if that were all there was to say, because to him it was just a fact of life, after all. Usually that was that, whether the girl decided to stay and see how it went – like that night – or whether she'd rather turn on her heels and go home (and some of them did, but my brother never ran after any of them).

I would almost always stay on the wagon, but that time it was hot, and it was a beautiful night. I wanted to feel the heat of the sand so I asked my brother to help me. I didn't have to repeat myself. He just hugged me tight – something I've only ever been able to try and sketch out with the hint of a humerus bone protruding from my left shoulder and my head tilted towards him, like a violinist towards his instrument – picked me up and let me fall delicately onto the shore.

"Thanks, buddy."

Then my brother goes back to the girl, and they start to make out vigorously. There's no moon that night, and the lake is the colour of dark petroleum. On the opposite shore in the distance the town lights resemble Ares City. After a while the two separate and start to talk. From how she's gesturing it seems like the girl is doing most of the talking. The shouting lets me know that something is definitely wrong, even if I try to concentrate on the waves slowly breaking on the water's surface [*crossing Saturn's orbit/nominal route and velocity/it can't really be called a fly-by, I'm too far away; but not that far – so I can hone in my senses and enjoy – I'm just a few billion arm widths away from the magnificent rings, I can even count them and imagine listening to them like an old vinyl/data memorization and transmission ongoing/and then the moons, hazy Titan, icy Enceladus, magnificent Dione/all Oval systems GO*].

The exchange doesn't last long before my brother gets up and comes to me.

"Sorry buddy, do you mind if I turn you this way?" I see what he's getting at right away. "Go for it," I tell him, it's not like I'm dying to watch them, and he takes me by the shoulders and rotates me one hundred and eighty degrees just as you would the head of a corkscrew.

"Thanks brother. And sorry," he says while patting the middle of my back. I tilt my head as if to nod yes, and now facing a bush, lose myself in my own thoughts. Except that after a few minutes I start to hear panting behind me. Those two have started screwing or something that sounds a lot like it, and I start to feel something move down there. Nature has been benevolent after all: it's taken everything from me, but my willy has always worked with a certain surprising audacity given my situation, even if using it has always been pretty difficult.

And so, in that moment on the lake shore a series of (unstoppable) events happened. While ten or so arm spans behind me the girl's yelling was becoming increasingly excited, below me the little guy was starting to call attention on himself, to the point where a hand would have been useful. Anyway, I did what I could, starting to move my pelvis slowly to try to do you can well imagine what, when the lake's humidity, a light breeze and the rustling bushes conspired against my nose making me sneeze. A second later, I don't know how, I felt that it would be impossible to maintain the position I was in. My centre of gravity was moving, and as if in slow motion and as much as I tried to tilt my head forward, I could no longer (oh, fuck) compensate. As my brother and I found out that the girl was pluri-orgasmic, I found myself like Gregor Samsa, but without the need to undergo a metamorphosis, on my back like a tortoise on its shell, only capable of swaying left and right, looking up into the dark night.

The stars.

The mystery.

I stopped swaying.

I stopped listening to them (but maybe a part of me continued to hear them gasping).

I stopped breathing (and thinking about the little pulsating guy down there).

I just contemplated. The galaxy.

It was like hanging out over the edge of a well, hoping to fall in by mistake, because maybe it takes too much courage to do it on purpose, and then actually falling in at the end and finding in that fall the answer to every possible question [*clock at its lower limit/Solar System exit is set from the end of the Sun's power, when interstellar medium prevails and the senses confirm it/data memorization and transmission ongoing/no Pluto, no trans-Neptunian object, not even a dwarf planet in range of perception/all Oval systems GO*].

It was only thanks to my brother's love and patience (and my father's sacrifices), who took care of me every day of our adolescence with a selflessness that I don't think I would ever have towards him – but that maybe was just a way of taking care of himself, of dealing with a sense of guilt – that I was able to finish high school with him. That was, without a doubt, what led me to fooling myself into believing that things would stay the same even afterwards. That nothing would change.

Instead.

Three scant lines from the Official Company Report stated that "the safety harness not being clasped correctly" was at fault. They would usually find a way to stick the blame on the victim to avoid paying compensation. So, our father ended up as part of the annual loss statistics included in the table on "Collateral Damages" downloadable from the Company website. My brother, in accordance with the Survivor Compensation Procedures, received an automatic message offering him the chance to take Dad's place, though at a lower level [*They said that it's like being frozen up here, no stars whizzing back like in science fiction TV shows, no space tunnels with arabesque designs, you just swim in a static blackness, which is why at the beginning you find yourself continuously turning on the guide system just to check your location and make sure you're not stationary, but then you get used to it and stop/all Oval systems GO*].

I knew that he had (obviously) accepted when he left his room. His eyes were red, and he was wearing my same Gagarin t-shirt, but without the safety-pinned sleeves. Faintly and without looking at me, but still patting me on the middle of my back, he said: "Sorry little one."

Then the supernova of our existence, the explosion of every certainty in every sense of space, but of time most of all, was in those three words. It was the destruction of our future, of any possible future, the decimation of the past we both (but especially me) had basked in regarding what we could have been. It meant no university for him, and thus neither for me. How could I have done it without his legs, arms and hands – he my Soyuz capsule, I his passenger? Not even counting how much it would have cost and that we could never afford again. Survival has always been priority and the following years were impossible to dispose of debris, dark cosmic clouds, all that was left of our hopes. Like when you're at the finish line of youth and, despite everything, you still believe that anything is possible, and then something makes you realize that you've got the short end of the stick and the ether never actually existed.

Within my domestic sphere time managed to definitively defeat space. I was placed on a self-propelled physiological needs platform provided at a subsidized rate by the Company, the waste was emptied every day at dawn and the food replaced by my brother before he left for his day on the construction site. I was left to watch a stillness pass me by that transformed the days into months and into years, in front of my computer for company and means of searching the web for even just the nebula of those stars that had exploded under my nose.

However, I don't think that's the actual reason why at this point my memory becomes flat and unremarkable. When I was offered my (only) possible future, one of the first things They explained was that the migration would have a strange effect on my memories. The result of the mental geography transfer would be more like an underground subway system than a bus. Mostly a few isolated episodes, really, as important as single stations separated by dark tunnels, than a time-space continuum of experiences linked by conscious panoramas [*today my stay in the starry blackness of the untouchable horizon has been rattled: something has entered within the detection range, some billion arm spans away, a cosmic vagabond, like a floating trunk from who knows where, at the mercy of the gravitational waves; since I can't possibly change course to see it from up close, I've simply increased the perception of my senses, opening my eyes and tasting this big lumpy dirty and compact snow potato/data memorization and transmission ongoing/some brilliant amino acid fragment, maybe even one, or even two DNA precursors, cytosine and guanine molecules/all Oval systems GO].*

The thought of deoxyribonucleic acid, of H_2O, of frozen mud – just like those winter Sundays Dad and I would watch from the rugby field bleachers as my brother ran with the ball held tight under his right arm, legs grinding out towards a breakaway try; and I would shout as if cheering for myself, trying to imagine what it would be like to run like that – has left me predisposed to some unexpected flicker of polarization, like a passing heart arrhythmia. If that comet ever gets near a star, it could at some point be transformed into a shining tail, if it ever has a planet it can slam into, it could fertilize an ocean.

Speaking of strange effects, the subway one is not all that different in the end, only more pronounced than what really happens in the human mind – picking and choosing memories. The really absurd thing about my Oval situation is the clock decreasing so that, by rule, every letter recorded in this diary corresponds to a little bit less than a year spent on Earth.

I'm taking it really easy, so to speak. They has decided to implement this function to minimize the instability risks for a ten-thousand-year voyage, but we will perceive it as lasting just half an hour, the time for a brief story more or less, since despite our current appearances we're (still) humans. It makes me smile, and I can do that, to think that all one thousand twenty-four of us could have said this at any moment of our lives.

Anyway, thinking that since I started recording this message eighteen thousand years have passed on Earth makes it impossible to not get vertigo and be overwhelmed by the most natural question: will there still be someone down there to listen when, once I've arrived at my destination, I'll have finished my recording and will leave it to the electromagnetic waves to carry away like a message in a bottle?

After all I have yet to meet anyone else out here, so all of you, my earthling compatriots, are still the only ones I can address in the hope of finding someone to listen. Of course, I have no idea what you'll look like when you get this message. What evolutionary heights you will have reached with the Shift and what technology applied to biology will have been able to do by then. Maybe it will be the other way around; maybe you'll all have become knick-knacks resting on top of furniture and it will be revealed that, rather than being *different*, I was just ahead of the times. The fact that I'm still here *now* and, all things considered in great shape, leads me to believe that it might be possible (hopefully) for even my brother to still be down there, in some way that I can't even imagine. Right, I don't think I've ever told you his name. Even my own name is a particle of dark matter...I know that it exists. Out there. Somewhere. Spread out over incredibly long intergalactic filaments, in its sidereal spiral weave. Keeping them together like two lovers. Making them dance around a stable centre of gravity. I believe it exists only because I can see its effects. Just like I'm sure that I exist [*initiate memory diagnostics/fragmentary positions 21%: within the norm of the physiological effects after millennia of exposure to the interstellar currents/importance principle ON/all Oval systems GO*].

It must also be said that after all this time it would make sense that, if the Shift is still somehow part of our history, it might have become part of a legend or mythology. Like the founding of Rome, the construction of the pyramids, or even worse, our expulsion from Paradise, but in this particular case it should, obviously, be called the return to Paradise. Maybe that's why the other one thousand twenty-three travellers and I, scattered throughout the galaxy, could be the last to still remember the moment that changed humanity's fate as something *real,* because for us it still seems to have happened quite recently..

Given the circumstances, it doesn't surprise me that I find myself here, at another subway station. I can't help but stop and look around, even if just to pass some time (and some space) since all of this has ended up involving me directly. Maybe it will end up surprising you too, when you read, listen, or let these words be projected directly into your brains, or whatever other ridiculous thing you'll end up using to understand this message [*as the Oval gradually moves through space, the stars change positions around me, but they do so extremely slowly, like when a new wrinkle is permanently formed through the flow of entropy and tears, but by the time you notice it, it's already commonplace/orientation system updated/so it doesn't matter if I'm already familiar with the Whale, Aquarius, Pisces, Aires and other Milky Way constellations I'm directed towards because they're similar to those I'm used to, or because I've become familiar with them in the meantime: they will nonetheless always make me feel at home/all Oval systems GO*].

I want to make something clear about this right away though: my disability wasn't to blame. In other words, it's not because I was stuck in the house for so long that I never noticed anything. *Nobody* noticed. Nobody on planet Earth lived through those years knowing just what kind of plot was being woven into humanity's future. Ok, so some rather minor voices, even well-known journalists and members of the scientific community, cried out and gave the alarm, but they were labelled as crazy and as conspiracy theory peddlers. They were ridiculed and insulted. Some lost their careers over it. Others, relegated to the margins of authority, but capable of producing books aimed at those who wanted to believe, even became rich. That's why the date is kind of arbitrary too. It was chosen by historians after the fact. Having to pick a date, they decided on (late?) 2049 as the defining moment when it all started. But that's not necessarily how it actually happened.

Certainly, who could ever have imagined that a self-driving car not stopping at a traffic light, not even braking, but instead accelerating and then mowing down a whole family would be the (first) symptom of something so huge?

Every day, all around the world, there were at least a dozen cars involved in mortal accidents caused by technical errors. Why should a tragedy that happened at a small, insignificant intersection on a seashore town road (in Italy?) be any different? Who would ever have thought to link that accident to those that, in the middle of the white noise generated by all the *normal* ones, started to happen according to a framework that was only apparently random, from Minneapolis to Saint Petersburg, from Marseilles to Buenos Aires, but never – for example – in Australia?

At my permanent station, inside a body that every year moved further away from the concept of humanity because of immobility and synthetic food, I immersed myself in obsessively studying the sky as much as I could through the web. One day the computer recommended the (must see) news on a few accidents that had happened in England, close together in space and time. All in the county of Kent, most of them in the Dover area, all involving Flat Earth Society.

The aggregators screamed: "The Flat Earth Serial Killer!" The news trended on the homepage for at least three hours, but then, as if orchestrated by an able hand, the strange accidents stopped and only started back up again once the media's attention was turned elsewhere, meaning nobody was ever able to connect the dots. It was as mysterious as a constellation-less sky. It just so happened that at a certain point nothing more was heard about the Flat Earthers, and no one worried about them any more [*Tau Ceti is no longer a punctiform object and is now just a small disk/it fills me with pride and joy; the absorption lines of its spectrum excite me/data memorization and transmission ongoing/only approximately eight thousand two hundred letters until arrival/all Oval systems GO*].

Just like in a grand orchestra, this was just one melodic line between the many being played simultaneously, all contributing to making a single global symphony nobody could hear, yet everyone unknowingly involved in its heuristic adagio. Maybe there are many others that nobody, not even in hindsight, has ever noticed, as if they were at frequencies to low or too high to be perceived. For example, what could be said when a little while later Pope John Paul the Third, the Restorer, fell victim to an automatic shutter that was supposed to stay up but that instead, despite every security system in place, suddenly came down on top of him and sent him to the morgue with a shattered neck? It would take another thirty years before scholars would place this, and other tiles, into the same mosaic, but by then so much time had passed and so many things had changed (for the better) that whoever came upon this hypothesis, or any of the many others, could do nothing but shrug their shoulders and say: "Nonsense! But then...even if it were true?"

If on one hand the progressive demolition, one piece at a time, of a certain vision of the world was in progress, on the other hand the void left by what was being destroyed, had to be – and was – promptly filled. For every end of a universe there is always the beginning of a new one, because the infinite balance is never up for discussion. Who could have thought that the AI (they were one but also many) was slowly (and silently) planning something strange, certainly, but also new and better? It had been able to guide the choices of the great multinational corporations thanks to its ever-growing presence on their board of directors. It had initially been employed as a consultant in various political cabinets and then even elected, not only at the local level but also the national due to its decisions always being revealed as the best outcome for all citizens and to the human candidates' increasing laziness.

After all, its programming was simply directed at optimization, at getting the *best* result. The fortunate thing was that, from the AI's perspective, the *best* for planet Earth still involved the presence of the human race [*a gamma ray blinded me for an instant and practically at the same time I was thrown about like a cork in a storm by a series of gravitational waves/ it's not the first time something like this has happened since I've been on my journey, but it makes me emotional every time when I think about two splendid neutron stars that, in only seconds, come together and become one/data memorization and transmission ongoing/all Oval systems GO*].

The statistical data outlined the ongoing change over time in every sector, but the climate was the first to be noticed. The annual IPCC report showed a clear trend inversion (there were even talks of a *collapse*) in global temperatures. This inversion was confirmed to have increased in the following years while the level of carbon dioxide in the atmosphere progressively diminished. Armed conflicts found stable mediation and defence budgets were steadily cut both in the west and in the east. Over a couple of decades the military companies that weren't forced to close, were converted to the aerospace sector. Investments in education, culture and science increased significantly, and global research partnerships were initiated that had been unthinkable just a little while before. In the projects and programs planned by the AI the word *competition* disappeared, and the word *collaboration* took its place. Over the course of those same years there was a noted collapse in the number of believers of all major religions. It was all there, black on white, and summarizing it like this makes it seem like the coming of a utopia, but it had got to the point that the accepted world view was such that to most global citizens it simply seemed like the right and most obvious thing to do [*diagnostic memory activated/positions fragmented by 14%: within the physiological effect norms after millennia of exposure to the interstellar currents/importance principle ON/all Oval systems GO*].

It's not like I had any doubts, but They knew my every move both inside and outside of the Network (given that nothing really existed outside the Network) which meant that They knew me better than I knew myself, so, They already knew that I wouldn't have any. It was like the question had already been asked, as if They had asked it every day for all of those years and I had answered it every day. Sure enough, when the time was right, They sent somebody to get me, not somebody to ask me.

I remember they knocked and had the courtesy to let me command the door to unlock and open on my own. I then saw four mosaic-eyed (I had never seen any in real life) androids enter the house and I asked myself immediately what the neighbours would say, since those kinds of machines had never been seen in that area.

"Congratulations, you've been chosen for the *Extrasolar Human Exploration Program 1.0*," announced the one standing in front of the others. I was aware of the existence of the project and its guidelines and knew enough to know that it was the most ambitious endeavour ever attempted in space, and this was why the chosen explorers would have to be human. Sending an AI, however sophisticated and self-aware, would be seen by the world as the usual, typical, robot mission, just the same as all the others over the last century, and this would have hopelessly compromised the reach, the meaning and the dream of the mission. It wouldn't have gone down as one of the great moments of history, and this, simply, wasn't the *best* thing for They [*the detection of Tau-Ceti's solar wind activates the clock increase, just like the beginning of the slowdown that will take me to my destination/I still can't resolve Tau-Ceti-j, but its star is so yellow – just a little bit more orange than the sun – it now unequivocally dominates my sky/ all Oval systems GO].* Of course, I was also clearly aware that there was no coming back.

"Me?" I raised my eyebrows, not possessing much else that I could move to show my disbelief. They hadn't released any details on its candidate selection process. Things were done differently now, and They didn't usually spend any time processing questions that were deemed unnecessary. That's also why none of the androids deigned to answer me.

"You won't need anything," continued the same machine, "we will take care of everything. You will be made comfortable, from now on we will take care of you."

Accompanied by a light buzzing, a magnificent latest generation floating platform entered my house. I'm not sure if my brother was there when I was taken away, but I remember his elderly face watching me from the other side of the glass (or was it a mirror?) in the migration room before the preliminary procedure. His smile and his *thumbs up* right before I gave in to the sedation. When I awakened (turned back on?) he was the first thing I saw. He was half-awake and slumped in an armchair next to me. I followed my new instinct (programming?) and got up and then sat down. Actually, I stood on my own two *feet,* and I watched him in silence from above. It was as if I were trying to reconnect something within me. Then he suddenly opened his eyes. He saw what I was, jumped to his feet and I (finally!) *hugged* him and *felt* him. Even if in a somewhat – so to speak – metallic way. We stood there. The sensation was so strange. I no longer had a heart that could accelerate, or a skin that could tingle and become warm. Neither did I possess eyes that could tear up nor a stomach that could fill with butterflies. Yet whatever it was, wherever it came from, in whichever way my new instinct (programming?) created it and made me feel the sensation – whether it was vector potentials, magnetic effects, calculated just for the occasion prime numbers – I still felt like calling it happiness [*Tau-Ceti-j is exactly where my calculations say it should be, shining in the middle of its habitable zone/active in all ways, like when all the lights in a stadium turn on/data memorization and transmission ongoing/clock increasing/all Oval systems GO*].

So, I'm (finally?) about to arrive at my destination and I feel *strange*. It could be because time has passed at a much quicker pace than I perceived or because of my malfunctioning memory, or because of both. Absolute time says thirty-one thousand six hundred twenty-two years have passed, but for me this journey has been just like a boardwalk stroll spent watching a different sun to yesterday rising [*clock at maximum value/propulsion activation on address coordinates #19C79A1 for orbital insertion in two thousand forty-eight seconds/all Oval systems GO*].

I am now as close to the planet as the distance from the moon to the Earth (how many arm spans was it?). I gather data just as cheerfully and enthusiastically as a kid searching for shells on the beach: slithering when he can, at times rolling around and using his lips. Each one was a victory. Each one had a story that could be heard by placing it close to the ears. Just by touching it with the tip of the tongue, each one said something about where it came from. The radius is about one and a half that of Earth and the mass is almost the same. Its density is however less than half and its resulting gravitational force is less than two thirds that of Earth. Its rotational axis is inclined by around forty-two degrees. And the day lasts almost twenty-nine hours. The dominant colour, at least on this side, is a slightly yellowish white criss-crossed by green and ochre pastel tones and shaped like fraying clouds, with intense light blue and precise brushstrokes where the sky is clear. I detect intense cyclonic activity in its vast tropical area.

Scanning the first data set from the spectrometer is like leaning your head back and opening your mouth to taste the snow on Christmas (is this a memory?). Oxygen and nitrogen abound, and the pressure at ground level seems satisfactory, as does the overall global temperature, at least on this side, with an average higher than on Earth and it never drops below zero. In fact, I can't make out the polar ice caps. The amount of ammonia, methane and carbon dioxide is not completely negligible, but I can't say that it's a crucial discriminating factor that makes it incompatible with human biology. In any event a workaround can probably be found, the same goes for the total absence of an ozone layer which means that radiation reaching the ground could be high [*further analysis requested/orbital insertion in twenty-eight hundred seconds/all Oval systems GO*]. The strength of the magnetic field is like a pat to the middle of the back. The (new) world observed on all wavelengths at the same time is a celebration of vibrations: optic, infrared and radio are only displays of frequency modulation. I think I can hear something emerging from the white noise. Something weak. Something recurrent. Something that becomes better defined the closer I get. Like placing a stethoscope on a man's chest to find out he's *alive*.

I cross the terminator and dive into the shadow zone, focusing my senses on the source of the signal [*routine auto programming activated/orbital insertion cancelled/adjusting route parameters/all Oval systems GO*]. I detect that the planet is (already) inhabited. There's no doubt, all the latest data points in that direction, and the electromagnetic emissions down there are certainly artificial in origin. Just like city lights on the other side of a lake (what's Ares City?). Even though I can't decode them, the automatic message that I received a few seconds ago was personally addressed to me (to me?).

[*Oval #273: planet Tau-Ceti-j has already been explored. Due to new technology I developed two years after your departure, the Extrasolar Human Exploration Program 2.0 was able to reach it in a time that was three thousand times faster than yours. The parameters were found to be compatible, and colonization was consequently undertaken with success. Your data will be maintained in the memory*].

That means that there is no longer any (necessary) need for me to stay here and so I won't stop. I no longer have any ties, only the ones I seek out for myself and the need to find a star about every forty thousand years to recharge. It's by optimizing this criterion that I have calculated my new route [*heating propulsion system activated in three…two…one…/clock decreasing/all Oval systems GO*]. I've combined it with the maximum number of possible stars to explore and therefore other worlds to visit. I have no objective other than the journey itself and recording information. I still have (once again?) a lot of memory space available, in any case I will continue to utilize the importance principle: as data is recorded, everything considered non vital will be deleted.

According to my calculations, I will reach the outer edge of the galaxy in a hundred million years, where the kingdom of the dried fig really begins. The trip will total around three months of travelling at a minimal clock. More or less like a summer vacation by the sea where Mum would cover us in anticancer protection first, and then Dad would buckle me into an orange life. The shoulders had been specially modified to make sure I always floated the right way up, just like an oval buoy. Then he throws me into the water, and they push me out towards the sea together, towards that untouchable horizon, and I laugh and wish it would never end.

Reward

by Franci Conforti

translated by Carlotta Codebò

Franci Conforti loves great characters, adventures in strong colors, nocturnal intuitions, dangerous points of view. She has always written, but started publishing in 2016. In addition to numerous short stories, she has five novels to her credit. Spettri e altre vittime di mia cugina Matilde, published by Delos Books (Odyssey Award 2016); Carnivori (Kipple, 2017) Kipple Award 2017; Stormachine, la macchina della tempesta (Delos, 2019) Vegetti Award 2019; Eden (Delos, 2021) Odyssey Award 2021. Spine (Urania Mondadori, 2022) Urania Award 2021.

1) The Nutcase

"Oh, it's that nutcase again. Be careful when you go outside, he likes to throw rocks."

We're in the company cafeteria. My colleagues are in the middle of breakfast but they stop to turn around. The chief forwarding agent, in his air force blue cyber coveralls, sips his coffee while keeping an eye on the situation from the glass window dominating the lobby. He's the one who gave the alarm.

Lia Tor, warehouse worker, coveralls the color of a cardboard box, stands up rather enthusiastically. "I bet it's Saito!" she says aloud. The moment they hear that name people leave their tables to go enjoy the show.

Only Pyotr Fedorov, blue cyber coveralls, security department, remains in front of the buffet. Smiling, he stares at the cold cuts behind the deli dispenser's plexiglass or, more likely, at Giulia Colombo, reflected in the shiny surface. She's also wearing blue coveralls and they used to go out. What else is there to say? He's cute, she's pretty and cheerful.

Pyotr grabs a bottle of soda by the neck, shakes his head and lazily walks up to the window. The nutcase is still there.

I've heard a lot of stories about Mr. Saito, even though I've never seen him because I haven't been working here long. So, when a few customer service reps in green coveralls request that the sliding door open, I follow them outside unconcerned about the small infraction I'm making. I've been assigned to Pyotr, and I'm not supposed to take my eyes off him because that's my job for today.

Right...my job. The new one, Human Resources. Before that, I was a green-coverall-wearing Customer Service Representative at the Milan company branch. It wasn't the right fit for me; I love people, but only from a certain distance. They moved me to the Archive Department, black coveralls. I thought they were so classy, but they were the only thing I liked about it. Otherwise, I felt more like a robot than the robots I worked with, and so, I ended up here, at the Peschiera branch. Well, more or less.

No coveralls, I'm still in my pyjamas. I work from home, through a mini-drone and an integrated 5-sense technology helmet. I swear, it's almost like I'm there. I love this new job. I'm tasked with observing interpersonal dynamics and figuring out how to supplement the salary of those who take part in the BENEFIT program. Just to be clear, we're not only talking about the company car, the happy hour with the famous guest or the discounted dream vacation, no, there are other things. Because what's truly important can't be bought.

After all, our department's secret motto is: *satisfied or fired.* I know it sounds funny, but if we can't find a way to make someone who works here genuinely happy, the Personnel Management Department puts in a recommendation to another company and then fires them, and that's just one example.

Meanwhile, Saito is still acting like a lunatic and we're enjoying the show from the balcony. The glittering city skyline can also be admired from here, at the edge of one of the great protective environmental domes. A magnificently green countryside interrupted by the gloomy softness of the woodland reflected in the reservoir lakes' surfaces. In the last fifty years Milan has expanded, it has become a fantastic babel of green spaces, multicultural neighbourhoods and solar bio-architecture. We're all quite proud of it.

"Bastards! Humans first! Damned sell-outs, traitors, slaves to capitalism! You're like the trees that vote for the axe because it's got a wooden handle!"

Saito, wearing a t-shirt and camoflage pants, has noticed us and is now yelling in our direction. He shows off the backpack full of rocks he's using to keep in check a couple of self-driving trucks and a dumb yellow gardener-bot, frozen in front of the gate with its sack of mulch to be disposed of in the bioreactor.

"He must have been drinking," comments a colleague wearing the pink coveralls of the Administration Department.

Saito pulls off his shirt and remains bare-chested. He has incredibly pale skin, a broad chest, square shoulders, and, maybe, a willingness to show off. A black and red tattoo takes up the right side of his neck and part of his back and chest. It's the old Japanese rising sun flag with sixteen rays.

"Fucking fascist, him and his tattoo. Look at him...It would be doing everyone a favour if he just disappeared off the face of the Earth."

"Now you're going too far, he's just a loser who's out of his mind."

"Oh, you really don't get it! Can't you hear what he's yelling? No mercy for..."

"Come on you two, stop it. Look at what he's doing."

"He's tying himself to the bars!" I yell out, but nobody hears me. I'm required to keep the mini-drone's microphone turned off. It's too late anyway; Saito has just cuffed himself to the gate.

I zoom in and notice that his hair is turning white and that his skin isn't as plump as it seemed. I look him up on the internet. Fabio Saito, second-generation Italian, drafting technician, ex-driver for our company. Eight years to retirement, no welfare payouts because he's in good health, yet the personal details are unforgiving: he'll be seventy soon, and after a hundred or so over the top protests, he's well-known to the authorities as a lunatic.

"Finish your breakfasts," says Pyotr to his blue coveralled colleagues, "I'll deal with it before that asshole hurts himself."

I hear some giggling and a harsh comment coming from the cardboard coloured coveralled warehouse colleagues. "He doesn't worry about us, but he does about *that guy*, our Pyotr."

"Must be his type; you know, between animals," spits out another one while I fly after Pyotr into the elevator.

That Pyotr Fedorov is a company anomaly is no secret, but I don't know much else about him.

Management advises us not to access the reports written by our previous colleagues, so we won't be influenced by them. That's why I only know the official details. Thirty-three years old, orphan, naturalized Italian at birth. Left the military academy at twenty when he failed the exams to become an officer. He's had fifteen different jobs and has been let go fifteen times in a row. He started working here at twenty-two years old and has never taken a sick day. Some general notes: undisciplined, troublemaker, not a union member. A hot head, but quick-witted and remarkably trust-worthy. Or rather: he won't accept any company benefits, yet he still participates in the BENEFIT program renouncing his right to privacy. Goodness! He's a hard nut to crack. That's why Pyotr is one of the few who can boast they have a living, breathing, human operator, me.

Following Pyotr, I leave the elevator and cross the paved quad that leads to the main gate.

The rocks rain down.

The self-driving trucks keep a safe distance, except for the stupid gardener-bot that's standing stock still, not far from Saito, risking his optics being destroyed.

Pyotr lengthens his stride and curls his fists. Oh shit...It'll take just one rock to break my mini-drone into pieces. I don't dare get any closer. But maybe I should? I don't know.

Rule number one: no physical, verbal or emotional violence.

What if those two start beating each other up? Would I also be held responsible?

Nothing like this was covered in the video lessons I took.

It's stressing me out. I call my supervisor, Charles David Johnson, ex-employee now consultant, living in Hawaii. They'll take it out of my paycheck seeing as, just my usual luck, the newbie support ended last week.

"Answer the phone, answer the phone, answer the phone..."

I'm on tenterhooks. Pyotr, hands on hips, weight on one leg, has come to a stop about ten yards away from the closed gate.

"Hello!" I don't acknowledge Johnson's greeting, and simply share my screen while dumping everything I know about the situation on him in real time, tripping over words and concepts.

"Relax, kiddo. Pyotr only ever oversteps boundaries when he knows he can," he tells me in an accent that makes his Italian sound strange.

"But procedure says..."

"Fuck procedure with Pyotr. Get out of his way and pretend you haven't seen anything."

It wasn't the answer I was expecting at all, especially knowing that these calls are recorded.

"Are you sure?" I ask unconvinced, "I really care about this job..."

Meanwhile, Pyotr has grabbed onto the gate with his hands, right where Saito has cuffed himself. They exchange a few words. They're probably provoking each other, or maybe trading insults. Pyotr sticks an arm through the gate, grabs Saito by the belt and pulls him towards him. No, it's not okay. Saito reacts as if he has been bitten by a snake. He wriggles around irritably, then he snaps open the cuffs and jumps back a few steps.

"Hey, where are you going? Come back sweetheart!" Pyotr yells after him. But Saito gives him the middle finger, spits out an angry *chikushou*! and strides off, cursing.

How the hell did he do that?

Johnson is still on the line, and he coughs slightly to get my attention, "Impressive, right?"

"But what did he say to make him run away like that?"

"Who knows? But I imagine that Saito is quite homophobic, and Pyotr has fun shocking guys like that. I'm not saying it's legal, but..."

"Oh, and we approve?" I simply comment, perplexed, not willing to go any further.

Johnson laughs raucously, laughing at me.

"Ha, ha, ha, my dear, wrong question: it's not up to us to approve. You're confused, but who isn't in our profession? Accept this piece of advice: think only of our mission, the rest isn't your problem. We don't judge, we take care of them. Our job is to understand what to offer them so that they can do their best and, obviously, be happy. That's what we put in the reports we send to Personnel Management. How and whether to make employees follow company guidelines and the respective policies is their job, not ours. Same with firings. Do you copy?"

I nod affirmatively and a pleasant sensation dissolves the knot I had at the base of my stomach.

2) Teamwork

Today I'm on shift with Giulia Colombo, Pyotr's ex. You should see her. She's tiny, a mass of bubbly energy behind two green eyes framed by a mane of red curls I envy, almost as much as I envy her ability to cheer up anyone she meets. It's part of her way of fixing things: she smiles at everyone, even when she doesn't feel like it. Well, at almost everyone.

Pyotr doesn't count and, when she meets him, Giulia darkens and rumbles like an incoming storm. Anyway, I like Giulia and I like working with her; everyone compliments her all the time and, it might seem stupid, but it's as if they were complimenting me a little too.

Giulia is easy, the algorithms know her wish list inside out: friendship, love, loyalty, social justice, solar ethics and caring for the environment. All stuff that unfortunately can't be bought, especially because, for her, LOVE is written in big capital letters and must walk arm in arm with all of the other above cited principles.

Is it wise to fall in love with someone who doesn't respect them, then? No. But it happens.

For instance, Pyotr happened to Giulia, and that's why, even in her case, the algorithms are useless. Lately her satisfaction and performance levels have dropped by thirty percent. It's not enough for Personnel Management that she pretend to smile. They want her to be genuinely happy.

"Colombo! Ah, how fortunate." A gangly guy wearing a pseudo regimental blue, black, and cardboard parcel paper coloured tie, typical of the Board of Directors, yells from the end of the hallway. The man waves an arm over his head, dodges secretaries and administrators to catch up with us. He's panting but he doesn't stop to catch his breath before he starts talking.

"You have to find that Pyotr guy who works with you right away. He's disconnected his coveralls and that lunatic is at the gate again. You have to come up with something, whatever you want, but you must fix the problem definitively, I repeat, *definitively*. He's gone too far this time. Mr....Mr. Baudrillard, my god I ran so fast, I'm out of breath...I was saying Mr. Baudrillard had the window down and...now he's in the gym, he's taking a shower. Eggs. Rotten. You don't know how bad it smells. His suit is ruined."

"But I'm on shift until evening, and Pyotr and I don't even get along any more."

"Even better! You'll keep an eye on him. I'll find someone to take your shift. Find Pyotr and badger him. You'll be a team. You'll be by his side until you find a solution to the problem. Definitively, I mean. No funny business. And your compensation will be doubled, promised. Can I count on you?"

Giulia screws her mouth up into a yes. Satisfied, the beanpole points his finger at me, hovering lightly around Giulia's shoulder.

"And the two of them can count on you, operator..." he says, coming closer and squinting his eyes so that he can make out the writing, "operator Ris. CfcmA27?"

I'm startled, usually no one notices me. I turn on the microphone.

"Of course, sir," I answer in a trembling voice because existing, at times, makes me emotional, "I request that an upgrade be enabled for the whole...team. And, thank you sir."

Only a little bit later and Giulia and I are standing in front of the bathroom door of a still-in-construction frozen goods warehouse. Pyotr has hidden himself away in here with Alberti, a blond contract lawyer. Giulia, arms crossed over her chest, yells at him from behind the door.

"You never change, huh? You're on shift and they're looking for you. Saito threw rotten eggs at the CEO."

"Ah," he says from inside.

"They want you to fix the problem. Once and for all."

"And how the hell do they think I'm supposed to do that?!"

"I don't know but figure it out or I'm going to have to stick to you like glue."

The door opens. Pyotr's hair is messy and he's adjusting his coveralls.

"And that would be just terrible, right?" He says in a low voice.

Giulia avoids him. Then she turns her back on him and heads down the hallway.

Pyotr fixes his hair and shakes his head as he watches her walk away.

"You'll never forgive me, huh?" He shouts as he goes after her.

I buzz along after them.

I'm once again in the infamous quad, at a safe distance from the gate where the usual crowd of curious onlookers and vehicles waiting to leave has gathered.

"I've got enough for all of you," Saito yells at us, showing us an old carton full of eggs.

"Open up," Pyotr orders the robot in control of the gate. Giulia holds him back by his arm.

"Hey, stop, stop, you can talk to him just fine from here."

"They said *definitively*, right?"

"Are you crazy? He's twice your size."

"But he's old."

"He'll sue you; guys like him want nothing more."

"My word against his. Stay here and take care of the drone while I clear that guy's head a little."

What does he mean by "take care of the drone?" A second later I can't see anything, Pyotr has quickly grabbed my mini-drone and is holding it tight in his fist.

"Let me go, let me go, you can't do that!"

He ignores me. See what happens when you're defenseless and only as big as a walnut.

"You can't do that," Giulia says as he places me in her hands.

"Too late, stick it in your pocket and distract the others for me."

Cursing under her breath, does as she's told.

I turn off the propellers. Shit, and now what? For the second time, on my own dime, I call Johnson. In just a few seconds I manage to stammer out an explanation of the situation.

He laughs, that evil Anglo-Saxon! We're all risking our jobs here and he's laughing.

"Uhm, kiddo, keep this between us, okay? Never worry about Pyotr. If they haven't gotten rid of him yet, they're not going to do it now."

"But why? They've just abducted me!"

He roars with laughter once again. "Various reasons, the first is that he works his butt off doing the jobs that others don't want to do, like taking care of Saito. The second is that he hooks up with basically everyone, even the big shot from the union. He's like that woman in the Archive Department, what's her name? Sandra, right These...*habitual relations* of theirs, enhance company benefits, but, as you Italians say, 'I've said it here, and I'll deny it here.' Do you copy?"

I give up asking him whether it's either legal or moral. I have other problems now. Giulia is taking me out of her pocket, and I have to assess the situation.

The gate is open, Saito is panting, and his face is screwed up in a grimace. He's holding onto his ribs with one hand and fixing his shirt with the other. Pyotr, carton full of eggs tucked under his arm, turns back towards us.

"Asshole," he says passing by us and going towards the outdoor showers, the ones used by truckers. He smells disgusting and he's covered in dust, egg yolk and sticky egg whites.

Giulia goes after him. "Listen, you massive idiot, if they threatened you and beat you up, you just wouldn't do it again?"

Pyotr keeps going without answering her. I think it's his way of admitting she's right.

"But I do have an idea, listen to me..." she insists, lengthening her stride to keep pace with him.

The same old stupid yellow gardener-bot turns on the nearby lawnmower and stops me from hearing the rest.

3) Hardware Graveyard

Two days after the egg throwing incident, Giulia has convinced Pyotr to put her plan into action. I follow them down the white hallway that leads to the IT lab.

"I miss you," he tells her, at a certain point.

"Go fuck yourself," she mutters, exasperated.

"Don't I do that enough?"

Kiss her, I think. Stop her and kiss her. I know, it's a stupid idea, worthy of immediate firing and pressing of charges. I know, this isn't the right way to go about things; it's like something straight out of an old movie and in real life there are other things you need to do to rebuild a relationship, but they keep circling each other like two animals and it's starting to give me anxiety.

I feel bad for him, and I feel bad for her. How is it possible that two adults can't figure out how to talk to one another and come to an understanding?

"Welcome, I was waiting for you," says the lab door as it opens.

We're in a big room with white, shiny walls. Shelves and counters made of the same material are covered in multicoloured cables, Q-motherboards, dismembered robots, mechanical arms, wheels, heads and so on. New and recycled, all arranged with maniacal orderliness.

"Do you want to have a look inside or would you rather talk about it here?" Fumagalli, the barely twenty-year-old computer engineer in white coveralls, asks. With *inside* he means inside the sterile area. Going in there, means being locked in a transparent booth, like the Pope mobile, but on a monorail.

"No, here's more than fine," Daniel Strauss, emerging from behind some shelving, decides for all of us. He's the social structuralist bio-economist that Giulia has involved in the plan. Daniel, with his views on social and environmental politics, is pretty famous and has been a part of the company's Technical Committee for years. He's wearing a pink suit, flower print silk shirt and sneakers. He has also shaved his head into a golden-haired mohawk. He's over seventy, but Giulia stares at him with infinite admiration and Pyotr can't stop side-eyeing them.

"First of all, thank you for remembering this robot integration project. Seeing it fail would have hurt me deeply," says Strauss, strolling back and forth in the space between white work counters. "I've modified it based on your needs and I've submitted it to the Board of Directors. They've approved it, but we will be working within the individual employee autonomy framework moving forward. In practice this means they'll give you the resources, but it'll be your own initiative. However, I can assure you they're all cheering for us. If we pass the first test, we'll begin the actual trial period by offering the service to every unemployed person in suburban area 52."

"So you mean that if it goes bad, it's all our fault and if it goes well, they'll take all the credit?" Pyotr spits out acerbically.

Strauss observes him calmly, making his sun-yellow mohawk wave back and forth.

"Yes, that's it exactly. As a freelancer I'm used to the risk but, of course, as an employee you're free not to adhere to the employee autonomy framework. If you want to withdraw, now is the time. I can personally request your substitution, so that you don't risk a negative write-up, if that's what you mean."

Pyotr clenches his jaw and grumbles a no, that's not what he meant.

"Good, I'm glad. So can I share my vision with you now?" continues Strauss.

Giulia can't realistically smile and nod any more than she's doing right now, while Pyotr merely grimaces. Fumagalli just looks like someone who's already heard this story too many times before.

"Well, then." Strauss says. "If you think about it, generally speaking, Mr. Saito isn't completely wrong. We're no longer in the early two-thousands, we have the technology and it's profitable for companies, which is why they're heavily automatizing. The problem is unemployment; resulting in alienation, crime, and market contraction due to part of the population falling into poverty. The recent pandemics and our new approach to sexual morality are only masking the phenomenon through a demographic contraction, but it's only a question of time and…"

Strauss pauses for effect and looks our way.

"Well," he continues, "as I've been theorizing for a while now, there is a solution: placing robots in every economic sphere and not simply limiting them to production. In other words, as subjects instead of objects because robots shouldn't be just producers but also consumers. If not all, at least some of them, and in this case, I'm referring particularly to hybrid robots, based on quantum neural networks, the ones we had to shelve because of the educational costs. We should instead compensate these robots for the jobs they perform, rewards they'll then spend to be updated by humans. A perfect cycle. Imagine it. They'll begin with simple jobs and then, for one or two hours a day, they'll go to their teacher's houses and pay to learn how to undertake more qualified roles. Oh, I can already see my grandmother teaching good manners to a robot or how to set the table or how to serve tea. Think of the artisans, cobblers, glassmakers, beekeepers, all the traditional knowledge that would otherwise be lost. Not forgetting the cumulative life experience of everyday people. The memories, the love stories, the trips, the movies..."

"And what in the hell would our Saito teach?" butts in Pyotr, rude and far too hostile.

"Nothing at all really, or anything, it doesn't matter for now. What matters is that they spend time together and communicate, but I think it'd be best to suggest that Mr. Saito teach something specific. I don't know, oil painting. Baking apple pies. For now, the robots just have to learn how to react correctly to human expectations and unpredictability."

"Why would a company shoulder the cost for all this?" Pyotr interjects once again, ignoring Giulia's elbowing.

"It would be a bargain for the company," Strauss replies, "if it works on a mass scale, it would remarkably decrease a robot's educational costs, it would ensure credit flow, new market openings, warehouse stock reduction. We reward the robots, they reward people who will in turn, use that reward to buy from the very same companies that put it into circulation in the first place. Think about it, it would supplement the universal basic income and wouldn't end up ensnared in bureaucracy because the rewards are taxed on input and detracted from company budgets. It would not only be decent work but also fun, free, and lucrative. Saito will like it. It's exactly what he's calling for after all: humans first. Without mentioning how gratifying it is for people to preach to an audience or, simply, be listened to and accepted unconditionally as robots do, something that shouldn't be underestimated."

Pyotr crosses his arms. "Uhm, maybe it'll work on normal people, but not with that lunatic."

"Well, then if it works on him, it'll all be downhill from there," replies Strauss turning affably towards Fumagalli, "And you? How far along are you with the modifications?"

Luca Fumagalli, engineer, is distracted. He's petting an arm ending in a pincer that, from behind the counter, is softly pulling on his white coveralls. When he notices we're all staring at him, he smiles embarrassedly.

"Uhm...it's a discarded prototype that hasn't been retired, it was intended for the customer service office front desk. Neural network, never used because its learning ability is much too slow and paying programmers just to talk to it didn't make any sense. I put it to work with the garden robots. Even if it thinks too much, it manages all right. Give me a couple of days and I'll have finished working on it. I've added a pocket for the rewards just in case Saito is a complete technophobe. Do you want to see the rewards?"

"That would be great," Giulia says enthusiastically, using her hands to fluff up her red mane of hair.

Fumagalli pulls some colorful, transparent gem-like objects from his pocket.

"Rechargeable microchips. The green tablets are for food and plants, the blue ones for IT, the yellow ones for clothing and so on..."

"Where's the catch Strauss? Because there always is one, right?" Pyotr says.

"Call me Daniel, if there's a catch then I haven't done my job well. If we do find one we'll make sure to get rid of it," he retorts. "I think that every situation can be a win-win and I refuse to believe that there is an 'us' and a 'them,' an enemy or an evil to eradicate. No enemies, no evil, only adversaries, and actually our adversary is our best ally. Only he can strengthen our capability for growth and to include our diversity. Our ability to absorb contradictions, the day and the night, good and evil to create something better, something that is continuously evolving. Our success can never be measured through the defeat of our adversaries, but rather in *their* success together with *ours*. For this operation to be successful I would like all of you to share this approach, I know it's not easy, but no one should suffer a defeat."

We're all silent. Is it really possible to act like that?

"What if Saito keeps the rewards and comes back to throw more eggs?" Pyotr asks, bringing the discussion back to more practical matters. Giulia glares at him, but he just mocks her by raising the corner of his mouth.

"Can I be honest?" Daniel asks rhetorically, "Who gives a damn about the eggs. Taking into account the huge benefits for both the company and for the disadvantaged, a handful of rewards and a CEO's wounded pride are hardly important."

Pyotr finally nods affirmatively. "Okay. Now can we look at this robot-*thing*?"

Fumagalli nods his head towards the recharging robot hidden behind the counter. It's still clinging to his coveralls with its pincer. "Come on, N68, come out. Let everyone see you."

It's about the height of a pony and slowly advances by raising skinny rubbery-hoofed legs. It sports a mechanical arm with a pincer instead of a head. Despite its appearance and its many eyes, it behaves almost like an animal.

I fly around it, its optics following me curiously. There's a nice dent on its custard-yellow thorax. Is this maybe the stupid gardener robot that got hit by Saito's rocks?

Pyotr, hands low on his hips, shakes his head. "This thing is too fragile; Saito will tear it to pieces."

"It doesn't matter, it was meant for the trash anyway. We're just using it for testing."

I feel bad. They shouldn't talk about it like that in its presence.

"What nonsense," Giulia says, "this robot is sturdy and beautiful. I like the eyes it has on the front, they're very expressive. You'll see, forget about dooming it to the graveyard, I'm sure it'll teach you all a lesson: it'll be the start of a new era."

Right, Giulia! I smile to myself, unseen by everyone else.

4) Mercy

"No, let's take that one. I feel like driving."

Moral of the story: we're in an old company car with manual drive and we're going to Saito's. It'll be a surprise.

"Relax, it has an automatic transmission, I don't have to do anything," Pyotr tells Giulia, who's gripping onto the grab handle over the car door with both hands.

"Automatic transmission, airbags, a 16-valve petrol engine..." he continues, almost enamoured.

"Petrol?!" she repeats, eyes wide.

I'm shocked too. Not only are we risking getting into an accident: we're polluting, and we could go up in flames! Incredible how some idiots insist on driving themselves.

Pyotr, meanwhile, has his hands on the wheel and a blissful smile on his face.

Passing by the Little Love Motel, he leaves Viale XXV Aprile, turns into Via Alighieri and then goes up an unpaved road. The robot's ocular lights flash furiously as they process data. The trip lasts fifteen minutes, including a U-turn because we'd gone down the wrong street.

Giulia , who has been holding her breath, only lets it out once Pyotr has parked between two poplars at the end of a dirt road, out in the middle of the countryside.

"Destination reached," says the robot in a syncopated voice. We turn to stare at it. It has got stuck in the seat and it'll take some time to pull it out. The car doors open and Giulia and Pyotr both get out, one from on either side. They're in casual clothing so as to not annoy Saito.

Pyotr is wearing a black t-shirt that shows off his muscles, his shoulders and also a streak of sweat down the middle of his back. Giulia lets out a huff because the day is already hot. She fidgets with her dress to let some air through. It's the type that's trendy nowadays: super short and covered with little flower appliques.

"What a ruin!" she says nodding her head towards a dilapidated farmhouse some fifty yards away. No door, Virginia creeper climbing all the way up to the roof and swarms of buzzing mosquitoes everywhere. On the right, two piles of debris seem to be guarding the rusted-out hulk of an old abandoned van. The only correct way to define it all is: poor and squalid.

Pyotr takes a moment to look around and take in his surroundings. We all notice right away that the first thing Saito sees, every morning as he leaves his house, is his former company: down there beyond the rice paddies, on the horizon.

The blue glass windows, the energy tower, the terraces full of flowers and the saplings growing on the warehouses' rooftops. They taste of hope, they smell of the future.

"Shit," says Pyotr, shaking his head. He goes back to staring at the robot stuck in the car seat and Giulia who's leaning over it and trying to get it out.

"Come on, move that leg, raise it, turn it, no, turn it this way..."

The robot struggles, but can't do it, and Giulia is too stressed out to notice that her skirt has risen. Pyotr sees it and just stands there dumbfounded, enjoying the view. I buzz around him, making my propeller spin faster to get him to understand that he needs to cut it out.

"Giuly, stop it," he says, "there's no point in making all this fuss, let me see if he's here first."

N68, Giulia, and I watch him walk away, confident and indolent.

Pyotr vanishes into the house's darkened entrance, but before we can even start worrying he appears again. He comes back towards us with his head down and his lips pressed tightly together. He avoids Giulia as she steps closer to him questioningly and goes straight for the car.

"No, we can't;" he says curtly, "not like this, let's go."

He sits in the driver's seat, his expression grim, hands gripping the wheel hard.

Giulia leans through the open car window. "What the hell's got into you?"

He doesn't answer. Giulia becomes worried. "Is he dead?"

Pyotr shakes his head.

"Drunk? Sick? A needle stuck in his arm?"

But Pyotr isn't the type to be shocked by those kinds of things.

"Ok, then if you won't talk, I'll go take a look myself."

He grabs her wrist and strokes it with his thumb, either to make her relax or to get himself to calm down. In any case, to stop her.

"No. If we wake him up, he's going to tell us to go to hell. If we make him our offer, here, like this, we're taking away the only thing he has left."

"Which is?"

Pyotr hesitates. He doesn't want to talk about it, but he has no choice.

"It's useless. Look, it's a matter of...of dignity. That man might be an asshole, but..." He shakes his head and hits his hand on the wheel.

"But what? We're here to offer him a dignified life. Not to take it from him, he's already got that covered, living as he does."

Giulia is pissed off; her red curls seem to come to life as she wriggles out of Pyotr's hold. "Take your hands off me," she says, voice hard.

He makes a show of raising his hand and places it back on the wheel.

"You couldn't care less about Saito, huh?" he says bitterly.

"More than you do. You run away every time there's a problem."

"Bullshit, get in." He feels around the dashboard, looking for the ignition.

Giulia crosses her arms over her chest and looks askance at him.

"You have no idea, I said get in, we're leaving."

"You're not the boss here..."

They're fighting. Again. I turn my audio on, and while I'm at it I add a little reverb to make my voice seem more authoritative.

"Hey, you two, stop it. What do you think you're doing?"

They both stare at the drone in surprise. Especially Pyotr.

"It's just that..." he tries to find a justification for his behaviour, "I didn't think Saito lived like this, I mean, it's 2081, Italy, what the hell!"

He pauses, but he knows it's not enough, Giulia keeps staring at him and I wait in silence.

"He sleeps on a mattress on the ground," he adds in the end, "he's nailed a plastic tarp over it to stop the mosquitoes and the drops of water that fall through the roof. He uses the fireplace to...cook. No electricity, no fridge. He's...he's got a mound of canned goods. That's what he eats, and in the other room are the rusty weights and equipment he uses to keep in shape. He has a three-foot-tall plastic blue bin. The kind used to transport oil. It's filled with rainwater, and he keeps... he keeps a folded towel on its ring handle. And all that shit is kept neat and tidy."

He takes a breath. "And don't tell me that he asked for it. Even if it's true, it doesn't change anything. In fact, what that really means is that the alternative for him is...worse. He's defending something that's precious to him."

"What?"

Pyotr shrugs. "I don't know. His war, maybe. Maybe without it he'd already be dead. He'd let himself go, I don't know, like other old guys. What would he have left? And then now...I don't think he wants us to see him like this, us and especially me."

I bite my tongue and keep my doubts to myself. Pyotr identifies with Saito? If they fire him, will he end up the same? In thirty years could he end up in his place?

Giulia taps the car window. "Fine, I get it. He'd say no. He's the enemy, or not, he's just an adversary and we should show mercy. We need to think of something else."

Pyotr purses his lips and nods. His eyes look suspiciously wet. He takes a hand off the wheel and offers it, palm up, to Giulia. Maybe it's his way of thanking her? To make peace with her without angering her? He stays frozen like that while Giulia thinks about it. His hand remains facing the sky until she places her own over the depths of his soul. He holds his breath at the contact.

"We're lucky, you and me, we're also both idiots," he tells her softly.

"Oh yeah? And what do you think I should do?"

He shrugs without moving the hand she's holding. He doesn't want her to fly away.

"You could...you could stop hating me and find a place for me too."

I spin my optics towards the scenery, put my drone on stand-by and take off my helmet.

I'm in my room.

I can finally see where I left my coffee which means I can stop clutching at the air over the table. As I bring the cup to my lips, I use the back of my other hand to wipe my eyes. Darn it, I hate crying, and I hate those two. Darn it all over again.

I redo my braid and open up my chest by taking a deep breath. I need to stay calm. Can I do anything for them? No. But I can find the right way to introduce the robot to Saito. If Pyotr identifies with him, maybe I can use the same techniques.

I think back to what Mr. Johnson said about Pyotr's hidden company benefits. At the beginning I'd thought it was nonsense, but he wasn't lying. I checked: I found his paycheck, the bonuses for his night guard shifts and for working as part of management's security detail. There were also benefits he had had been offered directly but that he had turned down, not just over the years, but even recently: season tickets, the kavra course, the car we came here with. About the hidden benefits, a colleague of mine had written: "In conclusion, Mr. Pyotr Fedorov has a need to break the rules, a need to let others know that he breaks them and to be accepted for who he is. My suggestion is that these benefits be reconfirmed because the infractions committed on my watch have always turned out to be pro-company. The tasks refused are always useless or potentially damaging and not those that he found disagreeable. On the contrary, the personal risks he incurs and the sexual favours he doles out to the benefit of many colleagues, make him a precious resource and an element of social enhancement. See attachment B."

All true, in black and white.

I remember reading all that and feeling particularly uncomfortable. The problem between Giulia and Pyotr was precisely his infidelity and there was a clear conflict of interest with the company. I spent a sleepless night checking if management had put into action strategies to manipulate Pyotr's behaviour in their favour, but nothing came up. The problem between Giulia and Pyotr was, and is, only between Giulia and Pyotr. But I'm going off on a tangent. My problem now is Saito.

Could I offer Saito a hidden benefit to make him accept the robot and the rewards?

If doing it to Pyotr is legal then it should be for him too. Whether it is morally acceptable I have no idea. Maybe it isn't in either case, and I find myself having to choose between idolizing the truth, and the pursuit of someone else's happiness. They pay you to satisfy them, Mr. Johnson would remind me if I consulted him on the matter.

This is where half-truths come into play.

Besides, Saito's war isn't against the robots. It's against us, against the company, which means he mustn't know the company is in favour of the initiative and that it would be a win for both. He'd never accept a win-win situation, he would never accept that the result could satisfy both. So, is it right for me to deceptively remove otherwise insurmountable obstacles? I don't have a sure answer, but I know that's what people like me are here for.

I put my helmet back on and reactivate the drone.

Pyotr and Giulia still seem to be frozen in their fragile, bitter moment of contact. They're looking anywhere but at each other. Time's up, I'm sorry lovebirds, but there's work to do.

I turn on the audio. "Hey, listen to me, I know what to do. N68 was built to work at the customer service desk. Let's teach it what it needs to know and then let it go by itself."

Giulia steps away from the car window and Pyotr places his hands on the wheel once again. I don't think he's understood what I said, but she has. She twirls a curl around her forefinger and thinks it over.

"Too risky, if Saito tries to break it to pieces, I want to be able to step in and try to convince him."

"I'll stay," I say, "many robots have a support drone."

"No, Saito used to work for the company, he'll figure out that it's a remote-controlled model. He'll catch you right away. Just think about it, as distrustful as he is."

Right, I hadn't thought of that. The alternative would be modifying the chassis to make it look like a robot-drone; it's easy, but illegal. Enough to press charges and fire whoever is responsible on the spot, and I care about this job.

So I try something different and address the robot directly. It's not like those two pay any attention to him anyway, same way they keep ignoring me too.

"N68 have you ever worked autonomously? Not as a gardener I mean, but in contact with humans."

It extends its mechanical arm, and its pincer-shaped face pops out from the car door. Just listening isn't enough, it wants to see too. It wants to gather data from our facial expressions, just as we would.

"Yes," it answers, its voice a bit syncopated, "I went to the Mezzate Farmers' Market for their gardening special offers. I bought twenty-five kilos of GREENBIG lawn seeds, a KIRKA shovel, three hundred BLUEBELL roses. I haggled with the traders. 6.389 percent discount. They delivered the goods on time, Luca was pleased."

"Luca?"

"Yes. The engineer Luca Fumagalli. We are friends, he told me so."

"Ah, any other experiences?"

"Not yet. But I've tried. Now I know that showering truckers don't want to chitchat."

The three of us exchange amused glances.

"If we give you instructions on how to behave with Mr. Saito will you follow them?" Giulia asks.

"Yes, of course. Following instructions is easy."

I interject. "Do you know who Mr. Saito is? Do you remember him?"

"Yes: Fabio Saito, seventy years old, *'Humans first, you bastards! Damn you all: sell outs, traitors'*..." it says, mimicking his voice perfectly.

"Shh! Are you crazy? Lower your voice, or he'll think we're aping him," interrupts Giulia.

"*Aping him*?" asks N68.

I interject. "Laughing at him, got it? You can't do that... now tell me, have you and Saito ever talked to each other before?"

"No, we've only thrown rocks at each other."

"You threw rocks at him too?"

"Yes, but the gate was closed. I have to improve my aim."

We glance at each other once again. This time we're perplexed. Giulia's expression changes.

"No, we can't do this. Imagine if he had actually hit Saito with a rock? What ever happened to the laws of robotics?"

N68 interjects with a certain enthusiasm. "One hundred and two laws of robotics on the books. The rocks were thrown from a distance of five metres from the target, purely for communication purposes. I was actually wondering if there was a human language based on rocks: rhythm, strength, direction... incomplete analysis."

We look at each other crestfallen. It's clear now why training a neural network hybrid takes so long and is so expensive, and why learning, just like for a human being, never ends for them.

"You're right, it's too risky," I admit, disappointed. I want to scratch my head, but I realize that it's stuck in my helmet, inside my dimly lit room.

Pyotr, on the other hand, who has yet to say a word, doesn't agree.

"They'll get along, they're both crazy. Saito isn't a helpless old lady, he'll be fine."

"But he'll provoke it and the robot might react," Giulia points out to him.

"We'll tell it not to do that."

"No, it's not enough, let's stop fooling around. N68 can't be controlled remotely. Who'll stop it if, when faced with a crazy guy, it goes crazy?"

Pyotr turns and stares into my camera. "What do you think? You could pretend to be a robot-drone. Are you up for it?"

I'm speechless. Then I stammer something out: "I don't know...the mini-drone weighs less than an ounce...how can I stop it?"

"We'll program a word, no, listen, a special sound. When N68 hears it, it must go into standby."

I can feel my panic rising. I have the hunch that everything is going to go badly: a total disaster.

"What if Saito destroys my drone? We're all here unofficially and I'll have to re-buy it and be paying for it for years...if they don't press charges and fire me first, that is. Just when I've found a job that I like." My voice is whiny and I'm not proud of it.

"If you have to pay back the drone, though, you'll have an advantage..." Pyotr blurts out, regretting it right away and lowering his gaze.

"That's what happened to me," he opens up, "they won't fire you until you pay everything back. I was working in the company for a month when I destroyed a crane, I'll finish paying for it in twenty years. I was lucky, without that accident they would have already kicked me out, I don't know how many times, and without this job, I don't know where I would have ended up."

Does Pyotr really think that's the reason why he hasn't been fired?

I bring up the file from his first year right away. I find the accident. The ruling says that he has ten percent joint liability, but they only collect a truly laughable amount every month: those two cents are surely not the reason they keep him around. They've also tried telling him so, but he doesn't want to believe it. He's convinced that they fudged the ruling to help him out, he believes that the crane falling was all his fault, and that, in his own way, he's repaying that debt and that favour.

I get back to the incoming remote images. Pyotr is standing terribly close and is staring at the drone, which means he's actually staring at me.

"So, what's your name?"

"Me?" I ask, confused.

He smiles. "Of course, who else?"

"Caterina," I answer, breaking yet another rule.

"If anything happens, all three of us will take the blame, promise."

Giulia nods her head affirmatively from behind him.

"Ok...ay," I stammer, not all that convinced, "then I'll explain to N68 what we're going to do. In the meantime, you guys pull him out of there."

5) No One Should Come Out the Loser

Speaking of breaking the rules, Pyotr was hungry. He's the type of guy who loses all sense of rational thought when he's hungry. They left me and the robot in front of Saito's door and went off to have lunch at Asina Luna, an old *trattoria* right behind a row of lime trees down there. It's a romantic spot, I'm happy for them. A little bit less for me who's stuck here. It's a beautiful day, the wind has picked up and is pushing the large white clouds away.

Mini-drones hate the wind, they're made to fly inside between desks and hallways. So I land on N68's custard-yellow back and use my suction cup to make sure I don't get blown away.

"Can you hear me?" I ask Giulia and Pyotr.

"Perfectly, they've just brought out the *antipasti*," he says, "you can go whenever you're ready."

"N68?" I say.

The robot emits a series of sounds reminiscent of the doorbells in old films. Ringtone, pause; ringtone, pause. Simple and effective.

Mr. Saito appears at the door, half dazed. The morning's muggy humidity is but a memory, and the cool breeze provides relief. He's barefoot, wearing track pants, and his beard is unkempt and white. He squints his eyes because of the reverb, and he rubs his buzz cut back and forth.

"What the fuck," he says softly on seeing the robot planted in the middle of his weedy yard. His expression changes once he recognizes the logo on its side.

"Oh, so that's how it is. Those assholes are sending tin hit men after me now. I'll show you…"

I hold my breath as N68, recklessly, takes a step forward.

"Hello, Mr. Saito," it says, but Saito kicks both of us, sending us off balance. We swerve to the side, N68's legs crossing together like a shrimp in an effort to stay upright.

"Hello, Mr. Saito," N68 tries again. Doesn't matter, he comes after us and kicks us again twice. This time the nutcase uses more force, and we end up pushed back by a few metres.

Don't be so polite! I want to yell at N68, but it'd be a mistake. I have to stay calm and avoid setting off the robot. I could suggest that it…

"Hel…"

There's no time for me to say anything at all. With a crazed grin, Saito attacks once more and I close my eyes just as I feel a series of punches rain down on me. But N68 dodges the punches by suddenly positioning itself to one side. Then again, and again, and again.

I'm stunned, I admire its speed as well as the elegance of the move.

Wheezing a bit, Saito laughs. He realises that the robot is fast and isn't just going to let him beat it up. So, he comes slowly closer, extending his hand, just as he would with a dog. He then brushes N68's pincer with his palm. The robot doesn't squeeze, it doesn't move, and so Saito grabs it by the neck.

Stalemate. N68 doesn't do anything, nor does it seem frightened.

"Who the fuck sent you?" Saito yells close to the microphone.

The robot's ocular cameras flash, and I keep my fingers crossed.

"Hello Mr., Doctor, *signor* Saito, nobody sent me. This is all part of my education and training."

"Huh, what the fuck are you blabbering about?"

"When I'm not working, I try to find people I can learn from."

"And you came all the way here? Right to me? Ha! Who are they trying to fool? I don't buy it."

"I like it, *I don't buy it. Ha! Who are they trying to fool?* I'd also like to learn, *Bastards, traitors. You're like the trees that vote for the axe because its handle is made of wood!* Will you teach me that too?"

Saito drops it as if it were a snake.

"What the heck are you? A spy? A rebel robot?"

"I don't know. I'd like to learn strange sayings, weird phrases, the ones that nobody uses any more. I'd like to...understand."

Saito stands up straight and pulls himself together. He looks around, trying to find traces of the enemy hiding nearby in the vegetation.

"Do they know you're here?" He asks, still looking around him.

"I don't know. I'm an autonomous robot, with a neural learning network, reconnaissance drone and no remote control. They no longer teach me anything. Teaching costs too much. But I can help in the garden. If I make a mistake, I'm only good for the dump and the recycling centre. If I learn, I'll make fewer mistakes."

"Hold on a second. What did you say you were?"

Here we go, the moment of truth has arrived. Everyone knows how these advanced neural network models were a failure. Is Saito taking the bait?

"Quantum neural hybrid, 2Gg4N68series, waiting for the landfill."

Saito circles around me and N68. He does it a couple of times. He thinks about it.

"Don't you have a normal name?"

"Not yet. Should I open the voice-recording program for names?"

Saito doesn't answer. He bends down, tilts his head, sees the paws and muddied abdomen. He squints his eyes and then looks off into the distance, towards the company. It's quite a walk from down there to here and it rained last night too.

"You're like a dog," says Saito, "Do you know how to say it in Japanese? Inu."

"Inu, for admin Saito? Should I record it?"

"Uhm, he mumbles, trying to hide a small smile, "do what you want."

"Thank you. Then Inu can stay here and learn? Can I?"

"And what do you want to learn?" Saito asks, still suspicious. But the robot recognizes his tone and lets out a pleased hum, starting from its abdomen, like a huge purring cat.

"Every man has knowledge that he deems important. I'd like to learn that first. Then *bastards, you and yours...too.*"

"Stop that," Saito protests, because hearing your own voice at that volume is genuinely annoying, "I got it. It's fine."

"Really?"

"Are you deaf? I said yes."

"Thank you, teacher, these are for you. For your time and for the...risk you're running teaching me. I hope they're enough for now."

Well done N68, adding the element of risk was a surprise. Saito is already looking at it differently, almost in understanding, while N68's thorax opens up to take out the rewards inside and offer them to the man.

"What the hell are these? Candy?"

"Compensation. Bearer bonds. Green for food, blue for IT and robotics, yellow for clothing and household items."

Saito stretches out his hand hesitantly, like a frightened child, but there's also traces of a smile forming on his face.

"Did you steal them?!"

N68-Inu flashes indecisively. "No, I earned them to pay the humans I take lessons from. I've chosen you."

I hold my breath; I can't understand whether the concept of profit is upsetting or attractive to our guy. Darn it, Mr. Saito, don't be difficult, you have nothing, you could really use those rewards, come on, take them.

"They've paid you like a human being..." Saito insists. "But whatever, it doesn't matter because I don't want them anyway," he says, turning around and walking back into the house.

I curse to myself, we almost had him. I just hope he hasn't figured out the plan and gone off to get a hatchet to cut us up into pieces. Fortunately, after just a few moments, he reappears holding a fruit crate.

He stares at the robot, as if trying to establish a sort of wordless interspecies communication. He sets the crate down vertically in front of N68-Inu and sits on it. His hands are a bit swollen and ruined. N68-Inu, in turn, crouches on the ground, like a sphinx: neck straight, pincer at the ready.

Saito's face hints at a smile and I notice that he's missing a tooth, maybe two, on the left side of his mouth.

"Listen, Inu," he says, "to see why they're all traitorous bastards, you must first learn the facts then understand them. Like, I don't know, a haiku. Do you know what that is?"

"I'll look it up on the web. Found it: form of poetry from Japanese literature, with only seventeen syllables, using a 5-7-5 pattern."

"Exactly, this is knowing but not...understanding. Understanding is reading a haiku like a human being and being able to talk about it like a human being would. That means having your own opinion and believing in it."

"If I understand haikus then will I also understand *you're like the trees that vote for the axe*?"

"Yes, if you can figure that out, then you can understand anything. Even what they're doing to us, *those bastards*. It won't be easy; it might take a long time."

"That's why I'm destined for the landfill, it takes me too much time and I can only learn from my mistakes," says N68-Inu, "will you still teach me?"

Saito gets up, throws away the fruit crate and sits cross-legged on the ground in front of N68-Inu.

"Thank you, Saito-san," says the robot sitting on its haunches. I, however, find myself latching onto its tilted back, and I'm forced to rotate every one of my optics or otherwise I'll be stuck staring at the sky.

"Good," says Saito, "now I have to figure out from where we should start."

He looks out towards the horizon, does some sort of gymnastics with his fingers, rolls his shoulders like before a race, half closes his eyes, and breathes in through his nose.

I don't envy him; I wouldn't really know where to start either.

Then he starts to recite carefully:

The strongest of ropes
Either it unites two men
Or binds only one

A few minutes later the sound of a chirp interrupts the training.

"Free time is over, Saito-san. My gardening job starts in an hour. Can I come back tomorrow? Statistically it's probable that with time...I'll come to understand. I already feel... *transformed*," it concludes with a small bow of its pincer.

We get up and leave, walking along the country roads, with this alien gait of ours. We'll return to the company on foot, at a modest pace.

Giulia and Pyotr, still in the *trattoria*, can't stop themselves from commenting.

"Good job Caterina, you did it!"

"And it was so scary when he attacked you, but then

look what happened! Let's tell Daniel right away, he'll be ecstatic."

"Daniel?"

"He said that's what we should call him."

"Oh, that Strauss guy, I'm not so sure about him. First, we should..."

I stop listening to them. My optics and sensors are all tuned towards Saito as we're leaving him behind. Hands on hips and toothless grin, he picks up the fruit crate again and tucks it under his arm as he watches us leaving.

"A rebel robot, we'll make history..." he murmurs softly to the nettles and the sky his only him witnesses. Then he picks up the rewards sparkling on the ground and goes back into the house.

Yes! We did it, I tell myself. He's happy and so are we. Mr. Johnson would be proud of me. Yet what if Saito discovers how things really stand, how would he feel? Used? Stupid? Defeated? No one should come out the loser.

I take off my helmet, it's hot.

I haven't eaten anything in almost a day and my head is spinning. I go to the sink, throw cold water on my neck, and find myself playing around with a half-formed idea. If the project works, we could ask something from Mr. Baudrillard, and I know just what to ask. A form of recognition that Saito might be willing to acknowledge: going down in history as the man who started a circular economy capable of including robots. It's only the first step, but it might reduce conflicts between human and artificial workers.

It might really work.

I pour myself a glass of red wine that tastes of hope.

Pony and Cow

by Alda Teodorani

translated by Sally McCorry

Writer and translator Alda Teodorani lives in Massa Lombarda, and works in Rome, where she teaches creative writing. She published novels and short stories with the most important Italian publishers (Mondadori, Einaudi, Bompiani, Stampa Alternativa). Her stories include E Roma Piange *included in the anthology* Gioventù Cannibale *(1996),* I sacramenti del male *(Mondadori, 2008)* Gramsci in cenere *(Stampa Alternativa, 2015). She's been a member of the commitee of Convegno Roma Noir at La Sapienza University of Rome and for Attilio Micheluzzi Award for comic books.*

> **Ox:** *What sort of animal was it?*
> **Horse:** *My grandma told me it was a kind of monkey.*
> *I think she thought it was a man, and that made me really scared.*
> **Ox:** *A man? What do you mean, a man?*
> **Horse:** *A race of animal. Haven't you ever heard of man?*
> **Ox:** *I've never seen any.*
> **Horse:** *I never have either.*
> **Ox:** *So where are they?*
> **Horse:** *They are nowhere to be found any more, it is the lost race, but my grandparents tell great tales about them.*
> *Giacomo Leopardi,*
> Dialogue between a Horse and an Ox

1.

The pony with a missing hoof walked with a funny gait, watching him you would be amazed he managed not to topple over. He was skinny, so skinny he looked like a sheet of plastic thrown over a heap of bones, or maybe more like over the armature for a papier-maché horse.

He was slowly leaving the city of Rome. It was a long time now since his adoptive family had left, he had little hope now that they would come back to get him.

"Leave the pony," the man said to the woman as they got into the lorry with the rest of the animals: two horses, two cats, and two dogs, "Letizia is a big girl now, she'll lose interest in that old nag. Anyway, when we get there she won't think about it any more, what with all the new things there will be to see. Come on. The ships won't wait."

Letizia was the baby of the house. She was crying so hard when she got into the lorry she didn't even look around. The pony couldn't see her face because of the gas mask she was wearing, but he heard her screaming until the lorry started moving and turned the corner and vanished from sight behind the boundary wall. He kidded himself she was crying for him.

Around then, as if released from the ether, hundreds of sirens ripped through the air and recorded voices yelled out, instructing people to go to the ships.

Pony wandered for days, months, years, and decades around the city. In all this time - since his family had abandoned him like a broken old toy - he had never stopped wandering the streets of Rome.

There was not one human left in the city, and while the sirens that nobody would ever switch off - and would never stop until the sun died - carried on sounding, he set off along the road leading to the sea, towards where, a hundred years ago, the ships had left for other planets.

2.

When, at the beginning of the twentieth century, a local nobleman decided to rehabilitate the land around Torre in

Pietra and re-establish the dairy farms, he might already have known about the legend of Pagliaccetto. Or perhaps not. In fact many years had gone by since the cow drover Pagliacetto had built his stone tower and ninety-nine water troughs around Rome. Despite his power to dominate animals, he lost a challenge against the swineherd Pocaciccia to tame two wild bulls, harness them to a plough, and see who could trace the straightest furrow. His arrogance, and confidence he would win, had betrayed him.

In shame, Pagliaccetto, drove his cows towards the sea and walked with them into the waters of the Tyrrhenian Sea, sinking together with his herd.

Many centuries later Pagliaccetto's tower was renovated, the land around it rehabilitated, new stalls built and milk production started.

Around when Pony was abandoned the stalls again belonged to a descendant of the old owners of the farm. The man, after making his fortune with a software company, had bought it back several decades previously.

He had neither children nor other relatives and coming back from the United States with a ton of money had decided to settle down in the country to make cheese. Thanks to his skills he had fitted his stalls with sensors and mechanical arms, and automatised cleaning and waste disposal systems that turned manure into fertiliser for the farm.

The calves, who should have been drinking the cows' milk, were slaughtered and turned into feed for their own mothers, and the cows who ran dry suffered the same fate. Other vegetable feeds came from the farm's crops. During the summer the cows ranged the fenced fields in the soft hills.

The owner loved to say he would run the farm without any employees; everything had to be able to work on its own. And he had, effectively, managed it: the stalls and the production of milk and cheese were completely automatised thanks to solar energy obtained from the large lighthouse that used to be a water tower. Drones and robot servants did the rest.

Then, one day, the man just didn't get up. That's how he died, peacefully in his bed, like a computer being turned off and slowly closing down all its applications, but without any backup being saved: his memory, what he was going to leave in the world as he faded, was outside, fragmented into hundreds of specimens, ruminating in the fields.

3

When Pony decided to leave Rome, Cow, one of the few of those specimens left, was at the front of the farm in a field bordered by the Via Aurelia. She had tried to go towards the snow covered peaks which she thought would be easy to reach. Her augmented reality visor, powered by solar cells, made her believe she was surrounded by huge fir forests, and she could see other cows around her grazing, they were all the colours of the rainbow, yellow, blue, orange ... but she couldn't see her son, Calf. Maybe she would find him when she went back to the stall, but she liked being here, the air was clear and further down there was a stream where she could go to drink.

But the grass tasted like dust, and if she tried to quench her thirst at the stream there was only sandy earth to lick. The panorama she could see around her though splendid was just a figment provided by the AR visor. She was monitored by a drone connected by sensors to a big GPS collar that prevented her from leaving the farm: as soon as she tried to the collar would vibrate, and when she got too close to the fence the electric shocks came, increasingly stronger until she realised the only way to get rid of them was to change direction.

The farm was full of rats and pigeons gorging on the feed enriched with supplements, continuously provided by the robots. The automatons were programmed to carry on doing this every time the food in the troughs dropped below a certain level, and would carry on doing so for ever.

With the passing of time the farm had become a place where seagulls from the two lakes came. These waters were now full of cormorants devouring fish and water snakes whose numbers were decreasing because of the rising temperatures of the water: there was not enough food for everybody. The gulls hunted any small bird or rodent they could find, they had even destroyed a few surveillance drones, mistaking them for prey or competitors.

The drone monitoring Cow was still safe though. Up till that moment at least. Until the eagle arrived, a descendant of the one that used to fly over stadiums full of yelling humans centuries earlier In her genes there were also other memories: ancestors used for hunting and tearing down illegal drones; clandestine fights between eagles and armed drones, organised in private marquees or abandoned shopping centres, before the humans left. Whether it was due to morphic fields[2] or collective consciousness, the eagle swooped on the drone and stripped it bare, ripping off its propellers and making it drop to the ground where she finished it off with a few well aimed pecks of her beak.

4.

Pony saw Cow in the middle of the road. She was behaving very strangely: she stopped to bite at the asphalt, then moved a little way over and tasted the road, she looked totally confused. Maybe the glasses she was wearing were the problem, thought Pony.

He zoomed in on Cow's visor, looked for it on net, and realised what it was. He turned and trotted towards her. She didn't appear to have noticed his presence, and before she

---

2 See Rupert Sheldrake, *The Sense Of Being Stared At: And Other Aspects of the Extended Mind*, London, Arrow Books, 2004.

could move he grabbed the strap holding the visor on, and tugged.

Cow felt her head jerk, the mountain tops vanished and she found herself looking into Pony's large purple eyes. She had never seen a creature like him.

She looked around. They were in the middle of the road by the farm that she knew so well. There was a picture of a cow's head on the white wall of the building.

Pony watched Cow compassionately. He knew all about her, he had often seen the image on the packets of milk the family drank, on little Letizia's tablet, he had even, thanks to the integrated projector in his eyes, displayed holographic images of her on the wall in Letizia's bedroom, when he told her goodnight stories.

Bovine language was easy for Pony to reproduce. He had found many verbal sequences online he could modulate with his vocal processor.

PONY: Hi, nice to meet you!

MUCCA: Who are you

PONY: I'm a friend, my name is Pony.

It seemed like Cow wasn't too keen on talking, and she headed towards her stall.

Pony followed, saw her take a long drink from a tap where water had started flowing as soon as she came close to it.

The stall was deserted, all the cows were out in the surrounding hills. Pony went to take a look at the tap, even though he didn't need to drink. The leg with no hoof dragged along the cement and lost a screw.

MUCCA: why are you missing a hoof?

PONY: the little girl wanted to see how it worked, so she took it off, but she never managed to fix it back on again. Then her father gave her a puppy, it was so small she had to feed it milk from a bottle. After that she had no time for me any more. In the end they left and I've never seen them again.

Pony projected the images of the day they had abandoned him, and of the day after for Cow to see, he also showed her the rockets rising from the ground and vanishing into the sky.

Cow didn't understand much of what he was saying; she saw the holographic images but now she had something else on her mind: Calf.

She looked around. Nothing.

She went into the neighbouring stall, it was empty.

She turned to Pony.

COW: they've taken my son away.

PONY: where have they taken him?

COW: I don't know. Come with me and see.

Cow took Pony to Calf's post, and he examined everything. On the wall there was a metal plaque with a QR code printed on it in red. Pony connected. Cow saw strings of data running across his big purple eyes.

Perhaps not everything was lost. Pony lifted his nose and pointed his scanner at the logo on the wall of the stalls. Then he dropped his head as if he didn't want Cow to see the results of his search. He was quiet, as if he was examining the ground in search of a bolt he may have lost.

COW: So?

PONY: They took him to the slaughterhouse this morning, with the community tele-driven transport.

Cow said nothing. She couldn't connect to the web, but she knew about the existence of the slaughterhouse, the history of that hellish place had been broadcast to her by a clandestine drone. The drone, bearing the symbol of pirates on its shell, had flown over their barn a number of times cracking the codes of all the AR visor receivers of the cattle, and had transmitted terrible videos before being brought down by the farm's drones.

COW: We have to save him. We might still be in time.

As she spoke she remembered the images Pony had shown her.

COW: Did all the men leave?

Pony nodded and lowered his head, the long cables of his mane touching the cobbles.

PONY: It's not far, let's go.

5.

The last functioning slaughterhouse in Rome before the people left Earth was run exclusively by droids, and even though it had to supply the whole city, it butchered only a very few beasts. The reduction of livestock farms to diminish impact on the environment, the spread of nutritional printers, the ever increasing awareness amongst people and therefore falling consumption of meat, had improved the situation.

From the images on the web, however, Pony was expecting a place of massacre, screams, and crying, with blood everywhere. He began to slow down as they went past the city's largest dump. Created with the Testaccio model in mind, or that of the preceding century in Bologna, it was made up of a number of hills with craters at their centres. Each hill was circled by a road which then led up its slopes, these were used by self-driving lorries to reach the tops.

He didn't want to see calves being killed, and he didn't want to see Cow cry. Then he saw monkeys who were coming down the hill with funny little carts,. He sharpened his vision and saw what they were carrying: bottles of milk. Packaged food. Pieces of metal and plastic.

What were monkeys doing there? He knew what they were from the images he used to project for Letizia when he told her the story of *The Jungle Book*, but these were different ...

The monkeys were taking their carts towards the slaughterhouse. The sound of lowing began to become audible in the distance. Cow began trotting. Pony was only just managing to keep up, he yelled at her to wait for him but she was no longer listening to him.

Then, all of a sudden, from the top of the road that led down to the abattoir, Pony saw it all.

Dozens of calves standing in line, but they weren't there to be killed. The monkeys were feeding them the milk that had previously been stolen from their mothers on the farms: the dairy industry had been continuing to run, thanks to the automated systems, but the unconsumed products were sent to the dump, where the monkeys went to fetch them back.

Cow had stopped by the fence and was furiously licking the head and eyes of her Calf.

Pony would have smiled if could have. He limped closer to one of the monkeys who, standing by a glass cubicle, was examining some pieces of metal. Pony scanned them: they were pieces of drones, tone of the pieces had a skull printed on it.

PONY: Ciao I'm Pony, what's your name? Where are you from? What are you doing?

It was his way of being friendly when he felt confused.

MONKEY: I'm separating out metals and bio-plastics for the 3D printers. I have to reprint ... something.

Pony was shocked to hear the monkey talk, she had kept her head down and hadn't even looked at him. Then the monkey threw the materials into two different bins and came over to him.

Pony took a step back fearing she wanted to jump on him, and staggered. The monkey bent down and took a look at his truncated leg. Pony felt a slight tingling sensation. Then the monkey straightened up and Pony saw strings of data running across her big purple eyes, and a slight red glow in the depths.

He realised they were the same.

MONKEY: Now, for example, with one of those bits of material I can rebuild your hoof.

She rested a hand, the one that tickled him, on his neck and guided him towards the glass structure. That was when Pony realised from now on in things could only get better.

TABLE OF CONTENTS

INTRODUCTION: CONTEMPORARY ITALIAN SCIENCE
FICTION by Francesco Verso   5
BEAUTYMARK by Linda De Santi   24
THE RACE OF CROWS by Francesco Grasso   62
BAD PARENTS by Andrea Viscusi   76
THE CATALOG OF VIRGINS by Nicoletta Vallorani   88
IN BLOOM by Clelia Farris   98
THE GREEN SHIP by Francesco Verso   130
THE LOVE ALGORITHM by Michele Piccolino   143
FLOWER QUEEN by Romina Braggion   156
THE MOBY CLITORIS OF HIS BELOVED by Ian Watson
and Roberto Quaglia   178
CHINA ON THE MOON by Alessandro Fambrini
and Stefano Carducci   191
BEING OVAL by Alessandro Vietti   228
REWARD by Franci Conforti   252
PONY AND COW by Alda Teodorani   285

Designed and typeset by Alda Teodorani
Cover illustration by Simone Alvisini